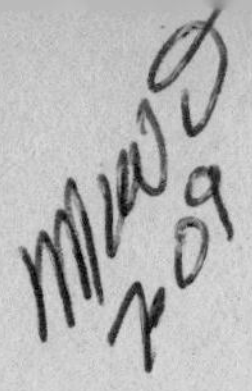

CATCH OF THE DAY

"Welcome back to the land of the living."

"I'll cut your liver out and eat it for lunch," Jeter snarled. He had never been caught like this before and it didn't set well with him. Straining against the ropes holding his wrists only produced a sluggish flow of blood.

"More likely, I'll cut out yours and feed it to you."

"Who are you?" Jeter had to ask, and found it hard to keep a hint of admiration from his voice. He had met his match after all these years. It was hard to believe it was some West Texas drifter. The man rode straight as a ramrod in the saddle, strands of lank black hair poking out from under the dusty Stetson pulled down to the top of his ears. There wasn't a trace of fat on his body—only whipcord muscle. But he was like a hundred other cowboys Jeter had seen—and killed.

He was like them all except for the cold green eyes. Jeter had seen eyes like that before, every time he looked in a mirror.

JAKE LOGAN
SLOCUM
AND THE
HANGING HORSE

J
JOVE BOOKS, NEW YORK

THE BERKLEY PUBLISHING GROUP
Published by the Penguin Group
Penguin Group (USA) Inc.
375 Hudson Street, New York, New York 10014, USA
Penguin Group (Canada), 90 Eglinton Avenue East, Suite 700, Toronto, Ontario M4P 2Y3, Canada
(a division of Pearson Penguin Canada Inc.)
Penguin Books Ltd., 80 Strand, London WC2R 0RL, England
Penguin Group Ireland, 25 St. Stephen's Green, Dublin 2, Ireland (a division of Penguin Books Ltd.)
Penguin Group (Australia), 250 Camberwell Road, Camberwell, Victoria 3124, Australia
(a division of Pearson Australia Group Pty. Ltd.)
Penguin Books India Pvt. Ltd., 11 Community Centre, Panchsheel Park, New Delhi—110 017, India
Penguin Group (NZ), Cnr. Airborne and Rosedale Roads, Albany, Auckland 1310, New Zealand
(a division of Pearson New Zealand Ltd.)
Penguin Books (South Africa) (Pty.) Ltd., 24 Sturdee Avenue, Rosebank, Johannesburg 2196,
South Africa

Penguin Books Ltd., Registered Offices: 80 Strand, London WC2R 0RL, England

SLOCUM AND THE HANGING HORSE

A Jove Book / published by arrangement with the author

PRINTING HISTORY
Jove edition / December 2006

For information, address: The Berkley Publishing Group,
a division of Penguin Group (USA) Inc.,
375 Hudson Street, New York, New York 10014.

ISBN: 0-515-14225-5

JOVE®
Jove Books are published by The Berkley Publishing Group,
a division of Penguin Group (USA) Inc.
375 Hudson Street, New York, New York 10014.
JOVE is a registered trademark of Penguin Group (USA) Inc.
The "J" design is a trademark belonging to Penguin Group (USA) Inc.

PRINTED IN THE UNITED STATES OF AMERICA

10 9 8 7 6 5 4 3 2 1

1

John Slocum tried to sneeze, but got a mouthful of dirt. He reached up to brush away the filth clogging his mouth and nose, and found his arms pinned to his sides. He struggled, then began thrashing about in growing panic when he realized his arms were held down at his sides by the wooden sides of a coffin. He blinked and tried to see that he was only having a bad dream.

The sound of dirt falling on the coffin lid mocked him.

"Help! Let me out!" His shout deafened him, but did nothing to stop the methodical dropping of more dirt on top of the coffin. Slocum worked his hands up past his sides and pressed his palms flat on the lid and heaved with all his strength.

The lid refused to budge.

His panic soared, and he felt energy surge through his muscles. He could have lifted a horse off the ground with the huge effort he put into pushing open the coffin lid. He heard a mournful creaking as wood began yielding, but the weight of the dirt was too great. Distant sounds as the grave digger continued to fill the grave filtered down to him and added to his growing fear of being interred alive.

"You can't bury me like this! I'm not dead!"

The echoes that had deafened him before were gone. The increasing burden of the sweet-smelling earth above the coffin effectively muffled his outcry. Slocum pushed harder, with growing need. The air within the coffin wouldn't last long. He had to escape. He had to!

Panting, he strained until the muscles on his shoulders cracked with the effort. In such an awkward position he couldn't bring enough pressure to bear—and even if he had the proper leverage, he wasn't sure he could have moved the hundreds of pounds of dirt and the still-secured coffin lid.

Sweat drenching him and causing his shirt to plaster itself to his body, Slocum kept up the pressure on the lid until he sagged back, momentarily exhausted. It took a great deal to frighten him. He had gone through the war and had seen friends get their heads blown off by cannonballs and bodies turned to bloody shreds from exploding artillery pieces. Men dying in vicious ways had only momentarily slowed him. What an angry Apache could do to a captured enemy was beyond description, but Slocum had seen the result and been unmoved by it. More than one friend had been trampled by a herd of cattle in full, frightened stampede. He might have seen every way of dying there was and had not feared such a fate would be his.

He was scared shitless now.

Slocum collapsed and rubbed his arms the best he could to get blood flowing through them again. If he flagged now, he was a goner. Wiping sweat off his forehead carried away a small mud slide. Dirt from the grave being filled had somehow filtered onto his face, and was now caking ominously on his cheeks and across his trembling lips.

Slocum sucked in a deep breath, and let it out slowly to force away the terror that nipped at him like a pack of wild dogs.

"How'd I get here?" he wondered aloud. He couldn't remember. His head hurt like a son of a bitch, and moving it from side to side made him wonder if something important had broken loose inside. Somehow, he had been struck on the top of the head. Rolling from side to side pressed a lump the size of a goose egg into the top of the coffin. But he couldn't remember how he had acquired that aching bump.

"Don't get all spooked," he said, trying to convince himself he wasn't in about the worst situation a man could find himself in. Buried alive. Waiting to suffocate. Waiting to die of thirst. Waiting for the maggots to begin eating his flesh. Would that happen before he was dead?

Slocum scratched at a sudden itch on his chest and panicked again, sure that the worms were already feeding on his flesh in the darkness of the grave.

He screamed and screamed until he was hoarse. Then he got control again. The air was still breathable. It might last for hours if he didn't do anything to burn it up. Slocum had been trapped in mine cave-ins and had survived because he had kept a cool head. More than once in those situations, however, other miners had been there to help, to dig him out, to get help that saved him. But there had been a time or two he had dug himself out. It was possible. He had to do that now, if he could figure out a way to do it while lying flat on his back, staring up into utter blackness, the rough pine coffin lid only inches above his face.

How had he gotten in this pickle? His head throbbed even worse now that he had discovered the lump, making it difficult to concentrate. He had been hit on the top of the head. Hard. Who had done it? Slocum couldn't remember.

"What do you remember?" he asked himself in a voice that was hardly a whisper because he had screamed until his voice cracked and his throat throbbed. The questions kept him from thinking too much of his fate. If he could figure out how he had been thrust into the coffin, sealed up, and then buried alive, he might find a way out. Who could have done this to him? Why? He had enemies. Plenty of them. As many as there were grains of sand in the Chihuahua Desert. But he couldn't remember any of them being close enough to do this.

He couldn't remember anything of the past few hours.

Snippets of names and faces fluttered tantalizingly close, but fear kept them from becoming solid memories. He reached down to his left hip and felt for his trusty six-shooter. The Peacemaker was still in its cross-draw holster. Fumbling, he pulled it out and rested it on his chest. Slocum started to fire it as a warning to the grave digger that someone was still alive in the coffin, then stopped. The smoke from the discharge might suffocate him. Worse, there might be too much dirt now for the report to be heard. Pressing his ear against the side of the coffin, Slocum heard distant sounds. Try as he might, he couldn't make out what he was hearing. Horses? Wagons? Something rhythmical and rattling like a carriage or a prancing horse pulling a buckboard. Firing the six-gun wouldn't draw any attention if people were in the wagons.

He collapsed and lay with his head pressing into the rough board making up the side of the coffin. With the Peacemaker, he could shoot holes in the lid or side. What would that accomplish? Slocum knew it wouldn't do anything for him.

"I'd choke on the gunsmoke," he said in his throaty rumble. He moved the six-shooter back so he could tuck it away in its holster where he would be able to find it again.

The thought flashed through his mind that a .45 slug in the head was a quicker death than suffocating. But Slocum wasn't the kind to kill himself. He had faced too much in his life and had never given up. Ever. He wouldn't succumb to his own hand now. He would get out of the grave and find whoever had put him here.

Then the tables would be turned. But Slocum wouldn't bury his foe alive. He'd make sure six slugs were in that bastard's foul heart. He would enjoy firing every single round, relish the sound of the man dying, thrill to the lifeblood trickling from one hole after another in his chest.

His?

"Ruth?" The name came unbidden, but he couldn't place it or put a face to it. Another crowded close. "Amy?"

He couldn't remember who they were, but the names were fresh and carried a brightness like a new penny.

Frustrated, Slocum banged away at the lid, and accomplished nothing but tiring himself. More sweat ran into his eyes, forcing him to work his hand up to wipe it away.

"Can't do that. Need to conserve my strength. Don't burn up the air."

He hardly listened to his own advice. His thoughts wandered back to the two women. Ruth. Amy. They meant something to him, but the memory was elusive and flittered just beyond his remembrance. And there were other names. Jeter and Killian and a lawman. More than a single lawman. A mob. A noose and a horse.

Slocum felt as if his head would split like a rotten melon struck with an ax handle if he tried to put everything together. He wiped away more sweat, and then ran his hand over his neck. All he felt was the usual grit that accumulated under his bandanna. The noose was a faint memory, but there weren't rope burns around his neck. Somebody else had been hanged. Or was that a memory intruding from some other time and place?

"Place. Where am I? What town is this?" He forced himself not to answer with words like "cemetery" and "potter's field."

He settled down and concentrated. The importance of figuring out how he had come to this sorry state was at the top of his mind. If he worked it all out, he wouldn't panic again and burn up more air and maybe think about using the six-shooter on himself.

"What time is it? Day or night?" He fumbled around to find his watch pocket. In spite of his vow not to panic again, Slocum did. His watch was gone. The watch that was his only legacy from his brother Robert. Gone! He patted every pocket on his vest, and then worked around to the bottom of the coffin as he searched for the timepiece. The watch might have fallen from his pocket.

He didn't find it. Whoever had put him into the coffin had stolen his watch but left him with his six-shooter. That didn't make any sense. Or did it?

Slocum closed his eyes, then opened them slowly. Not a speck of light showed anywhere, so it didn't matter if he kept his eyelids open or not.

"Time. I was robbed of my watch," he said. "And buried. Buried in San Esteban."

The name of the West Texas town triggered more memories. Slocum tried not to rush them. He might scare those precious recollections away like a greenhorn would frighten away a deer that might feed him for a week. Coax the memories. Tease them closer. Like a timid rabbit, they approached him, and he tried not to appear too eager, fearing they would race away to a hidden burrow.

"San Esteban," he whispered. "I was on the stagecoach from San Antonio and . . ."

2

Slocum tried to sleep in the Butterfield stagecoach, but was tossed about due to the rough road. Every time the stage hit a rock, the entire Concord was tossed into the air and landed with bone-jarring force. He coughed, then sneezed as a fresh cloud of gritty brown dust blew through the open window. Slocum pulled his sweaty bandanna around and wiped the dust from his eyes and nose, then tied the blue cloth so it made him look like a road agent ready for action.

"Do you have to do that?" The man sitting across from him glared. His dark eyes were twin, glassy marbles that didn't seem to have pupils and peered at Slocum without blinking.

Slocum tried to figure the man out. He went from being friendly to nasty and back again every other minute. He was dressed like a banker, but the shabbiness of the coat—the threadbare lapels and the worn-out elbows—showed the man had fallen on hard times. There had been an attempt to shine the boots, but not recently. From the bulge in the man's dirty coat, he wore a pistol in a shoulder rig. Slocum considered how likely the man was to use his gun, based on his cold look and steady hand. He wasn't a gunfighter, but he wasn't a banker either.

"Scare you?" Slocum asked.

"You look like a damn road agent. Out in these parts, they hang the road agents they don't shoot outright."

"I'm not going to hold you up, and the driver has no worry either. I just want to get to El Paso." Slocum tried to settle back into the corner of the compartment, only to jerk around when a sharp splinter poked into his shoulder. His sudden movement prompted the not-a-banker to reach for his six-shooter.

"Settle down," mumbled the other man in the compartment. This one was sleepy and had been dozing in spite of the West Texas heat and jarring movement of the stage rumbling along the rocky road. He was better dressed than the man on the seat beside him, but hardly a gunman or banker. Slocum pegged him as a proprietor of some kind. It took no imagination to see this man wearing an apron as he swept out a general store or worked to sell yard goods to eager frontier wives.

"Who're you to tell me what to do?"

"I paid my money same as you," the sleepy storekeeper said. "Let him travel in peace. Let *me* travel in peace. We all got to endure this damn heat for another hour or two until we get to San Esteban and change teams."

"It's another couple days of hard travel beyond that to reach Fort Davis," Slocum said. "If we're going to ride together, we should get along or at least hold our tongues."

"Who're you to be givin' me advice?" The first man

thrust out his chin truculently. If Slocum hadn't been so miserable from the heat and dust, he would have taken a poke at that tempting target.

"Nobody," Slocum said, not wanting to rile the man further.

"Then pull down that bandanna so I kin see yer face."

Slocum did as the man requested. His expression made the man reach for the six-gun holstered under his left arm. He froze when his seatmate grabbed his wrist. The storekeeper must have been stronger than he looked because the man not only stopped reaching for his gun, but winced as the fingers clamped down hard enough to make the knuckles show white.

"Peace," the storekeeper said. "Let's all be peaceful. Won't kill us." He spat out the window, then turned back. "And if we're not real neighborly to one another, it *can* kill us."

Slocum wiped his face again, but did not return the bandanna to protect his mouth and nose. The roiling clouds of brown dust were dying down as the coach rolled over a rockier stretch of road. The stage bounced harder now, but the air was more breathable, and not pulling up the bandanna made the man seated across from him subside with ill grace.

"Better," the storekeeper said, releasing his grip and closing his eyes again. Slocum saw the dust had irritated the man's eyes to the point where tears ran constantly down his cheeks, leaving muddy tracks behind.

Slocum leaned out and chanced a quick look ahead. The road was going into hillier territory, forcing the four-horse team to pull harder up the slopes. Already tired from hours of desperate, dry travel across the desert, the horses were in no condition to make good speed. Slocum didn't care. He wasn't out in the sun and rode in relative comfort. Eventually they would reach the small town of San Esteban, where he could get a mug of beer to wash the grit from his mouth. A beef tongue sandwich or two would go down mighty good too.

From San Esteban it was only a couple days' travel north to the more prosperous town of Fort Davis, where Limpia Creek poured fresh, clean water out of the mountains and into the town cisterns. The cavalry post there kept the region safe and prosperous, or as prosperous as it could be with the perpetual lack of money from soldiers. With the Warm Springs Apaches off the reservation in New Mexico and Arizona, raiding deep into what had been Lipan Apache territory, the cavalry was always in the field on patrol.

That made his trip to El Paso all the more likely to be uneventful. Slocum cast a gimlet eye at the man sitting across from him. It would be uneventful if this yahoo would ever shut his pie hole.

"It's the damn weather," the man said. "Too hot. Not enough to drink. And the dust! How do you endure it?"

"There's no choice, that's how," Slocum said. He pulled up his bandanna to see if the man would protest again. He didn't. This suited Slocum just fine as he tried to catch a few winks in the lurching, creaking stagecoach.

Slocum jerked awake when the driver applied the whip to the team. The horses protested, and their resistance to pulling faster was answered with several more cracks of the whip. Slocum stuck his head out the window and looked up to see the driver on his feet in the driver's box, putting his shoulder into cracking the twenty-foot black whip directly over the horses.

"What's wrong?" Slocum shouted. The driver paid

him no heed. The man reared back and sent the whip singing out to land hard enough on a lead horse's rump to raise a welt.

Slocum knew a driver never intentionally harmed a horse, not out in the desert this time of year. If they ended up stranded because a horse died, they might end up buzzard bait themselves. Craning his head around, Slocum looked behind the stage. He saw nothing but the churning cloud of dust kicked up by the spinning wheels. Popping back into the compartment, he slipped the leather thong off the hammer of his six-shooter.

"Why are we rattling along like this? Is that fool driver tryin' to kill us all?"

Slocum ignored the shabbily dressed man. There could be only one explanation for the driver's sudden need for speed. Someone chased them. Considering Victorio and Nana were miles off and being hounded by the U.S. Army, that meant road agents were intent on robbing them.

"I said, what's going on?"

"I heard you. Ain't it obvious?" the storekeeper answered, as if he had been the one addressed. "If you got any valuables, you'd better hide 'em somewhere that the road agents won't find 'em."

The stage suddenly slewed to one side, killing all forward motion. For a heart-stopping instant, Slocum thought they were going to topple over onto their side. As it was, he was thrown hard against the door. The latch sprang open and spilled him to the sunbaked road.

"Don't reach for that hogleg, mister, not if you want to keep on keepin' on."

Slocum wiped dirt from his eyes and peered up at the road agent sitting pretty in the saddle. He stared down the double barrels of a shotgun.

"No argument," Slocum said, moving his hands far from his sides.

"Grab some sky. It's a real purty blue. You'll like it. You'll like it even more when you get to brag about not gettin' killed."

"What does this mean?" the shabbily dressed man demanded.

"It means you're addlepated," the highwayman said coldly, "and that you're gonna be dead if you don't lose that pistol you're fondlin' like you would your dick."

Slocum glanced back in time to see the man toss the six-shooter from his shoulder holster to the ground. The man jumped out, and then was shoved out of the way by the storekeeper as he climbed out of the stage.

"It's too hot out here to spend the livelong day in the sun," the storekeeper said. "Why don't you get on with it so we can go get a beer? If you're inclined to leave us the price of a brew, that is."

"You won't find any cold ones at San Esteban," the masked robber said. "You. Up there in the driver's box. Climb on down and bring the strongbox with you."

"Ain't got—" The driver ducked when the road agent fired one barrel in the air.

"It's bolted in the rear," the driver said. "In the boot, under the luggage."

"Why don't you start workin' your way down to it then, while I relieve these gents of their possessions?"

The outlaw took off his hat and tossed it to the storekeeper. "You're the only one with good sense. Put ever'thing in the hat. Rings, wallets, bankrolls, watches, ever'thing."

The man grumbled, but emptied his pockets. Slocum

knew he had hidden something in the compartment of the stage. He finished with the shabby man and came to Slocum.

"Go on," the storekeeper told him. "You heard what he said."

Slocum dropped his roll of greenbacks into the hat. He hated to part with almost a hundred dollars, but the second barrel of the shotgun was pointed in his direction. He could always find another cowboy who didn't understand the odds at poker or who was too drunk to care if he lost his month's wages.

"Keep on goin'," the road agent said.

"What do you mean?" The storekeeper had his back to the outlaw and looked Slocum squarely in the eye as he spoke, but the outlaw's meaning was clear.

"It was my brother's. It's all I have to remember him," Slocum said.

"Get me that there watch," the road agent said. "I don't like sittin' in the hot sun any more than you do."

"I'm sorry, mister," the storekeeper said, reaching for the watch in Slocum's vest pocket.

Slocum moved faster than a striking snake, grabbed the storekeeper's wrist, and swung him around.

As quick as he was, the outlaw was faster and had seen the resistance coming. The road agent leaned over and brought the long barrel of his shotgun down hard on the top of Slocum's head. Slocum went to his knees, pain flaring as his vision blurred. The second blow, to the side of his head, caused him to topple facedown onto the ground, unconscious.

The next thing he was aware of was pain radiating from the top of his head and going all the way down his spine. Every breath he took drove a knife into his ribs, and something was wrong with his legs. Slocum jerked and heard a loud *yip*!

Rolling onto his back, he saw a coyote with part of his pants leg in its mouth. Slocum grabbed for his Peacemaker and fired point-blank at the coyote. The animal reared on its back legs and then fell to one side, the bullet having blown out the top of its skull. Slocum sat up, rubbed his leg, and saw that the coyote hadn't actually bitten into his flesh. The tough denim pants leg had saved him from the first nip, and there hadn't been a second.

Slocum looked up at the sky and wondered why it was late afternoon. Then bits and pieces fell together as he remembered what had happened. He rubbed the lump on his head and winced. His fingers came away bloody, although the thick Stetson he wore had saved him from more serious injuries.

"Son of a bitch," Slocum said, getting to his feet. He took a few unsteady steps, then looked around. As far as he could see was empty, heat-shimmery desert. No trace of the stagecoach or its occupants remained. This made him even madder. It was bad enough that the outlaw had stolen the one thing in his life that meant anything. It was worse being left on foot in the middle of the deadly hot West Texas desert.

He held up his six-shooter and stared at it in wonder. The outlaw hadn't bothered taking the pistol. Just the roll of greenbacks—and his brother Robert's watch.

Slocum had a score to settle. Two scores. The outlaw would regret the day he stole that watch almost as much as the driver would rue leaving behind a passenger to die of thirst and exposure. Slocum rubbed his leg where the coyote had begun its meal. He had come really close to never waking up. The hungry canine could as easily have ripped out his throat first before going on to other spots for its afternoon meal.

Looking up, squinting at the sun and pulling his hat down enough to shield his eyes, Slocum got his bearings. The sand in the twin ruts that passed as a road had been disturbed in both directions, telling him that the driver had gone on to San Esteban rather than backtracking after the robbery. Putting one foot in front of the other, Slocum began slogging along in the stifling heat. He should have found a cut bank or deep arroyo that provided a modicum of shade and waited for the sun to sink, but his anger drove him to keep walking. Overtaking the stage wasn't likely, but every minute he wasted put it and its driver another few yards farther away.

He walked for almost ten minutes, reached the crest of a steep hill, and then stopped dead in his tracks. Without realizing it, his hand went for the butt of his six-shooter. At the base of the hill stood the stagecoach. Slocum didn't see either the team or the passengers, but did see the driver.

This was one bullet he could save for the road agent. The driver was sprawled across the roof of the stage, arms dangling down and obviously dead.

Slocum slipped and slid down the dusty road to the stage. He climbed up to be certain. The driver looked to have been dead for an hour or more from the condition of the body. Bits of his flesh had been pecked away by buzzards, leaving the white bones poking from torn shirt and ripped pants. Buzzards were quick to come, quick to eat, and even quicker to leave. Their meal had taken less than five minutes, forcing Slocum to guess at how long the driver had dangled over the side after his flesh had been stripped away.

Slocum jumped to the ground and opened the compartment door. He noticed a new hole the size of his fist in the door panel—a shotgun blast. Inside looked like a slaughterhouse with blood spattered in all directions. But the body belonging to the blood was gone.

Going around, Slocum saw that the bolted strongbox in the boot had been forced open. Whatever had been inside was long gone with the road agent. He heaved a sigh, went back to the door, and looked around the hard, dried ground for any tracks. A few drops of blood had caused the dirt to form what looked like obscene raindrops. Someone bleeding badly had staggered away from the stagecoach. Slocum found the storekeeper—or what was left of him—in an arroyo a few yards away.

He drew his six-gun and began hunting for the shabbily dressed gent. Slocum returned the pistol to his cross-draw holster when he found him on the far side of a creosote bush. It wasn't obvious right off how he had died. It wasn't from a shotgun blast like the storekeeper, but he was still deader than a doornail.

"Reckon I was luckier than I thought," Slocum said aloud. Whatever had gone on after he had been slugged had proven deadly for the three men. The outlaw was more dangerous than Slocum had thought when he first laid eyes on him. That knowledge of such cold-blooded killing didn't deter Slocum in wanting to get his watch back. It only meant he had to be just a tad more vicious and not too squeamish about pulling the trigger first.

The driver and the storekeeper had been unarmed, and that hadn't stopped the road agent from murdering them.

Slocum cocked his head to one side when he heard a distant neigh. Turning slowly, he homed in on the sound. He wanted to whistle or shout, to call out to the horse roaming in the desert, but any sound might scare it. Walking as silently as any Indian, Slocum crossed the hard-baked desert, keeping low and finding which way the wind blew so he could get downwind from the horse. Only then did he work his way into the tepid breeze until he caught the horse's scent.

From behind a bushy, thorny mesquite he stared at the horse. It had been one of the team and had somehow broken free. Why it hadn't started running and kept up the pace until its heart exploded, Slocum didn't know, but he was grateful. Riding meant the difference between life and death.

Especially since he intended to go after the road agent rather than continue along the road to San Esteban. He had a score to settle, and nothing and no one in the small Texas town was likely to be much help.

He slipped around the mesquite and stripped off a handful of seed pods. The sound alerted the horse.

"Here," Slocum said softly, holding out the bean pods. "Have something to eat. It's all right. Come on over. Come on, come on."

The horse warily approached, its nose working hard to sniff at the beans. Finally hunger overcame fear, and it began eating from Slocum's hand. He reached out and slipped his fingers through the bridle remaining on the horse's neck. When the horse was done and tossed its head, trying to pull free, Slocum leaped onto the horse's back. The animal had pulled a stagecoach, not been ridden as a saddle horse. Slocum had to use all his skill to keep his seat as the horse reared and bucked, but to the Butterfield Stagecoach Company's credit, the horse had never been mistreated and was used to strange men around it. Slocum eventually gentled the horse and got it walking back toward the stage.

The horse tried to shy away, probably scenting the spilled blood, but Slocum kept it moving until he came to the front of the stage where he could study the tongue and what remained of the traces. From the look of the harness, the road agent had cut the team free with a sharp knife.

"Why'd he want to steal a team of stage horses?" Slocum wondered aloud. He patted his new mount on the neck. "Not that you wouldn't be a fine saddle horse. But why would he steal the others in your team?"

Slocum searched in an area around the front of the stagecoach and found a muddled trail where the outlaw and the team had run. He started to follow, then wheeled the horse around and returned to the stage. His gear had been stashed in the boot. It took a few minutes to locate his saddle and other belongings where they had been discarded in the outlaw's haste to get down to the strongbox. Careful of his skittish horse, he dismounted and secured the bit of bridle to the stage's wheel before throwing his saddle on and securing his bedroll and saddlebags. Clearly uneasy with this added weight, the horse tried to bolt more than once. Slocum kept a firm hand on the bridle, and eventually mounted.

It took a few tentative attempts to buck for the horse to get such foolishness out of its system. Then Slocum warily returned to the trail left by the other horses—and the outlaw. Less than a quarter mile later Slocum realized what the road agent had done.

"You're one clever whore's son, I'll grant you that much," Slocum said. He tried to find the proper trail, and couldn't make out which was the outlaw and which were the other three horses.

The road agent had ridden in the midst of the other

horses to cover his own trail. One by one he had let the horses go. The one Slocum rode had probably been the first, but hadn't acted as the outlaw had hoped by running until it died of exhaustion. Slocum couldn't tell about the other horses. They might have been more frightened and were still running out in the desert, leaving a false trail.

"Where'd you go?" Slocum looked around and couldn't come to a good decision. Ahead lay the Davis Mountains, but farther south was a clear trail leading across the Rio Grande into Mexico. If Slocum had been responsible for the robbery, that was where he would have gone to get away from American lawmen and especially the Texas Rangers. But one trail went that way, another toward the distant mountains, and two others almost due north.

Slumping, Slocum knew how hard it would be to find the outlaw without a canteen filled with water and several weeks of provisions. He straightened, took a good look at the lay of the land, and then headed north until he crossed the road leading to San Esteban. Giving in to the inevitable, he rode into the sleepy little town to report the robbery and murders to whoever passed himself off as a lawman here. If nothing else, the Butterfield agent would want to know his stage and driver wouldn't be making the next leg north toward El Paso.

3

It was always the same. The driver thought he could outrun a man on a good, strong stallion. Les Jeter sneered as he watched the stagecoach driver stand and begin using his long whip to goad on his team. Jeter was no fool and had picked this spot along the road into San Esteban for a reason—the best reason in the world. The Butterfield driver's team was about ready to drop in harness from the long pull across the hot West Texas desert. This stretch of road was barren, yet far enough from town that there wasn't a chance in hell that a lawman would wander out.

Jeter wiped his face. No fat-bellied deputy would ever come out in this heat. He mopped up more sweat from his forehead, then settled the bandanna so it hid his nose and mouth. He knew it wasn't much of a disguise after he had worked this road so aggressively for the past couple months, but he liked to do things all proper-like. It wouldn't do to have a road agent hold up a stage and not wear a bandanna.

He chuckled to himself. The instant any of the passengers saw his face, they'd panic. It had to mean one of two things. Either he was out to build a reputation or he would gun them all down. Jeter had all the reputation he wanted and had fought off lawmen in three different states. And cutting down the passengers depended a whole bunch on how well they obeyed him. But not wearing the mask complicated the robbery, and he wasn't in any mood for that today. Too hot.

"Giddyup," he said to his horse, kicking his heels and getting the powerful black stallion moving after the stagecoach. The driver had about tuckered out his team, and all because he had seen a solitary rider on a rise near the road. Jeter trotted along in the heavy cloud of dust kicked up by the team and the stage wheels, vowing to come up with a new plan for his next robbery. Eating dust like this was a pain in the ass.

The trot turned into a gallop when the stage suddenly slewed to one side and stopped. One of the doors popped open and a tall passenger with the look of a gunslinger fell out onto the sunbaked road. Instinctively Jeter knew he had a passel of trouble on his hands if he didn't take charge right away. He swung his double-barreled shotgun around and trained it on the dark-haired man with the cold green eyes.

"Don't reach for that hogleg, mister, not if you want to keep on keepin' on," Jeter warned. He had to keep the driver in plain sight, but the passenger would give him a bellyful of lead if he was distracted for even an instant. Jeter trained his shotgun squarely on the man.

"No argument," the passenger said. He slowly moved his hands out to either side of his body until they were level with his shoulders.

"Grab some sky," Jeter said, still tense in spite of

things going slick as silk so far. "It's a real purty blue. You'll like it. You'll like it even more when you get to brag about not gettin' killed."

"What does this mean?" cried a second passenger. As the man moved to the stage door, his coat flopped open to reveal a six-gun hung in a shoulder holster. Jeter kept the shotgun aimed at the gunman, who was still doing as he was told but looked like a coiled spring ready to explode in some unexpected direction.

"It means you're addlepated," Jeter said, wanting to be done with the robbery as soon as possible. Things were under control, but felt as if they might slip away at any second, and all because of the gunman. ". . . and that you're gonna be dead if you don't lose that pistol you're fondlin' like you would your dick."

Jeter watched as the man dropped the gun and then jumped out to the ground, followed a third passenger, who pushed him out of the way. This one had the look of a worldly gent who had seen and done it all. He was perfect for what Jeter intended.

"It's too hot out here to spend the livelong day in the sun," the third man said. "Why don't you get on with it so we can go get a beer. If you're inclined to leave us the price of a brew, that is."

"You won't find any cold ones at San Esteban," Jeter said, appreciating how businesslike the man was about the robbery. He wouldn't give any trouble. But trouble could spring up unexpectedly unless he got on with it and stopped lollygagging. "You. Up there in the driver's box. Climb on down and bring the strongbox with you."

"Ain't got—"

Jeter fired one barrel to shut the driver up and get him moving. The driver flinched and put his hands up as if he wanted to cover his face and make the world—and robber—go away. He wasn't going to be that lucky. When it became obvious to the driver that the second barrel would be centered on his belly, he started making all the right noises.

"It's bolted in the rear. In the boot, under the luggage."

"Why don't you start workin' your way down to it then, while I relieve these gents of their possessions?" Jeter reached up with his left hand, grabbed the brim of his dusty hat, and tossed it to the one most likely to help things along. The man snared it and stared into the sweaty interior.

"You're the only one with good sense. Put ever'thing in the hat. Rings, wallets, bankrolls, watches, ever'thing."

Jeter was pleased to see the man obey without a lot of foolish questions or protests. He dropped in a thin wallet, a ring, and fished out a key dangling on a gold chain and held it up just long enough for Jeter to get a good look at it. Jeter almost laughed. The man was a Freemason, but that didn't hold any water with him. Jeter gestured for the man to get to work collecting the valuables from the other two.

The gunman reluctantly dropped a thick roll of greenbacks into the hat. Jeter considered asking him to drop his six-shooter, but didn't want the gunslinger's hands anywhere near the weapon's trigger. Better that he kept his hands up high and away from the butt of that well-used six-gun.

"Keep on goin'," Jeter said when he saw his unwilling accomplice hesitate.

"What do you mean?" asked the man.

Jeter motioned for the man to take the watch poking

out from the gunman's vest pocket. There wasn't any reason not to pick them all clean, including the gunslick.

"It was my brother's," the gunman said. He turned his cold green eyes up. Jeter felt them boring through to his very soul and repressed a shudder. He had seen all kinds in his day, but none had this man's intensity. That didn't matter a whit to him, though.

"It's all I have to remember him," the gunman said. Jeter knew then and there he had to be ready for trouble. Big trouble.

"Get me that there watch," Jeter ordered. "I don't like sittin' in the hot sun any more than you do."

"I'm sorry, mister," the man who had done the collecting just fine so far said. He reached for the watch in the gunman's vest pocket.

Jeter reacted instantly because he knew what was coming—what had to happen after he'd heard the gunman's words. He bent over and swung his shotgun as hard as he could. The gunman had spun the other passenger around to use him as a shield while he drew his six-shooter. That was what he'd intended. He hadn't counted on the hard steel, strip-wound Damascus barrel smashing down onto the top of his head.

Jeter had to give it to the man. He was a tough hombre. Even the hard blow to the head didn't take him out. Leaning down low, Jeter swung the shotgun a second time. This time the gunman went down and stayed there.

The other passengers and driver were too stunned to react. They stared at their fallen fellow traveler, mouths open, saying nothing.

"Keep on collectin'," Jeter ordered the man who had helped him. "Be sure to take that watch he was so intent on keepin'." He pointed the shotgun at the man he had laid out cold.

The one holding Jeter's hat jumped to obey, then handed the hat up to the outlaw. Jeter made a mistake then, taking the contents and turning to stuff it all into his saddlebags. The passenger dressed in the threadbare coat picked up a rock and threw it. Hard. His aim was bad, and he missed his target, but did almost as well when the sharp stone hit the stallion's haunch. The horse reared, forcing Jeter to fight to keep control. He was tossed off and hit the ground hard. The impact stunned him, but not so much that he dropped his scattergun.

Through a roar in his ears Jeter heard the driver yelp like a scalded dog.

"Git in. We gotta git outta here!"

The two passengers still on their feet jumped and crowded inside, leaving the third on the ground. Jeter sat up in time to see the driver grabbing the reins. His vision was blurry from the fall. He intended to blow the damned driver's head off, but when the shotgun discharged, the muzzle pointed in a different direction. Jeter saw splinters fly when the load of buckshot tore through the side of the stagecoach and then a mist of blood erupted. He had shot one of the passengers. Then it was too late for him to grab for his six-shooter. The driver snapped the reins and got the frightened team pulling hard.

"Damnation, it don't ever get easier," Jeter grumbled as he got to his feet. He checked to see that the passenger he had buffaloed with his shotgun barrel was still out like a light. The outlaw pulled down his mask, put his fingers into his mouth, and let out a shrill whistle. For a moment he was afraid the stallion would still be running, but the well-trained horse came trotting up, looking contrite at what it had done to its rider. He vaulted into the saddle and lit out after the stagecoach.

Jeter had no trouble overtaking the stage and its exhausted team. Their condition didn't prevent the driver from brutally using his whip.

"Pull over, dammit!" Jeter shouted. The driver ignored him. He didn't ignore it when Jeter drew his six-gun and fired. The slug caught the driver in the left arm. From the way he stiffened, the bullet had gone completely through his biceps and into his chest. He toppled over, dead.

The team, without the whip cracking above, lost all will to run.

Jeter slowed and peered into the blood-splattered interior in time to see the remaining passenger fumbling for something. Knowing he'd had a six-shooter before, Jeter had to remove any threat. He thrust his own six-shooter through the window and fired three times. One of the slugs killed the passenger.

"What a day," Jeter said, slowing and then moving to the rear of the stagecoach. He pulled back the canvas flap over the boot. Some of the stashed cargo had fallen out as the stage tried to outrun him, but the driver had been telling the truth about the strongbox being bolted down. He aimed his six-shooter and fired a single round. The lead whined off the lock but broke the hasp.

Jeter bent low and flipped open the lid. A slow smile came to his thin lips.

"This makes it all worth it, don't it, old boy?" He patted his stallion's neck, then dismounted to better scoop out the contents. Over the past few months he had held up more stagecoaches than he could remember. The banks had tried transferring money in a variety of ways, but simply sneaking it past had been most effective since he couldn't hold up every last stage, no matter how much he wanted to. This was a shipment to a bank farther along the Butterfield route, maybe in Fort Davis. He hefted the bag of gold coins and, from long practice, jiggled the leather bag and estimated more than five hundred dollars. So much would have kept a dozen businesses running.

Or it could keep Les Jeter rolling in clover for a year.

He tucked it away in his saddlebags next to the rest of the loot, then mounted again. Jeter was a cautious man, for all his boldness when it came to holding up stagecoaches. He rode around to the team of horses, whipped out a sharp, long-bladed knife, and slit the harness.

"You four, come on along with me for a little while. Ain't nobody in this state, Texas Ranger or Indian, that'll be able to track me if your hooves are all mixed with mine." Jeter looked up in surprise as the two passengers he had thought to be dead lurched from the compartment and stumbled off into the desert. He started to use his shotgun on them, then decided there was no need to waste ammunition. They wouldn't last long in this heat.

He led the horses in the direction of the Davis Mountains and his hideout there, but one got feisty. He let it run, knowing it provided another false trail for any posse to follow. As he rode straight for the mountains, he let another horse have its head. It bolted toward the Rio Grande. Jeter watched it disappear with some longing. More than a year had passed since he'd been in Mexico. With the money he had stolen during his reign of terror along the San Antonio–El Paso road, he could live like a king across the border.

Jeter wiped the dust off his lips, remembering the taste of tequila and lime. And the milky, fermented juice of the agave—pulque. And the soft kisses of lovely señoritas.

That thought made him increasingly uncomfortable as he rode. Jeter rocked forward in the saddle to relieve some of the pressure, let the last two of the team race off northward, and kept up his arrow-straight trail for the mountains and what lay there.

It took two days for him to make his way through the mountains and into a grassy valley nestled between gently sloping hills. A couple of cattle lowed as he approached the small farmhouse. A barn stood some distance away, a large door partially open, hinting someone had passed through it recently. Jeter looked around for any sign of habitation, and smiled slowly when he saw a woman come from the cabin lugging a large basket of laundry. She went to a clothesline and began hanging up the wet clothes.

Jeter began responding as he saw what the young woman was hanging up. Simple dresses, frilly undergarments that must have ridden close to her most intimate flesh, other things he paid no attention to. The woman worked diligently and never saw him as he rode closer, then dismounted to advance on foot. He didn't want to spook her. She was about the prettiest filly he had ever laid eyes on. Shoulder-length brunette hair swayed seductively as she worked. She lifted the wet clothes to the line and fastened them with wooden pins, giving Jeter a delightful view of her figure. Trim waist, firm, full, flaring breasts that would be less than a handful but more than a mouthful—

And those legs! Now and then a vagrant breeze whipped up the hem of her skirt and showed trim ankles and shapely legs. Jeter felt himself growing harder by the instant as he stared at the woman. He knew he had to have her. Now.

Jeter moved on cat's feet, coming up close behind the woman. He reached out and grabbed her around the waist. She let out a startled yelp, looked over her shoulder, and then twisted away hard, dropping her laundry and running for the cabin. Jeter staggered from the unexpected flight.

"So, that's the way you want it, that's the way you're gonna get it!"

The brunette reached the cabin, grabbed the rough wood support holding up the porch roof, and looked back at him, eyes wide and breath coming in deep gasps. Jeter couldn't take his eyes off the way her breasts heaved under her crisp white blouse. If she were any more out of breath, the buttons would pop.

He intended to do more than make a few buttons pop off.

"Don't make it any harder than it is," he called, advancing.

"You . . . you can't!"

"Watch me. No, you won't be able to watch me because I'm gonna take you from behind. I want to feel your milky white butt rubbing up against my crotch."

She let out a gasp of disbelief and shot into the cabin. Jeter ran after her. The latch had been secured. He was too hot and bothered to take the time to open it any other way than kicking in the door. It slammed hard against the inner wall and rebounded. Jeter caught it and slammed it open again.

"This isn't the way," the woman gasped out. The top two buttons of that prim blouse had opened, giving him a hint of creamy white flesh heaving beneath. As the brunette turned, she gave him a glimpse of what awaited him when a third button came free and revealed almost all of her left tit.

"I want you," Jeter said, "and I'm gonna take you. Here. Now. I can't wait."

She dodged left, but Jeter was ready for the feint and captured her as she tried to go right. His strong arms caught her up and swung her around. She recoiled, but he kissed her. For a moment she yielded, then fought back. He enjoyed the play of her skin across his, her muscles, the passion she showed him. He kissed her again, then spun her around so fast that she sprawled across the table, bent at the waist.

He grabbed at the hem of her skirt and pulled it up.

"You were ready for me," he said, his hand stroking over the naked half-moon revealed. "None of them frilly things for me to rip off. This is better."

She gasped as he thrust his hand between her legs and stroked over the deep cleft he discovered. A finger sneaked up into her moist tightness.

"All ready for me, are you?"

"No, yes, oh!" She gasped when he tugged at her hips and pulled her back into the circle of his groin. His heavy, aching manhood penetrated her and slid easily upward—but only for an instant. With a deft twist, she worked her pelvis away and half-turned toward him.

Fingers snaking out faster than a striking rattler, she grabbed his jeans and pulled them down hard around his ankles. Shifting her weight, she shoved and sent him stumbling backward.

"You got to do better than that," she panted. "You have to catch me!"

With that taunt, the brunette dashed from the cabin, her skirt swirling around her ankles. Jeter caught sight of those luscious legs as she jumped from the porch and ran full-out for the barn. Cursing, Jeter pulled up his pants, stripped off his gun belt and tossed it onto the table, and then went after her. She led him a good chase, but he was hurting something fierce now for the feel of her all around him.

He saw the barn door swinging slowly, showing where she had gone. He walked with a long stride to the door and peered into the dim barn. No horses were in the four stalls, but a goat in one let its displeasure be known. Jeter ignored the goat and looked around for the woman. He didn't see her, but he heard her heavy breathing.

Spinning, he grabbed a bridle dangling from a hook and pulled away one of the leather straps.

"You're gonna rue the day you ran from me. Come here and get what you deserve."

He walked slowly toward the last stall, where he heard the heavy breathing. With a swift spin around, he confronted the woman. Her blouse had come entirely open, letting her milky white breasts tumble free. The sight of them momentarily mesmerized him, but not so much that he didn't move fast when the lovely brunette tried to duck past him and escape.

With a nimble move, he swung the leather strap around and circled her wrists, fastening them together. Jeter took another turn, then tossed the free end up and over a hook above the stall so that she had to stand on tiptoe.

"I told you not to run," he said. "Now you're gonna pleasure me." She tried to kick him, but he sidestepped and caught her leg at the thigh, pulling it up. He stepped forward so his crotch pressed into hers.

"Oh, ohhh," she moaned. Her brown eyes closed as he dropped his pants again and raked his manhood back and forth along the delicate pink chasm between her legs. Unbidden, her other leg rose and curled around his waist, drawing him in even tighter.

"This is what I've been dreamin' of out on the trail. This is what I've wanted."

"No, yes, oh, do it, do it!" she cried out.

He slid full-length into her seething interior, surrounded by clinging female flesh. The dampness turned to an oily flood as he stroked back and forth, causing her to swing slightly as she hung from the leather strap. He bent down and kissed her bouncing teats, licking and sucking and tonguing until she quivered. But lower where they were joined generated the most intense sensations. He moved faster and faster, his need for female companionship smothering everything else.

Face-to-face, he stared into her desire-glazed eyes. Then his hips exploded in a wild frenzy of movement he could no longer control. The carnal heat built and then he gasped, arched his back, and tried to drive himself even deeper within the woman's heated core.

He spilled his seed as she shuddered and began twisting and turning from the strap. Her legs clamped around his waist like steel bands to prevent him from leaving—as if he wanted to. Or could.

Then he sagged down, spent. Her legs fell down, and she once more supported herself on tiptoe.

"That was mighty special, Mr. Jeter," she said, a soft afterglow of a good loving on her face and extending down to her exposed breasts.

"Yes, it was, Mrs. Jeter," he said.

4

It had to be San Esteban. There weren't many towns along the road, but Slocum had hoped for more. As he rode down the main street, he counted the businesses. A dozen, maybe one or two more, and that was it. But the town wasn't a complete void in the vast West Texas desert because it sported not one but two saloons. There might be only one general mercantile, one pharmacy, and a single bakery, but the two saloons looked to have a monopoly on the real business.

Slocum knew this was being a mite unfair. It was past sundown and most businesses other than a saloon would be shuttered and their proprietors gone home for the night—or gone to belly up to the bar and quaff a few brews. He doubted many in this sleepy little town could afford whiskey. Hardly realizing he did so, he reached up and touched his shirt pocket where his bankroll had been. He was in the majority, not being able to afford a whiskey or even a beer unless he found a nickel tucked away in some other pocket.

Seeing the marshal's office, he stopped in the street and wondered if the lawman was inside. No light burned in the solitary slit window of the adobe building. Slocum dismounted, securely fastened his occasionally balky horse, and went inside.

He reached for his six-shooter when he mistook the deputy's snoring for a rattler ready to strike. The man had his feet hiked up on the desk and his head was tipped far back. He jerked about as his snoring disturbed even the man causing it.

"Hello," Slocum said. When he got no response, he rapped his knuckles hard on the door. The deputy's feet slid off the desk and crashed to the floor, bringing him awake with a start. The man grabbed for his pistol, but he was still enough asleep that he was clumsy. All he did was fumble and drop the weapon.

"I want to report a robbery. You in charge?"

"Who're you?" The deputy peered at Slocum in the gloom, then reached out and worked until he lit a coal-oil lamp on the desk. A warm, yellow light suffused the small room. Slocum saw a solitary jail cell that looked like it was easier to get out of than the office itself. The door hung at a curious angle, and rusty spots showed on the inch-wide steel straps making up the cage. For anything to show rust in this waterless desolation meant the cage had come from somewhere else, possibly Galveston or some other seacoast town.

"I was a passenger on the stage. We were robbed about ten miles outside of town."

"Stage is overdue. More than eight hours late," the deputy said, squinting at the Regulator clock methodically ticking off the seconds from its spot on the wall.

"That's because it was held up. Two passengers and

the driver are dead and everything worth taking's been took," Slocum said.

The deputy shrugged and looked increasingly peeved that Slocum had disturbed his sleep.

"Nuthin' I kin do. The marshal's out serving process." The way he said it, he resented being left alone in town. Or maybe he resented the marshal making a few dollars serving legal papers for some judge while all he had to do was sit and wait for animals to keel over in the San Esteban streets. It was probably his job to be sure all the dead animals were removed before they rotted too much in the hot sun.

"You don't care that three men are dead?"

"I don't know 'em, so why should I care?"

"You're wearing a badge, that's why." Slocum ground his teeth together to keep from saying what he really thought. Three men had died, and he had lost his brother's watch in a brutal robbery.

"You git a good look at the varmint?" the deputy asked. He gestured toward a few wanted posters tacked onto the adobe wall. Dust had piled up on the floor under each, showing that the nails had done more damage to the wall than to the posters.

"He wore a mask. And he knocked me out with a long-barreled shotgun." Slocum saw the deputy recoil as if he had been struck. "Who is it? You know the outlaw, don't you?"

"Yer description's mighty vague, mister. If you want, I'll take down some notes and leave 'em for the marshal. I only work here when he's not in town. He'll be back in a day or two."

"Where's the Butterfield office?"

"What you want—oh, you think Ole Man Sanford's

gonna give two hoots and a holler. Well, he might. The stage line's been losin' a fair amount of cargo over the past couple months."

"To the same road agent?" Slocum saw that his question had been answered without words by the frightened expression on the deputy's face.

"Down the street, across from the Drunk Camel."

"The saloon?"

"What else? Now, if you don't mind, I got serious work to do." The deputy opened a desk drawer and searched inside for something official-looking. All that was inside were old newspapers and a penny dreadful with a garish cover. He hastily closed the drawer and grabbed a stack of papers and began shuffling through them. Slocum knew he wasn't going to get any satisfaction from the part-time deputy. The man did nothing but keep the seat warm, not that the marshal probably did any more than that himself when he was in town.

Slocum stepped out into the cold night and looked around. Both saloons were doing better business now, but the Drunk Camel looked to be the more populated of the pair. Across the street where the deputy had said was the stagecoach office. The door stood open to let a sliver of light spill out in a pie-shaped wedge onto the boardwalk. Slocum hitched up his gun belt and went over.

He peered inside. A wizened old man hunched over a desk as he scribbled a long letter. A six-shooter lay on the desk close at hand.

"Are you Sanford?" Slocum got the reaction he expected. The old man's skeletal hand went to the six-shooter with remarkable speed for someone who looked half-dead.

"Who're you?"

"One of the passengers on the stagecoach that's not going to arrive," Slocum said. Sanford sagged even more, turning himself into a human question mark burdened by more than age now.

"I figured that was the way it was," the old man said. "Since I didn't hear the stage come rattlin' in, that means you walked?"

Slocum looked over his shoulder in the direction of the horse he had taken from the team.

"We were robbed about ten miles outside town. The driver and the other two passengers were killed. I got slugged and left for dead. There was only one road agent who did it all. He had a shotgun." Slocum saw that nothing after the part about the driver and passengers being murdered came as a surprise.

"He's a one-man terror. A regular horde of outlaws all rolled into one."

"Does he always kill everyone?"

"Not always. Sometimes he just shoots 'em up so they can tell the marshal about it."

"Why hasn't he been caught? The deputy said he's been at it for months."

Sanford spat and missed the brass cuspidor in the corner of the room. From the way the wall was stained with tobacco juice, he didn't often hit his target.

"Deputy? Just 'cuz he wears a badge don't make him a lawman. He's the town drunk when he's not sittin' in the office fer Marshal Benbow."

"If there's enough trouble, why isn't there a vigilance committee?"

"Mister, folks in San Esteban are peaceable and mind their own business."

"You mean they're scared shitless of the road agent."

Sanford laughed without a trace of humor and nodded. "Might say that. Hell, I *do* say that. All it gets me is stared at. They drift off then, muttering to themselves. I been sendin' letters to the home office, but they got other problems."

"The Apaches?"

"Don't get me wrong. Colonel Grierson's the finest man what ever sat astride a horse, but he got nothing but them black soldiers. They fight just fine, but they slack off when they got to ride down the Apaches."

"That's not what I've heard," Slocum said.

"Whatever you heard, they's not interested in catchin' a lone outlaw holdin' up stagecoaches out in the middle of nowhere. And mister, in case you didn't notice, San Esteban is the middle of nowhere."

"A mile from water, ten feet from hell," Slocum muttered.

"How's that?" Sanford finally took his hand off the six-gun. "Don't matter what you think. I got another report goin' in to the main office. You say Jethro's dead? And two passengers? The road agent got the strongbox too, I reckon?"

Slocum nodded. Jethro must have been the driver.

"You want a job? Soon as we get the stage back, we'll need a driver. You got the look of a man who can handle a team. And you know what you'd be up against."

"I've got other plans," Slocum said, resting his hand on the empty vest pocket where his watch had been.

"There ain't a reward on this varmint. There ought to be. A big one. Maybe a hunnerd dollars."

"I'll get him for nothing."

"You'll only end up like the rest if you cross him. We don't even know his name, but he blowed into the territory three-four months back and has been a regular Texas tornado whippin' up dust ever since."

"That's too long for a town to let an owlhoot like him keep on robbing and killing."

"They're scared, mister. Hell, I'm scared and I'm older than dirt. I been through Injun wars and even them Warm Springs Apaches don't frighten me much, but this fella, he's pure evil."

"He'll be pure dead."

"Good luck then. And in case you don't make it, it'll ease your mind to know that we got a real nice cemetery outside town."

"Hope there'll be room for one more grave," Slocum said. He didn't care if the outlaw was buried there or left for the voracious buzzards, the way he had left Jethro the stagecoach driver. As long as the outlaw was dead and Slocum had his watch back, everything would be fine.

Slocum patted down his pockets, but the storekeeper had been too thorough in obeying the road agent's orders. Every single penny had been dropped into the hat. Still, Slocum went to the saloon and stopped in the doorway, studying the crowd inside. They were a boisterous and happy-looking bunch. He went to the end of the bar and shoved his back against the wall as he leaned on an elbow.

"You got the look of a man with a powerful thirst," the barkeep said.

"I've got the look of a man who's been robbed of everything," Slocum said. "I was on the stage." He saw how the bartender backed off a pace.

"That's a crying shame, mister," the barkeep said. His hatchet-thin face paled a little under his weatherbeaten hide. "D-did he k-kill anyone?"

"Everyone else. He left me for dead."

"H-here, on the house," the barkeep said, sliding a beer down the bar to stop in front of Slocum.

"Much obliged," Slocum said, tasting the beer. It was surprisingly good, or maybe he was just thirsty. "You got any idea who it is doing the robbing?"

"D-don't care to find out neither," the bartender said, turning and hurrying to the far end of the bar. He talked quickly with several men there. Slocum watched their good nature drain. They all looked as if they would bolt and run, just from the telling of the story.

"How many robberies have there been?" Slocum asked a man who had been eavesdropping from a nearby table.

"More 'n I kin count," the man said. "He's bad medicine. Real bad. Got everyone in town afraid to even go to the outhouse without packin' a six-shooter. Rumor has it he rode with the Zaragosa *bandidos*."

"He didn't look or sound Mexican."

The man shrugged. "Might be he killed all of them and went out on his own. Or he might be like Luke—he's the barkeep—thinks, a Texas Ranger gone bad. It happens. And when it does, they turn mean. Meaner than when they wore badges."

"So nobody knows who this owlhoot is?"

"Lot of guesses, no answers."

"You could form a posse and track him down."

"Hell, mister, as long as he don't come into town, we're willin' to let him be. He don't bother us none, we won't tempt fate goin' after him."

"He's choking off travel to San Esteban. Won't be much longer until the railroad is built and there won't even be a stagecoach coming this way. The whole town'd dry up and blow away then. Looks like he's speeding that up by robbing every stage that comes here."

"He's killed a passel of folks, but none of them's been residents. That keeps it from being our direct concern." The man downed his beer, wiped his lips, and considered another. Then he decided against it. "You'll be better off ridin' on. Tangle with him and you'll end up dead."

"Yeah, out in the town cemetery," Slocum said angrily. "That's already been suggested by the stagecoach agent."

"Old Man Sanford's got it right this time. You heed him, mister, you do or that son of a bitch will kill you."

"He tried once and failed. He won't get a second chance," Slocum said.

"Suit yourself." The man pushed back and hurried from the saloon, probably headed for the other saloon, and left Slocum stewing in his thoughts.

He finished the beer and saw Luke wasn't likely to come back to ask if he wanted more, already knowing the answer. Slocum simply being in the saloon reminded everyone of the danger out on the road. He had seen fear clutch a town by the throat before, and it wasn't pretty. San Esteban would die long before the railroad choked off the traffic along the San Antonio–El Paso road because they refused to grab the nettle and pull it out, no matter how painful such an act might be. In the long run, they would all be safer and better off, but not a one of the citizens of this hellhole town would admit that.

Slocum stepped out into the street and shivered. When the sun went down in the desert, it got cold mighty fast.

"They call it the Drunk Camel because there used to be camels up at Fort Davis. They all died."

Slocum turned and saw a petite woman sitting in a

chair, shawl wrapped around her shoulders. She had long blond hair, eyes the color of the West Texas sky, and a smile burning brighter than even the noonday sun.

"You were wondering about the odd name, weren't you?"

"Among other things," Slocum said.

"My name's Amy Gerardo." She stood gracefully and came to him, her delicate hand outstretched. Slocum didn't know if she expected him to shake it or kiss it. Amy proved to be almost a foot shorter than his six feet, but the old saying about good things coming in small packages looked to be true. She was about the prettiest woman he had seen in a coon's age.

"Pleased to meet you. Mine's John Slocum."

"Mr. Slocum, I happened to overhear much of what you said inside the saloon."

"Do you always spy on men in saloons? You don't look like the type."

"Oh, thank you, sir," she said, feigning embarrassment and pleasure that he would think well of her. "News travels fast. I followed you here after I spoke with Mr. Sanford. Of course it was improper for me to actually enter, so I positioned myself here where I could overhear and be sure I saw you when you chose to leave."

"The barkeep gave me a beer because the outlaw stole all my money."

"I know. Les Jeter is a terrible man."

"You know his name?" Slocum tensed. The beautiful woman easily divulged a name that no one else in town admitted to knowing.

"He is the foremost outlaw in Texas," she said almost breathlessly. A flush came to her cheeks and her breasts heaved with—what? Excitement? It wasn't fear.

"How do you know of him?"

"I work for Mr. Ambrose Killian," she said. "And it is my job to learn as much of Jeter as I can. Please, Mr. Slocum, tell me what happened out on the road."

"Is there somewhere we can sit down? It's mighty cold out here."

"What? Oh, yes, of course. Why don't I buy you dinner? While you eat you can tell me all the details of this horrendous crime. There's a small restaurant down the street that serves quite good food."

"Most anything would set well with me. It's been a spell since I had anything to eat," Slocum admitted.

"I am sure I can get them to open up. They usually close before now." She waited with some expectation until Slocum realized she waited for him to offer her his arm. He did, and they went down the street past the Prancing Pony Drinking Emporium to a small adobe. As Amy had said, the restaurant was closed, but she arranged for the proprietor to open. Slocum saw how much money changed hands, and wondered anew at his lovely companion.

"Please, sir, sit. Eat."

"You're not having anything?" Slocum asked when a plate of stew and three-day-old biscuits was placed in front of him.

"I've eaten already."

"With Ambrose Killian?"

Amy took out a small notebook and pencil. She licked the tip before applying it to the paper.

"Tell me everything, Mr. Slocum. Don't leave out a single detail."

"Are you a reporter?"

"You might say that. Now, when did you first realize you were under attack by Les Jeter?"

The meal went quickly and pleasantly enough, but Slocum wondered at the volume of notes Amy took. She detailed every comment he made, no matter how offhand, and helped him get a fuller picture of all that had happened during and after the robbery.

"So he used the other horses from the stagecoach team to cover his tracks? How inventive," Amy said. "How perfectly diabolical!"

"I would have tracked him down, but I needed supplies. All I had was what had been in the stage."

"I believe you would have," she said, eyeing him boldly. Amy broke off the appraising look, closed her notebook, and stood. "Thank you, Mr. Slocum. You have been most helpful. If there's anything more you'd like to order, feel free. I'll see that the bill is taken care of."

"Wait," Slocum said, but Amy was already through the door and gone.

He settled back, ordered more coffee and two pieces of peach pie. His hunger was sated, but not his curiosity about Amy Gerardo.

5

"When did you first realize you were under attack by Les Jeter?" Amy Gerardo looked hard at Slocum, trying to worm her way into his brain and soul. He was an intricate man, far more than he appeared. He was observant and either very lucky or extraordinarily skillful. Amy nodded as she leaned forward across the small table, careful not to get any of the food spotting the table on her crisp blouse. That wouldn't do, though it might intrigue John Slocum. She was keenly aware of the way he watched her, much as a hungry cat eyed a bird.

She was no flighty thing, but it wouldn't hurt to let him think so if it gained what she wanted from him. Anything to help out Ambrose. Even if it meant disappointing a man as intriguing as Slocum.

Slocum muttered around a mouthful of stew. She noted several things he had mentioned earlier, tiny clues where Les Jeter might be headed, while Slocum swallowed and dabbed at his lips. He had more than a hint of the Southern gentleman, but she knew he had been out on the trail for some time. And it wasn't simply from his lack of bathing. His manners were atrophied, but at one time he had possessed a full set. Cleaned up and those gentlemanly ways unleashed, John Slocum could be a charming, deliciously dangerous companion.

"So he used the other horses from the stagecoach team to cover his tracks? How inventive," she said, scribbling frantically to keep up with both what Slocum said and her own observations. Ambrose would want to hear it all. Everything. And she would gladly pass it along. "How perfectly diabolical!"

"I would have tracked him down, but I needed supplies. All I had was what had been in the stage."

"I believe you would have," she said. She studied his stubbled chin, the deep emerald eyes that missed nothing, the set to his body. His determination was second only to Ambrose's. Amy wrote a concluding note to herself about how Slocum might be useful, then closed her notebook and stood amid a swish of skirts. "Thank you, Mr. Slocum. You have been most helpful. If there's anything more you'd like to order, feel free. I'll see that the bill is taken care of."

"Wait," Slocum said, half-standing. She hardly noticed. Her mind was aflutter with details, clues, possibilities that had to be related to Ambrose right away. He would want to know everything.

Amy stepped out into the night and walked away from the two saloons. Filthy places. Not fit for man nor beast, though both frequented them. More than once she had ventured inside to find out tidbits Ambrose demanded. Getting information about Jeter from the drunk who had ridden his mule into one saloon up in Fort Davis had been her most difficult task, especially since only *that* kind of woman ever set foot inside a drinking establishment. But she had fended off rude advances and found what she had been sent to unearth.

She clucked her tongue a bit at the thought of John Slocum in such a place. He fitted in perfectly—and yet he didn't. He was a hard drinker from the look of him, but he didn't go into saloons to socialize. She tried to imagine him with a soiled dove, and found it difficult. Such a handsome man had no reason to go to them for his pleasure.

Amy closed her eyes for a moment and got a firmer grip on her emotions. He was a commanding man, that John Slocum, but he was no Ambrose Killian. She hurried around the side of the stables at the edge of town and climbed into her carriage. She snapped the reins and got the horse pulling. It was a long way to the hacienda, almost to Fort Davis, but she had no fear of traveling alone in the desert at night. Her lucky star would shine on her the entire way home.

Amy sighed. *Home*. That was the way she thought of where Ambrose lived.

Amy dabbed at the sweat on her forehead as the hot noonday sun beat down on her. She was tired to the bone from the long trip from San Esteban, but she was also excited. She had important information for Ambrose that he would certainly appreciate receiving. With deft turns, she made her way through the partially opened gate a few yards off the main road and kept moving. There was no need to close the gate. Ambrose Killian's riches did not come from running cattle. The only reason he had the fence along the road and the gate was to discourage two-legged varmints rather than to keep in vast herds of cattle.

He had never been quite clear what the source of his family fortune was, but it had to be considerable. He might be an English lord or come from nobility or have ties to the Queen of England. Amy didn't know, but from the way Ambrose carried himself with such confidence, he was no peasant. His upbringing had included the finest of schools, judging from his diction and knowledge of the vast world. Amy admired it all.

The hacienda had been abandoned some years earlier before Ambrose had found it, moved in, and renovated it. The furnishings were exquisite, all imported from the Continent at considerable expense. Seeing such finery out in the middle of the West Texas desert always brought a sharp intake of breath and, depending on people's sensibilities, a tear to their eye at beholding such grandeur. Ambrose had worked constantly to make this an oasis of gentility, and had succeeded.

Amy let out a sigh as she tugged on the reins and stopped the horse in front of the carved wood entryway. With a lithe move, she dropped to the ground and entered the courtyard, where a small fountain bubbled up. It had taken her some time to find out how Ambrose had built a reservoir on the roof of the house to supply the bubbling, leaping water. It soothed her with its gentle rush. A scraping sound caused her to pause and look up to the tank. A servant worked to add more water to keep the fountain functioning. She averted her eyes. It was something like learning how a magic trick was done. Once she knew, the magic turned into something tawdry.

"Miss Gerardo," Ambrose said in greeting. He opened the ornate door and beckoned to her. "So good to see you once again."

"I have great news, sir. Great news about Les Jeter!"

Amy felt a rush of excitement when she saw how Ambrose's face lit up like a child receiving a new toy. It pleased her to please him.

"Excellent, my dear. Come in. Please, sit down." Killian motioned to a chair across from the love seat. Amy hesitated, wondering if she would be too bold to sit on the love seat and hope that Ambrose joined her.

She sat in the chair facing his huge chair, which seemed to engulf him with its bulk, wings rising high on either side of his body and head as he sank down.

"Wine?"

"Yes, please," she said. "It was a long, dusty ride from San Esteban."

"Ah, San Esteban," Killian said, tenting his fingers and resting his chin on the tips. He stared at her with gray, fathomless eyes that seemed to suck her down into a vortex and hold her enthralled. She wanted to go over and kneel next to the chair, reach up, and—

"Jeter," he prompted quietly.

"Oh, yes, sorry. I am so tired from the trip. I hurried, but it still seemed to take forever."

"Perhaps we should see into getting a double horse team for you, although that would be difficult for a woman of your stature to handle."

"I can handle such a team," Amy said, distracted. The servant put a small stemmed glass of blood-red wine on the table beside her, then backed away. "You aren't having any, Mr. Killian?"

"No, my dear, it's too early to imbibe. I want to keep my senses fresh and alert for this news. What did you learn?"

Amy rushed through the recitation of her dinner with Slocum and what had happened to the stage.

"So," Killian said, pursing his lips as he spoke, "Jeter is going to run dry holding up the stagecoaches soon. They will either force the Army to send along a trooper or two to protect their cargo, or simply stop sending anything of value."

"The railroad is nearing completion," she said, watching her employer. He was so well built, muscles rippling under the smoking jacket he wore. The bright red silk ascot hid a powerful neck with a vein on the side that throbbed when he was agitated. Amy had only seen Ambrose in such a state twice, and he'd had a towering anger that was not to be denied. She wanted him to be happy and never respond to her with even a small, dark piece of that hidden rage.

"He might consider train robbery. Nothing is past this criminal mastermind," Killian said, warming to the idea. "The railroad would send detectives. Perhaps hire Pinkertons to track him down—"

"But they would fail," Amy said between sips of her heady wine. "You haven't been able to track him and you are the best. They would have no chance."

"But Jeter might fall into a trap they laid. With enough men and resources, even the cleverest of the Texas *bandidos* would succumb. He has a secure hideout in the Davis Mountains, but they are a maze of canyons and deadly precipices. Apaches hid there for years before the cavalry routed them. Jeter is ever so much cleverer and far more dangerous."

Killian snapped his fingers for the attentive servant and ordered a glass of wine for himself. Amy took this as a small celebration. Ambrose had an idea on how to find Jeter.

"Tell me more of this Slocum fellow," Killian said,

looking at her over the glass. He quickly drained it and held it, his left index finger slowly circling the rim. It began making a ringing sound as he moved in the circle faster and faster. He abruptly put the glass on the table beside him. "Tell me everything."

"Why," Amy said, flustered, "I don't know anything about him. He wears his six-shooter like a gunfighter, but he was the perfect Southern gentleman. From his accent he hails from Georgia or perhaps South Carolina. Otherwise, I found out nothing about him."

"On the contrary. There is much you learned, if you would only think about it."

"I'm sorry, sir," she said, frightened that she had displeased him.

"Don't be. Consider this instructive. Slocum was the only one to survive the robbery. That means he is unique in this regard, for this robbery. Jeter savagely gunned down the others, but Slocum escaped."

"But—"

Killian held up his hand to forestall her objection.

"I know what you are going to say. Jeter thought Slocum was dead. But he wasn't. That is important. You call Slocum a gunfighter. He probably is, but he is also an expert tracker. He immediately understood the trick Jeter played by running the horses in all directions to confuse the actual escape path. Slocum did not waste time, but went to San Esteban to enlist aid. That means he is, in part, a law-abiding man."

Amy wasn't too sure about this. Slocum was bold and confident, but to call him law-abiding meant Killian had never spoken to him face-to-face. Amy knew Slocum was a dangerous man. Perhaps more dangerous than Les Jeter, if that were possible.

"You want to use Slocum to find Jeter?" she asked. "But you wanted to hunt him down yourself and capture him."

"The trial would be spectacular. No outlaw in the West would have a more important trial. I could sell the memories and reminiscences of the hearings in Europe and become famous overnight."

"You're already quite famous, I am sure," she said.

"This would mean lionization on the level of Oscar Wilde, that poseur. All would come to my readings and lectures. The crowned heads of Europe would beg me to give private audiences." Killian had flushed with excitement at the notion of such notoriety. He settled back into his chair.

"Slocum can capture Jeter for me. I will see that the outflaw is put on trial somewhere important. San Antonio perhaps. Or Austin. Wherever there would be considerable newspaper coverage. And I would be at the center of the trial because I am the foremost authority on Lester Evan Jeter!"

He breathed heavily now. Amy had never seen him more handsome.

"What will it take to hire this Slocum? Oh, never mind. I am sure you will find the proper combination of inducements, monetary and otherwise, won't you, my dear?"

It took Amy a few seconds to understand what Ambrose wanted from her. She nodded slowly that she understood. Anything that got her closer to Ambrose's heart—his bed!—would be done.

"While you were out finding these tidbits of data, I have been diligently working on the collection. Come. You must see it." He stood and held out his arm for her.

Amy gratefully took it, feeling the play of muscles under the jacket sleeve. He was so strong that she almost swooned in hope that he would catch her, scoop her up, and carry her in his arms. Instead, he walked briskly, forcing her to hurry to keep up with him as they went into the next room.

Many a museum would have been proud of such a display. On the walls hung rifles and pistols, all used by Jeter over the last three years of his criminal career.

"This one, this pistol. It is the one he used to kill his first man."

"The saloon owner?"

"Yes," Killian said with a hint of reverence in his tone. He lifted the six-shooter and held it out. She knew better than to touch it. Ambrose only wanted her to admire it, and she did.

"A Remington," she said. "A black-powder-and-shot model."

"But quite deadly in a determined outlaw's hands, and Jeter is most determined. He shot the bartender through the heart. One shot, one dead man. His first."

"How did you come across this?" Amy asked. "It must have been very difficult."

"I am not without my sources," Killian said, chuckling with pleasure at her recognition of his expertise. "A lawman in Austin had found the gun after Jeter dropped it fleeing his crime. It wasn't until sometime later that the sheriff identified Jeter as the killer and this as the murder weapon."

"I see that you have already built a case for it." Amy looked at the handsome walnut case with the glass lid. Inside was a wine-colored satin bed with the outline where the six-gun had been placed. The entire case stood on its own display rack in the center of the room. Ambrose obviously thought this was the keystone to his vast collection of memorabilia.

"I have a second case ready for the last six-shooter he'll use. I'll have them side by side with my biography of the West's most notorious outlaw between."

"Bookends to a deadly career in crime," Amy said.

"Well put, well put, my dear. I'll need you to go over the new manuscript pages I've written while you were gone. They need some tidying up. My writing is ever so atrocious."

"I'll get to it right away, after I've freshened up from my trip. It is so hot and dusty," she said, letting the last syllables trail off in hope that Ambrose would see fit to help her out of the dress and corset—and join in her bath.

"You look flushed. Perhaps you took too much sun. Sunstroke is a constant hazard out here," he said.

"I'm all right. Will there be anything else?"

"Yes."

Amy thought her heart would explode as he turned and looked down at her. He wasn't as tall as John Slocum, but he was as commanding. She was ready for him to command her to do . . . anything.

"I also located the sheriff's reports concerning his pursuit and attempted arrest of Jeter," Ambrose said. "I need you to go through and excerpt the most salient points for my biography."

"Oh, yes, of course," she said. Amy felt as if she had walked to the rim of a vast and gorgeous vista, only to have slipped and fallen over the edge.

"If you think my penmanship leaves much to be desired, Sheriff Oldham's is far worse. He has a crabbed script that I can barely decipher. And his spelling! Well, you'll have to cope with that yourself. Think in terms of what he said phonetically." Ambrose reached under a table, pulled out a small wooden box, and handed it to her. "If there are any pages missing, note that also. I might be able to replace them from the sheriff's widow."

"Widow? He's dead?"

Ambrose Killian looked as if someone had lit him up. He smiled and said, "Why, yes, my dear. Jeter killed him. With his own six-shooter. I am trying to track down that weapon also. His *second* murder. This will be the finest tribute to the most dangerous man west of the Mississippi!"

Killian spun and gestured grandly, taking in the entire room and its contents.

"Yes, yes, it will, Mr. Killian," she said. "If you don't mind, I'll repair to my room, get cleaned up, and . . . and get to reading the sheriff's reports."

"Do that, my dear. Yes, do that. I expect you to have considerable work done by dinner. And do consider how best to employ this John Slocum to track down Jeter for me."

"Yes . . . Mr. Slocum," Amy said absently, her mind returning to the tall, rough-hewed Southerner. "Mr. Slocum."

She left the room, hoping that Ambrose would call her back and give her a kiss for all her fine work. She hoped it would happen but did not expect it, since he was lost in the history of all the artifacts left behind by Les Jeter.

6

"No, Les, don't do it," pleaded Ruth Jeter. "It's too dangerous!"

"Hell's bells, that don't bother me much. Everything I do's dangerous. There's not a Ranger or lawman in this part of Texas who isn't lookin' for me."

They sat side by side on a rock looking out over the grassy valley where the cabin stood. From here the barn was hidden, down a slope and beyond the cabin, but other than this, the lookout point allowed a clear view of anyone coming up the valley. This suited Jeter just fine. He worried about being snuck up on as much as he worried that Ruth would take it into her head to leave him.

"You can't rob a bank all by yourself. It's suicide to do that. They've got guards in banks willing to shoot anybody who looks cross-eyed at a teller."

"Might be I don't intend to waltz on in and shove a gun under some scared teller's nose before askin' for money. Might be I got other plans."

"You thinking on tunneling in, coming up in the vault,

and emptying it that way? All by yourself, it wouldn't take more than a month of Sundays. And think about your back. You threw it out when that horse almost kicked you."

"I'm doin' all right," Jeter said irritably. Ruth didn't understand. It wasn't as much about the money as it was showing the world how good he was. And proving to her that he could provide for a family. One day he would have a son to follow him around. So far, and it wasn't for lack of trying, that hadn't happened. But it would, and Ruth would have to be proud of him and his son.

Jeter laughed ruefully when he realized another fact of nature. It *was* about the money too. He liked money, and the easiest way of getting it was to steal from those who already had it.

"What's so funny? The notion you might get your head blown off by some itchy-fingered guard? You've got them all so stirred up they might shoot you when you walked in the front door, no matter if you have your six-shooter out or not." Ruth drew up her knees and circled them with her arms. Jeter had seen her do this before when she withdrew into her own thoughts. It was best to let her be. Eventually she'd come around to understanding that he had to do this. It was for her. For her and their son, whenever he came into the world.

"I've got to hit the trail," he said, reaching out and stroking over her tangled locks. He used his fingers to crudely comb her brunette hair until it was less snarled and gleamed in the late afternoon sunlight. "You're so purty it makes me ache, darlin', but I got to go. It's for you."

"No, it's not," she said, turning away and burying her face between her knees. "You say that, but it's all about the money. Les, stop the robbing and come work this place. It's not ours, I know, but we got rights. Whoever abandoned it's not coming back. They would have been here by now if they hadn't left for good. A few head of cattle, maybe some more goats and sheep, and a crop of alfalfa and we can make a good living here. It'll be safe."

"Safe?" He shook his head. "There's no such thing, Ruth."

"Not now, not after you shot up about every stagecoach rolling through West Texas. There must be a powerful big reward out on your head. If the Rangers don't come looking for you, some bounty hunter will. I'm begging, Les. I don't ask for much, but I want you to stay here. Work here and forget the bank."

Jeter said nothing as he looked out over the pleasant green valley from this aerie. This was the sort of place he had dreamed of homesteading once—before he got the taste of adventure from robbing and killing.

"They won't be back," she said. "The people who upped and left won't come back. And if they do, you've got money from all those robberies. You can buy this place for us."

"They won't be back," Jeter said. He knew the man and woman who had built the cabin and barn and plowed up a few acres to the east would never be back. He had killed them both and put them in their graves less than a mile from where he sat with his wife. He hadn't wanted to kill either of them, but the man had fought when he tried to rob him. The killing had been an accident, but the woman wouldn't see that. She had tried to skewer him with a knife. It had been her or him. Jeter wasn't the sort to let a woman cut him up.

"Then stay, Les. Please. For me."

"I'm doing this for you. When I get back, might be that'll be enough for us to live on the rest of our born days." He stood and dusted himself off. It was a long ride into San Esteban to rob that pathetic little bank there.

Nobody knew what he looked like. That made his entry into San Esteban all the easier. Les Jeter rode past the bank and gave it a quick once-over, then rode on to the Drunk Camel Saloon for a drink. He went inside and found himself a table near the door where he could look out into the street, past the marshal's office to the bank.

"What'll it be?" asked Luke the barkeep.

"A half bottle of whiskey," Jeter said. "I think I got enough for that much." He rummaged around in his pocket and found a gold coin—one taken from the last stagecoach robbery. He dropped it onto the table. The tiny disk spun, shining gold and bright before falling flat.

"That'll do more 'n a half bottle, mister," Luke said, scooping it up. He returned a minute later with the whiskey, a mostly clean shot glass, and a handful of change. He dropped this on the table, where it formed a small mountain of silver. "Sorry 'bout all the nickels and dimes, but I ain't got any silver dollars fer change yet. Too early in the day."

"You could go to the bank and get the change," Jeter said.

"Or *you* could. I can't leave my customers."

Jeter looked past the barkeep to the only other patron, passed out on a poker table in the back of the saloon.

"Yeah, I can see that. Reckon I'll have to take it to the bank myself, but after I finish this."

"You must have worked up a powerful thirst for that much whiskey this early in the day," the barkeep said.

Jeter only stared at him, his gray eyes cold and empty. "I'll let you git on down to serious drinking," the barkeep said uneasily, backed off a pace, and then hurried behind the bar. Jeter heard him rummaging about, probably making sure his six-shooter or sawed-off shotgun was close at hand.

Jeter had robbed saloons before, but not today. It was like the man said. There wasn't whole lot in the till yet. And maybe even after a good week there wouldn't be, since San Esteban split their money between this and the other saloon. The Drunk Camel and the Prancing Pony. He wondered how they'd conjured up names like those. Jeter sipped at the surprisingly good whiskey and considered if it would be worthwhile to take a barrel of the fine rotgut. He shook off the notion of such an audacious theft. He might load a barrel or two onto a wagon and get away with it, but his sights were set on a bigger target. The men going into the bank weren't bowed over with bags of money, but they looked prosperous. The area around San Esteban was festooned with rich cattle growers. More than one had a string of horses that he sold to the Army, in addition to supplying beef and other foodstuffs. The desert made it difficult for the Army to transport much in the way of food, so it was cheaper to buy locally.

Cheaper, but not too much so. The ranchers gouged the Army unmercifully, and it showed in how prosperous a town like San Esteban was. And a well-to-do rancher had to keep his money somewhere.

The bank was an easy target that might yield a thousand dollars or more. Lots more. Jeter kept drinking as a plan formed in his head. His wife had been worried about one man holding up a bank, but Jeter was up to the chore.

They weren't too bright when it came to protecting their wealth in these parts.

He drank, he thought, and finally when the level of alcohol reached the point where it overcame his natural caution and Ruth's worry, Jeter stood, hitched up his gun belt, and left.

"Hey, mister, you gonna drink the rest of that whiskey? Kin I have a nip?"

Jeter paused at the door and looked to the back of the saloon. The cowboy who had passed out earlier craned his neck around like a prairie dog hunting for food. Only this one had spotted the few drops of whiskey left in the bottle.

"It's yours, partner," Jeter said. "But I almost forgot my change." He scooped up the pile of change. "You sure they'll give me a couple silver cartwheels for all this?" he asked of the barkeep.

"Sure am," the man answered. "They do it all the time for me, and I don't have that much in the bank."

"You mean you have an account there?"

"Yeah," the barkeep said warily. "What's it to you?"

"Nothing," Jeter said, laughing. He left, clutching his pile of coins. How stupid he had been! Thinking of robbing the saloon was a waste of time when the barkeep said all his money went into the bank. He'd rob the bank and get the revenue from both saloons!

Jeter made his way across the dusty street, aware of the sun in his eyes. It was getting toward afternoon. Siesta time. He wasn't sure if the bank closed for a couple hours and it didn't matter, since the kind of withdrawal he intended didn't require them to be open to the public.

"Just open for my six-shooter," Jeter said, stopping at the front door to the bank. It was dim and cool inside the big adobe building, and it took a few seconds for his eyes to adjust to the change in light.

Two guards, one snoozing in a chair to the right and the other standing with his hand resting indolently on his six-gun as he talked to the teller. Jeter looked around for the bank president or some other officer, but didn't spot him. He might be back in the vault. That would be good because it meant the heavy door would be open.

"A cornucopia," Jeter said to himself as he walked inside. He had always liked the sound of that word ever since he was a kid, and the way it rolled off his tongue made him feel good, big, intelligent. The bank was his cornucopia!

"Good day, sir," greeted the teller. "What do you have there?"

"I need some of this changed into greenbacks or even a silver dollar or two," Jeter said, dropping the pile of change onto the counter. He made sure a few of the coins bounced off onto the floor. The sleepy guard started and shifted position, but never opened his eyes. The other bent to pick up the change Jeter had dropped. When the guard looked up he was staring up the barrel of the outlaw's six-gun.

"Lose your hogleg," Jeter said. "And none of you folks get frisky and try anything dumb. If you do, your friend here gets a hunk of lead in the brain."

The teller blanched and stepped back from his window, hands going up.

"No, you stay where you are. Gather up all the money and put it into a bag for me."

The instant Jeter's attention shifted to the teller, the guard reacted. He put his head down and drove forward, catching the outlaw just above the knees. Jeter let out a screech of surprise and jerked the trigger hard. The recoil pressed the butt of the gun into his palm—and the guard died instantly. The bullet had smashed his spine.

Jeter sat heavily on the floor and swung his six-shooter around to cover the now-awake guard in the chair. Before the man could go for the rifle leaning against the wall beside him, Jeter fired. Twice. A third time, making certain the guard was dead.

"Don't, don't!" Jeter shouted, but it was too late to stop the teller from grabbing for a small-caliber pistol hidden under the counter. Jeter aimed and fired. His bullet caught the teller just above the bridge of his nose.

"Damnation," Jeter grumbled as he got to his feet. Things had turned sour mighty fast. "You should never have made me kill you all. They aren't gonna pay you a dime more for dyin' tryin' to protect the money in the vault. Hell, they aren't gonna have to pay you at all now."

Jeter kicked open the low gate between the president's vacant desk and the lobby and went around to the teller's box. He grabbed a moneybag and began stuffing what he could find in the teller's drawer into the bag. There was hardly enough to make the robbery worth his time. Less than a hundred dollars and three men dead? There had to be more.

Jeter heard people out in the street, mumbling and whispering among themselves, wondering if anything inside was wrong. He reckoned he had plenty of time before some intrepid soul poked his head in—

It happened sooner than Jeter had expected.

"Any trouble in here?"

Jeter recognized the part-time deputy who took over when the marshal was out getting drunk in other towns. He barely remembered lifting his six-shooter and firing.

The deputy's head exploded in a red mist as the bullet tore through the skull and came out the top. Jeter fired again, but his pistol came up empty. Grumbling at the inconvenience, Jeter knocked out the spent brass in his Colt and reloaded from cartridges stuck into loops on his belt.

Nobody followed the foolish deputy inside, so Jeter grabbed his moneybag and went to the vault. The door had been pulled shut, but had not locked because a large hunk of cloth jammed the locking bolts. Putting his back into it, Jeter pulled open the door and saw that the cloth had been ripped from the bank president's coat. The man cowered in the rear of the vault, hands up to protect his face.

"Don't kill me. Take what you want but don't kill me like you did the others."

"You know me?" Jeter asked.

"N-no," the bank president said, staring at Jeter with frightened eyes.

"Then you're gonna die not knowin' who shot you," Jeter said. He fired three times to make certain the president wasn't going to identify him later. It had been a mistake coming into the bank without wearing a mask. As the thought occurred to him, Jeter pulled up his bandanna. He had to make an escape through what might be a big crowd of townsfolk.

He went to the boxes on shelves and hurriedly emptied them onto the floor in the middle of the vault. The vault wasn't large enough for both the dead president and the loot. Jeter considered dragging the portly man out of the way, but he relieved his exasperation by shooting into the dead body a couple more times. It accomplished nothing, but made him feel better.

Humming his favorite song, "The Two Corbies," as he worked, he quickly finished searching the vault for valuables and did a quick tally of more than two thousand dollars.

"I'll show you, Ruth," he muttered to himself. "You won't doubt me when you see this much money." He swung the moneybag over his shoulder and left the vault and its grisly contents, but stopped when he reached the president's desk.

This time people outside weren't foolishly poking their heads inside the lobby. They shoved in rifle barrels. Lots of them.

Jeter looked around for another way out of the bank and realized there wasn't one. He had entered by the only door and had to leave that way. Even the windows were high in the walls and small—too small for a man his size to wiggle through. He might dump the money outside through a side window, shoot his way from the lobby, pick up his loot, and escape.

Jeter realized how hard that would be to do just as someone sighting down a rifle barrel spotted him and fired. The man had buck fever and missed by a mile. That was the goods news for Jeter. The bad news was how the other scared gunmen all reacted by firing their own weapons. They didn't have a good target in their sights, but it didn't matter. The lobby suddenly filled with dozens of rounds, all ricocheting around and forcing him to drop down behind the desk to keep from getting ventilated.

He poked up his head and waited for what would inevitably follow.

"You git 'em?"

"Had to. Nobody could live through that many bullets," someone else answered.

"Don't know. We wasn't aimin' at them, not exactly."

"We got them," the first voice said firmly, bravely, boasting at his own prowess. "Let's go drag the snakes outta there."

He knocked open the door using the butt of his rifle and stood silhouetted against the afternoon sun, making a perfect target. Jeter should have waited for the second or third man to enter, but the temptation was too great with the first. He fired smack into the middle of the shadowy form. The man dropped his rifle and sagged to the floor without making a sound.

"What happened?" demanded someone farther back in the crowd.

"Jackson got shot. They killed Jackson!"

Jeter ducked. He knew what had to happen. And it did. Everyone in the crowd opened fire at once. Splinters from the desk flew all around and he heard glass shatter. The pungent odor that followed caused him to look around. The kerosene lamp on the president's desk had been struck by a bullet and had shattered, sending its volatile contents all over the papers strewn about.

"Did we git him this time?"

Jeter bided his time and fired a single shot when a head poked around the doorjamb to look in. The man slid straight to the ground, dead. Jeter cursed quietly at his bad luck. The bodies were stacking up in the only way out of the bank. He'd have to vault over them to reach safety outside. If he killed any more of the crowd, he would be pushing a wall of dead flesh in front of him.

"Hmm," he said to himself, thinking about the possibilities of hoisting a body and using it as a shield against the crowd's bullets. Then he decided that would never work. Enough lead would rip the flesh off a body and quickly remove all protection. He had to get out of here and do it fast. If he ran out of ammunition, they would rush him and put an end to his career, which wouldn't do when he had other stagecoaches to rob and banks to hold up.

Jeter slipped along behind the desk and shoved the president's chair under one of the high windows. Risking someone hitting him with a wild shot, Jeter jumped up on the chair and studied the window. The situation wasn't as bad as he had thought. The frame held a window too small for him to wiggle through, but if the frame were knocked out, he might escape this way.

He began hammering away at the frame using the butt of his pistol, occasionally taking a shot or two through the front door to keep the crowd at bay. Jeter grunted when one side broke free and took a considerable hunk of adobe mud with it. Using the twisted frame as a lever, he worked away the rest of the window, then hopped up and thrust his head through. He saw the edge of the crowd, but everyone had their attention fixed on the front doors of the bank, not its side windows. They probably thought these windows were too small for escape too.

"Dumb asses," Jeter said, dropping back to the chair. He fired a couple more times, then fumbled in his pocket and came up with a tin of lucifers. With a quick scratch of the head of one across the rough wall, he had a blazing match to work with. He dropped it into the tin, which flared into a fire so intense he had to squint. With the tin turning fiery hot, he wasted no time tossing it onto the desk where the spilled coal oil had puddled.

The sudden eruption of flame scorched his clothing. Even better, it caused confusion to pass through the crowd outside.

"Fire! They set the whole damn place on fire!"

Jeter twisted agilely and got through the window, falling headfirst into the alley beside the bank. He twisted as he fell and rolled onto his shoulders before coming to his feet. Jeter slipped his six-shooter back into its holster and brazenly slung the moneybag over his shoulder before walking out to join the crowd.

"What's going on?" he asked a man in front of him standing on tiptoe and trying to get a better look at the flames gusting from the opened bank doors.

"Got a whole gang of robbers in there. We got 'em trapped! If they don't burn first, we're gonna hang 'em!"

"Good luck," Jeter said. "I think I'll ride on. I don't cotton much to necktie parties."

"Your loss," the man said, never turning to see to whom he spoke.

Laughing, Jeter returned to the Drunk Camel, slung the moneybag over his stallion's rump, and mounted. He considered riding past the burning bank, then turned in the other direction, giving a jaunty salute as he left San Esteban.

7

"You want me to go with you?" Amy Gerardo's eyes were wide. Ambrose had never asked her to be his personal secretary on such a trip before. She could hardly restrain her joy. "I can be ready to go whenever you wish, sir."

"Good, it's what I expect from you, Miss Gerardo," Ambrose Killian said. He paced back and forth in his trophy room, agilely missing the sharp corners on the display cases and occasionally stopping in front of a particularly toothsome item in his Jeter collection. He reached out and let his fingers brush across a buckskin shirt that had two small holes about where the wearer's heart would be.

"He killed an Apache chief who wore this shirt. Two shots from more than fifty yards away. Using that Remington, the one he took off the lawman," Killian said. "Jeter is a remarkable shot. None better, and I have seen the best."

"When?" Amy asked before she could restrain herself. She knew so little about Ambrose and his background.

Try as she might to unravel the reasons he was so intent on the career of one specific gunman, and not a particularly famous one, they remained closed to her. Ambrose wasn't the sort of man who encouraged questions about himself. That lent an air of mystery to him, and made her lie awake nights wondering about his childhood and even his more recent years. She had met him only six months ago, and that had been sheer coincidence. She had been down on her luck trying to make a living on railroads, stealing tickets and food, cozying up to conductors until they took pity on her, drifting like a rudderless boat in search of an anchor.

Ambrose had given her that when he had seen her aboard a train from Galveston to San Antonio and had quizzed her at length about her background. She was glad she had studied hard and knew all the things Miss Fotheringay's Finishing School instructors had tried to force into her insolent, rebellious young skull. Perhaps Amy hadn't learned everything, but she had learned enough to convince Ambrose she would make a reputable, efficient secretary and general factotum.

"Recently I went to an outpost some distance away," Ambrose said. "His name is Dalton and he might be related to those in the Doolin-Dalton gang, though that remains to be proven."

"Why are you interested in him? Does he know Jeter?"

"I am always on the lookout for the best in everything, my dear. Les Jeter might well be the foremost criminal of this era, and I am fascinated with every aspect of his life, but what if there is another, more dangerous outlaw worthy of my attention? Wouldn't it be fascinating to pit Dalton against Jeter and see who triumphed?"

"How do you mean, Ambrose?" Amy bit her tongue.

She had called him by his first name for the first time. She had always tried to maintain the formality he obviously desired, and such an intimacy might vex him sorely. Amy put her hand to her lips and waited for what might be an eruption of anger on his part for her careless familiarity. He didn't seem to have noticed because he was so wrapped up in his mental journey to find Dalton.

"Perhaps this Dalton can be hired to have a showdown with Jeter. Of course, he has to find him. If he can, he will have done something neither Ranger nor sheriff has done. By simply locating Jeter, this Dalton fellow will have proven his mettle."

"But you wouldn't—"

"I want to see Jeter's final minutes and experience them, record them, *feel* them. How better to do this than to put a known gunman up against him? If Dalton is a faster draw and more accurate, I will have seen Jeter's final instant of life. If Dalton fails, it will reinforce my opinion of Jeter and his skill with a six-gun."

"Is this Dalton a bounty hunter?"

Killian snorted in contempt. "I have no truck with such swine. They feed off carrion rather than accomplishing anything on their own. Lawmen hardly perform their jobs for money. No, they do it for justice."

Amy started to point out the many exceptions she had personally witnessed, but Killian rattled on.

"Dalton will be a perfect foil for what I need. Be ready to ride in a half hour. We'll be on the trail for some time, so prepare appropriately." Killian spun about and walked from the trophy room without a backward glance. Amy sighed and left through the door leading into the main sitting area and from there down the hall to her room. She wondered if she ought to keep a valise packed at all times for Killian's sudden impulses like this one.

"There's nothing here, sir," Amy said. She craned her neck as she looked around to find whatever it was that drew Killian to this spot. Mostly desert spotted with a few larger clumps of mesquite, the entire area looked like a good place to die. "Unless there are Indians lurking."

"This is the spot," Killian said positively. "Dalton was last seen at a watering hole and was supposed to have encamped there."

"How long ago?" Amy grew increasingly nervous as she listened to the soft whistle of the incessant breeze working its way over the dunes, creating new wrinkles on their windward foreheads. "Wouldn't he water his horse and ride on?"

"He has nowhere else to go. So said my source." Killian snapped the reins on the buckboard and drove over a rise and down the far side. The road was hardly more than a pair of ruts. This, at least, heartened Amy. Something more than a lone horseman had come this way often enough to leave the twin tracks in the desert.

"There he is," Killian said, urging the horses to more speed. His guidance was hardly needed once they scented the water waiting for them. They trotted to the edge of the pond and began drinking. Killian let them have their fill as he jumped down and looked around. Amy hesitated, not sure if she should wait for Ambrose to help her down. She appreciated the feel of his strong hand in hers, the way he sometimes placed his free hand on her waist to guide her—but he wasn't interested in such chivalry today. He was too caught up in his hunt for the gunman.

She climbed down on her own and pulled the horses

back to keep them from bloating. The horses resisted, but she had learned to handle them during the last four days when they had traveled across some of the most desolate land imaginable. Every mile had been a trial promising Apaches and sidewinders and road agents along with the heat and biting wind.

"See? See, my dear? He was here. He must have left only hours ago. The tracks are still fresh."

"How do you know it was Dalton?"

"Who else could it be?" Killian asked with absolute certainty in his abilities. Amy felt a moment of doubt, then smiled when Killian took off his broad-brimmed hat and waved it in the air as a man trooped back over the rise, leading his horse.

"Hello!" Killian called. "Are you Dalton? I have a business proposal for you, if you are."

Amy wasn't sure it was good to put all his cards on the table right away. This might be someone else. For all she knew, it could be Jeter himself. She straightened at the thought, and reached up to the buckboard where Ambrose carried a rifle. It had never occurred to her before that she had no idea what Jeter looked like. She had spent hours in the trophy room looking at the artifacts left by the outlaw. She was as expert in the debris of a violent man's life as Ambrose, but she had never seen a picture or heard more than a superficial description. She realized that Ambrose's vivid depictions had taken away the need for more photographic representations. She felt that she knew Jeter intimately, and hadn't ever asked what he looked like.

"Who wants to know? And do I have any business with you?"

Amy despaired at the exchange. The man had admitted to being Dalton and had gained nothing in return. These negotiations would be painfully open, she feared.

Killian went over and shook hands, then launched into a long description of crime in West Texas and how he sought Jeter.

"Hold your horses," Dalton said, shaking his head. "I've heard of him. Who hasn't? Not a stage driver in the state that's not heard of Jeter, but I ain't no lawman. I'm not huntin' for him unless I got a damn good reason."

"One thousand reasons, Mr. Dalton," Killian said, "ought to persuade you."

"You offerin' a thousand dollars for his head?"

"Nothing so crude, sir. I want him brought to justice. I want a long trial that details every crime he has ever committed and reveals to me those I have no idea about."

"I don't understand."

"You are the perfect man to accompany me on this hunt. Your fame precedes you."

"What's that?"

"You are an expert gunman and a brave fellow, by accounts."

"Well, reckon so," Dalton said, hitching up his gun belt. "You pay me a thousand dollars just to ride around huntin' for Jeter?"

"Something like that. As you can see, I am no expert gun handler, unlike yourself."

"That's a thousand right now? In advance?"

"Oh, hardly. Expenses now, the balance when we capture Jeter."

Amy saw Dalton working over what this meant to him and how he could gull Ambrose out of his money. She left the rifle where it was and went to stand beside Ambrose to give him support. She saw from the expression on his face that he was entirely caught up in his notion of what Dalton would do when faced with Jeter in a gunfight. Nothing else mattered.

"You gotta give me some show of good faith," Dalton said.

"You have camped here for some time," Amy said. "You aren't employed and don't have much to do, except possibly to prey on stray cattle to stay alive."

"How'd you know that?" Dalton looked sharply at her.

Amy had taken a wild shot and hit her target.

"That's of no concern. Fifty dollars a week until we find Jeter," she said. "That is more than fair."

"Fifty? Well . . ." Dalton pretended to think on it, but Amy saw the greed flare in his bloodshot eyes. Fifty dollars was probably more money than he had seen at any time in the past six months. "You look like decent folks and this outlaw's a bad customer," Dalton said. "Sure, I'll be glad to help you out."

"For fifty dollars a week," Amy added with some satisfaction.

"Word is, he's been around these parts," Dalton reported. He took off his hat and wiped his forehead using his sleeve. "Ain't many willin' to talk about him. He's got the lot of them yellow-bellies scared."

The small town wasn't far from the Rio Grande and, beyond its raging torrents, Mexico. Amy thought this was a perfect spot for Les Jeter to hole up. He could conduct his illicit business along the San Antonio–El Paso road, and then slink off to hide here until the law no longer actively sought him. The mud hovel of a town might have a name, but neither she nor Dalton had heard it.

"This is a gold mine of artifacts," Ambrose said unexpectedly. "We must locate all we can."

"What are you lookin' for? I kin help you out. I speak the lingo a little from time I spent over in Mexico."

Amy said nothing about this. She'd heard more than a few hints from Dalton about how desperate a man he was, how the law wanted him, and how he was on the run from a dozen different Rangers. All of it had been a tale spun to impress her, but it had not worked. Why Ambrose had sought him out was a mystery. Dalton might have been a gunfighter of some renown, but he didn't act it. She couldn't help comparing him with the man she had met in San Esteban—John Slocum. Ambrose hadn't been overly interested in having her do more than interrogate Slocum again. This trip had taken precedence over a return to San Esteban for that purpose, more's the pity.

"Where would a man like Jeter stay while here?" Ambrose spoke to himself, walking back and forth, his keen eyes flashing from one mud hut to the next. "He wouldn't stay in the finest place. That would be reserved for the *alcalde,* who must have some power over the locals."

"Family ties, more 'n likely," Dalton piped up. "You don't meddle with family in these parts. And nobody gets to be head man without having family to back him up."

"So he'd stay at a more humble dwelling. Like any of those." Ambrose pointed, and Amy found her attention following his arm to his finger and then to the cluster of adobe houses.

"Why those?" she asked.

"Let's ask and see," Ambrose said. "Be alert, Mr. Dalton, for any sign of him."

"What are we looking for, sir?" Amy moved a little closer to Ambrose when Dalton drew his six-shooter, spun the cylinder, and then slammed it back into his holster. She wasn't afraid of the gunman, not exactly, but felt better close to Ambrose.

"We never can tell," Killian said loftily. "We might even find Jeter himself, though I doubt it. See how peaceful the town looks? It would have a certain air of tenseness about it if a killer like Jeter were present."

"You want me to ask around?" the gunman said.

"Go on, Mr. Dalton. See what you can uncover."

"You lookin' for his loot? You think he buried it here? Or left it with a partner?"

"Oh, a man like Jeter is a solitary animal. There isn't any partner. There can't be."

"All right," Dalton said, not sure what Killian said. "I'll be back in two shakes of a lamb's tail."

"How quaint," Ambrose said when Dalton was out of earshot.

"What do you expect from a man like that?" Amy asked. "He's going to turn on you the instant he thinks you'll withhold his wages."

"He'll earn every penny. This is part of Jeter's range. I can feel him here. Can't you, my dear?"

Amy shook her head. All she smelled was the stench of garbage rising from the town. And all she felt was increasing uneasiness being around Dalton. The man was a real sidewinder and would strike when they least expected it. She vowed to remain alert, for Ambrose's sake as well as her own.

"There, he's motioning for us to join him."

Ambrose offered her his arm, as if they were going to a fancy-dress ball. Amy tried not to look apprehensive as they made their way to the house where Dalton stood impatiently at the open door, shifting his weight from one foot to the other as he watched them advance. Amy saw the way the man's left eye twitched. Nerves. Not a good trait in a gunfighter. This made Dalton all the more unpredictable should they find Jeter lurking here.

"What is it? Have you found where he stays when he's in this town?" Ambrose asked.

"I can't understand the yammerin' all that well, but the woman says a man who might be Jeter comes through here now and then. Last time was about a month back."

"What else did she say?" Amy asked, listening to the woman's constant flood of Spanish. She saw how Dalton turned cagey and knew he was going to lie.

"Nothing more."

"Except he left a few items here," Amy said. Dalton jumped as if she had stuck him with a pin. He hadn't expected either her or Ambrose to be able to understand Spanish. From what she could tell, Amy believed she spoke the language better than Dalton, except when it came to curses and the more lurid sexual descriptions.

"A shirt, I think she said. And a belt. Can't say that she mentioned anything more," Dalton said lamely.

"Señora," Ambrose said, "allow me to offer money for the items left behind by your unwanted houseguest."

"How'd you know she didn't want him?" asked Dalton.

"She has children," Amy said. "She wouldn't want a thief and murderer like Jeter staying around them unless she had no other choice."

"You take his things? If he comes again . . ." The woman looked distraught.

"Tell him Ambrose Killian took them and give him this." Ambrose pulled a card from a vest pocket and handed it to the woman with a flourish and a small bow.

She took the card and looked skeptically at him. "How much?"

"How much will I pay for the clothing? Let me examine it."

The woman vanished into the house and returned a few minutes later with a shirt, belt, and pair of pants that had been expertly mended. When Ambrose looked at Amy, the woman handed them to her.

Amy examined them carefully, turning over each item until she satisfied herself that they were not from local sources.

"Definitely not Mexican or handwoven around here," she reported. "There's some blood, but it could be anyone's."

"It doesn't matter if Jeter spilled it or it is his own shed blood," Ambrose said. "These belonged to him."

"You sure?" Dalton asked. The gunman looked increasingly contemptuous of the entire transaction, but he recoiled when Killian took the clothing, held it to his nose, and sniffed deeply.

"They're his," Killian said, heaving a great sigh. "I recognize his scent as well as any bloodhound could."

"The hell you say." Dalton rested his hand on his six-gun as if he might have to use it.

"Pay the woman for these items, Miss Gerardo," Ambrose said, walking away. He clutched the discarded clothing to his chest as if he had rescued a loved one from drowning and now feared to ever turn the person loose.

"Is he touched in the head?" Dalton asked. Amy ignored him as she haggled with the woman over the value of the clothing. If Ambrose hadn't shown such fondness for and attachment to the clothes, she might have been able to drive a better bargain. Still, she felt that eight dollars was a fair enough price to pay, and handed the money to the woman.

"You're givin' her that much for dirty, bloody rags? Hell, I'll sell you the shirt off my back for less than that if you want something dirty and blood-soaked," Dalton said. He leered at her, after making sure Ambrose was out of earshot. "I'll take off more than that just for you."

Amy glared at him.

"That won't be necessary," she said haughtily. Amy made a quick turn, letting her skirt flare out to keep him at least a pace off as she started after Ambrose. She wished she had the rifle with her now. Or a whip. That would suit a cur like Dalton. She stopped when the Mexican woman called to her.

"What is it?"

"There is more," she said to Amy.

"What? Where?"

"Not here. In a village two days' ride to the south, near the big bend in the Rio Grande."

"Big Bend?"

"*Sí,* there. He has left much there. A saddle. Spurs. Valuable things."

"Thank you," Amy said, returning to give the woman a silver dollar for the information.

"You will find much, very much."

Amy smiled as she trailed after Dalton and Ambrose. This find had to go to Dalton, but spurs worn by Les Jeter? If she returned with those, she would win more than simple gratitude from Ambrose. Thinking with great anticipation on what reward she might get, Amy hastened up the slope to where they had left the buckboard and horses.

8

John Slocum saw the smoke rising a mile out of San Esteban. He put his heels to the horse, but the animal wasn't in any mood to trot along. It kept up the same slow, steady pace it had since he had gone out scouting for any sign of Les Jeter. In a way, the slowness of the horse suited him fine since he had found nothing to show where the road agent had gone. Having to admit this to Sanford or even the good-for-nothing deputy didn't please him much. Slocum cursed, but knew the former team horse wasn't going to be rushed. It had spent too much of its life in a harness next to at least one other horse and usually three others. He was lucky to have any mount.

He still fumed as the horse took its sweet time ambling along into the confusion that had seized the town. Slocum sat straighter in the saddle when he saw the flames dancing high above the bank. The townspeople worked to snuff out the blaze, but it was a losing proposition for them. The interior of the bank finally burned to ashes before the flames died down. The heat had been so intense that some of the adobe in the walls had begun to crack because the straw holding the mud bricks had caught fire.

"Mighty nasty fire," Slocum said, swinging down from the saddle and going toward the smoldering ruins. "What happened?"

"Robbery," one man said. His face was sooty, showing he had been in the front line of firefighters working to extinguish the blaze. "He waltzed in, held up the bank, then started the fire."

"Who?" Slocum went cold inside. He had a good idea who was brazen enough to do such a robbery.

"Cain't say, but he was caught inside. Had to be. First off, we thought there was a whole damn gang of 'em, but it don't look so much that way now. There was only the one door in and out and nobody came out after the fire began. Reckon there was four employees, counting the bank president, inside. Can't see a passel of robbers anywhere, so it must have been one fella what done all the dirty work. Damned shame. I don't usually cotton much to bankers, but he was always square with me. Loaned a lot of folks money when they didn't have much in the way of a ranch or business."

"A prince among men," Slocum agreed. He had little truck with bankers, and knew the president of this bank had to be making plenty of money, or he would have been foreclosing on widows and throwing orphans into the street to make his profits.

Slocum left the men to continue their thankless task of tossing buckets of precious water onto the embers to cool off the ruins enough to enter. He wandered around to the side, and saw how the high window had been knocked out in such a way that part was in the alley and the rest remained inside the bank. He hopped up, grabbed the crumbling edge of the window, and pulled himself high enough to look inside. The stench of burned human flesh almost made him gag. The man out front hadn't been lying when he said there were people trapped inside, although Slocum couldn't identify any of the lumps left inside as ever being human. Looking around, he saw that the window had been hammered at and then forced out of its frame. He dropped down and brushed off his hands.

The robber might have escaped this way. The window was narrow, but Slocum thought he could wedge himself through, given enough goad. Having the fire licking at his ass would be more than enough incentive to get out of the building. Especially if he had already killed four people and faced an angry mob outside the only real door to the bank. Slocum had started back around to see how the crowd progressed in entering the bank when he saw a jagged chunk of metal with a piece of cloth caught on its sharp edge. He plucked it off the metal and held it up.

He had seen a shirt with a similar pattern before. During the stagecoach robbery.

"Jeter," he said with enough force to make several men turn to look at him.

"What's that, mister?"

"I think it was Jeter who robbed the bank," Slocum said. "He was wearing a shirt like this when he killed the driver and two passengers. Where's the deputy? I ought to tell him."

"The deputy's dead," someone closer to the door said. "Got his damn head blowed off when he tried to get into the bank. I didn't think he had it in him." The man looked around and snorted. "He don't have much at all in his head now, no matter what I thought of him before." The man pointed out the bits of bloody gray matter spattered into the dusty street.

"What about the marshal? He ever get back to town?"

"Cain't say. Benbow makes himself mighty scarce. Don't much blame him, not now. San Esteban is becoming a real dangerous place."

Slocum considered going to the stagecoach office and talking again with Old Man Sanford. He decided this wouldn't do any good. If the station agent had contacted the main office in San Antonio as he'd said, they might send Pinkertons or they might not, depending on what the managers thought. Slocum knew it wouldn't be long before the entire route was made worthless by the railroad being built some distance away. When the locomotives began chuffing along, not only would the Butterfield Stagecoach Company be out of business, but the entire town of San Esteban would have no reason to exist.

"Anybody see a rider leaving town about the time the bank was burning?"

One man stroked his chin and scowled. Slocum went to him and stood silently, waiting for the slow mental processes to work through all the details.

"Yup, I saw a gent. Talked with him. Real friendly fella. Had a bag slung over his shoulder when he come out of the alley."

"A moneybag?" asked Slocum, already knowing the answer.

"Coulda been. Didn't get a good look. There was a whole lot of confusion, you gotta know."

"A whole lot," Slocum agreed. "Did he ride east or west when he left?"

"That way. Away from the fire. That was sensible, and I didn't think nuthin' 'bout it."

"Thanks," Slocum said, in a hurry now to find Jeter's tracks. The outlaw could have circled, or maybe he kept riding. Slocum had to find out. This might be the only chance he had of getting onto the man's trail.

The horse protested a little, but it had been used to long, hard days in harness. The horse walked, but Slocum couldn't urge it to any greater speed. Content to just be moving along on anything other than his own feet, Slocum left town and began watching for any new set of hoofprints. He was in luck. San Esteban didn't see much traffic on any given day, and the only clear prints were left by a man riding to the west, toward the Rio Grande. Slocum wondered if he had been wrong not pursuing the trail going in that direction before, but in his gut he had felt the one heading into the Davis Mountains was the real trail.

Slocum began following the tracks the best he could on the sunbaked desert. Some shifting sand had obliterated the trail, but he kept on, getting a fix on a distant mountain peak and going for it as he suspected Jeter had. When he was despairing the most that he was following a will-o'-the-wisp, he saw a sheet of paper fluttering, trapped on a mesquite thorn. Reaching down, he snared it and held it up.

"Scrip," he said to the horse, to prove he was about the best tracker in this part of Texas. "Issued on the Fort Davis bank. Loot from the San Esteban robbery." How the solitary bill had come to escape the bag Jeter had used to carry the loot in didn't matter. It confirmed that the outlaw wasn't far ahead. The wind and weather would have destroyed the paper money if it had been impaled for very long on the mesquite bush.

Slocum had to work harder on following the trail when

he hit a rocky stretch. The Davis Mountains were not far off. The foothills presented a constant challenge to him, but Jeter wasn't heading in the direction he had been before. Angling away, heading through a pass in the mountains to the northwest, Jeter might have decided to take his stolen money and disappear into Mexico. But as Slocum rode and thought on the matter, he knew that wasn't likely. Eventually, Jeter would die in a robbery. Everything about the man said he had a death wish. He challenged fate by thumbing his nose at local lawmen and even the Texas Rangers. When news of the San Esteban robbery reached Fort Davis, it would bring out a company of soldiers fresh from fighting Apaches. A lone outlaw like Jeter wouldn't stand much chance after the soldiers had had their skills and courage honed by Indians on the warpath.

Slocum rode faster through the pass, and came out on a broad plain stretching green and tempting. A town even smaller than San Esteban was situated smack in the middle, beside a creek that ran down out of the higher elevations in the Davis Mountains. He sat with his leg curled around his saddle horn, taking time to roll himself a smoke. Slocum lit it with a sudden flare of his lucifer, then puffed in deeply, letting the smoke fill his lungs and calm him a mite. After being on Jeter's trail this long, he had gotten himself wound up tighter than a two-dollar watch.

The thought of Jeter stealing the watch during the stage robbery caused Slocum to tense up all over again. He kept puffing and settled down. He couldn't face a man with such an obvious need to make a spectacle of himself. Jeter might want to face off in the street and have a shoot-out. Slocum was quick, but had no idea if the outlaw was a real gunslinger able to hold his own with the fastest. If Slocum could avoid such a confrontation, he would do it. But he would get his watch back, one way or the other. If it took shooting it out with Jeter, he'd do it.

Finishing his smoke, not seeing anyone coming or going in the small village, Slocum lifted his leg off the pommel and slid his foot back into the stirrup. He gently kicked his heels against the horse's flanks and got it moving to the town.

Alert as he rode, Slocum knew he might already be centered in Jeter's sights. It was late afternoon, hotter than Hades, and the residents were likely taking their siestas. Anyone stirring wouldn't have Slocum's best interests at heart.

He entered the town and dismounted in front of a cantina. A Mexican sat beside the door, a huge sombrero pulled down to shade his face from the sun. As Slocum started inside, the man looked up.

"Hola," Slocum said in greeting. The man nodded. *"Ayudame?"*

"I speak English," came the answer. "What can a poor man like me do for a rich hombre like you?"

"Not so rich," Slocum said, sitting next to the man in the dirt, his back to the thick, cool, rough adobe wall of the cantina. "But you might be able to earn some money if you can tell me about an hombre." Slocum described Jeter the best he could, then reached into his pocket and held up the piece of fabric he had found back in San Esteban. "He's wearing a shirt like this."

Slocum saw the man pale under his swarthy complexion.

"A dollar," Slocum said, fishing out the solitary piece of scrip he had found along Jeter's trail. In a place like this unnamed border town, such a large sum would be magic.

"No," the man said, shaking his head vigorously enough to cause the tassels around the brim of the sombrero to bounce like hailstones on a roof. *"No sé."*

"I think you do know. All I want you to tell me is if he's in town right now. Nothing more."

The man's eyes went to the paper dollar. The greenback ended up flat on Slocum's palm. The man reached for it hesitantly. Slocum closed his hand, then turned it over and pressed the bill into the man's.

"Gracias," Slocum said. He had read what he thought was the truth in the man's frightened eyes. Jeter was no stranger here, but he wasn't in town right now. Slocum climbed to his feet, ducked under the low lintel, and found himself a chair near the bar where he could watch the doorway. He doubted Jeter was in town, but he wasn't taking any chances.

"Tequila?" asked the barkeep.

"Why not?" Slocum waited for the drink, then asked before the barkeep could return to his post behind the crude bar, "I'm looking for Jeter. Where can I find him?"

"You got business with him?"

"I'll kill the son of a bitch," Slocum said, not trying to keep the anger from his words.

"He is gone, but I wish you luck. Everyone in this town wishes you luck."

"I got that impression," Slocum said, seeing the man outside peering in, his head bobbing in agreement. The man in the sombrero clutched the dollar Slocum had given him as if it would turn into a bird and fly away. Slocum gestured for the man to join him, but he ducked back out of sight.

"He's a good-for-nothing," the barkeep said, pointing to the door. "But he's a prince among men compared to

Jeter." The bartender fumbled in his pocket and dropped a cartridge onto the table. "Use that on him. Back, head, chest, it does not matter. Just use it well."

"I will," Slocum said, pocketing the bullet where his brother's watch should have been. It would remind him of why he wanted Jeter, as if he could forget easily.

Slocum downed his tequila and let it burn away some of his anger, but not enough to forget why he had come here.

"Where would I find Jeter?" he asked the barkeep.

"Don't know, don't care. He comes here, spends a few days lording it over everyone, and then leaves like he came—a thief in the night."

"But not this time," Slocum said. He knew Jeter couldn't be more than a few hours ahead of him.

"Just passing through, that's all." The bartender looked hard at Slocum for a moment, then said curtly, "Drink's on the house."

Slocum saw that, for all the barkeep wanted Jeter dead, he wasn't going to be too talkative. Jeter might kill anyone asking too many questions—or answering them. Without another word, Slocum stood and went back into the afternoon heat in time to see Amy Gerardo's blond hair glinting like gold in the sun as she drove a buckboard into town. Supplies for a week or more bounced about in the rear, but she paid less attention to anything that might fall out than to the houses she passed. Slocum bided his time. It wouldn't be long before she saw him.

She drew back on the reins and sat on the hardwood seat, staring at him.

"Mr. Slocum," she said. "I had not expected to see you here."

"I keep turning up like a bad penny," he said. "What brings you to this fine town? Out for a constitutional?"

"Something like that," she said. "I am on an errand for Ambrose—for Mr. Killian."

"He sends you out alone when there are Indians off the reservation and dangerous outlaws like Jeter prowling the countryside?"

"Is he here? Was he?"

"You mean Jeter? Just missed him," Slocum said, watching her closely. He saw an entire rainbow of emotions play across her pretty face.

"I wanted to . . . see him," Amy said somewhat lamely. Slocum knew there was more to it than that, but he couldn't fathom what it might be that had brought her all the way from San Esteban to this desolate spot. "Perhaps, Mr. Slocum, we could join forces. You want to find him as much as I do."

"Can't see that would gain either of us much," Slocum said. "He's a dangerous man, but you know that." He fell silent to let her reply. She didn't give him anything more to speculate on.

"I must see to other business here," Amy said. "If you'll excuse me, I'll get to it. Perhaps we can talk business later."

Slocum touched the brim of his hat and waited for her to drive on. She went to the edge of town, looked back to see him watching her, then came to a decision. She got out of the buckboard and luckily went into the right house, only to emerge a few minutes later. An older Mexican woman came to the door and waved good-bye to her. Slocum saw the woman clutching what appeared to be a handful of greenbacks. Amy had given her a considerable amount of money. Why?

Slocum ambled down the street, passed through the

cloud of dust kicked up by the buckboard's wheels, and knocked on the door. The Mexican woman answered immediately. The hopeful expression on her face faded when she saw Slocum.

"Sorry to bother you, ma'am, but my lady friend was just here. Miss Gerardo. Amy Gerardo. I was supposed to join her, but we seem to be crossing paths without ever meeting up."

The woman only stared at Slocum with weak brown eyes.

"You'd do me a great favor if you could tell me what she asked of you."

"No, I cannot," the woman said. "She tole me not to tell."

"But Miss Gerardo and I are friends. More," Slocum said, smiling just enough to give the wrong impression. This shocked the undoubtedly devout woman.

"She not say anything 'bout that," the woman said. "All she asked was 'bout spurs."

"Spurs?"

"*His* spurs."

"Thank you, ma'am," Slocum said. "You've been a great help." He returned to the cantina and went back inside to sit.

Amy hunted for whatever Jeter left behind him. That much was clear. Spurs? Slocum didn't understand that, but he knew she wasn't out here to hunt down the outlaw himself. She hadn't even seemed to know of the bank robbery and Jeter's part in it, or she would have mentioned it. He finally came to a decision.

Again he left the cantina, and this time he also rode from the town, following Amy's twin ruts cut through the grassland. He had given her enough of a head start so she wasn't likely to spot him on her back trail.

Hunting for spurs made no sense, but meeting Jeter did. When she found the outlaw, Slocum would be there with his Peacemaker drawn and ready to take the man down.

9

Slocum was glad that his horse walked so slowly and refused to hurry. It kept him from overtaking Amy Gerardo as she made her way through the valleys and hills of the Davis Mountains—and it afforded him the chance to look around at the nearby ridges. While Amy was certainly worth following—she was dynamite wrapped up in a small package and appealed to Slocum a great deal—the silhouette of the lone rider along a ridgeline intrigued him more. Who would be out here riding alone in the middle of a rocky wilderness?

It was cooler in the hills than out in the desert, but there was precious little among the rocky, barren stretches to attract a rider. The small towns like the one Slocum had just left existed for no good reason amid the larger ranches with thousands of acres of sparse grazing for a handful of cattle. Some valleys were green and inviting, but growing anything in them would be a fool's pursuit for anyone other than a hermit. It was too many miles to town for what necessities couldn't be grown.

Amy began driving at a right angle to the road, heading down a lane toward a partially hidden cabin in a stand of trees. Slocum reckoned this was her destination since she showed no hesitation once she spotted it. If she had gotten lost, she might take her time going to ask for directions. Men on the edge of civilization tended to shoot first, even at women as pretty as Amy.

But the rider on the ridge? Where did he go? Slocum put his heels to the horse's flanks and got it struggling up the steep hill to pick up the trail. It might be a dead end or the trail might peter out. Slocum might even overtake the rider and find he had some legitimate reason for riding along all by his lonesome in the middle of the mountains. But Slocum thought the rider's shirt would have a piece ripped out of it and match with the scrap of cloth he had found back at the San Esteban bank.

"Giddyap," Slocum called, convincing the horse to not stop on the steep incline. It took more than a half hour to get to the summit, and less than a minute to pick up the other rider's trail. Slocum stood in the stirrups and peered ahead. The rider had vanished. A feeling in his gut told him this was no stranger. Slocum was certain he had found Les Jeter and was close to a shoot-out with him. He settled down and checked the rounds in the Peacemaker's cylinder. All six chambers were loaded. Slocum usually rode with the hammer resting on an empty chamber, just to be sure it didn't jostle around and discharge when he wasn't expecting it.

Slocum let the horse pick its way along the rocky path, which looked more like a game trail than one pioneered by a man astride a horse. The ridge curved away from the direction Amy had driven. Slocum barely cast a look her way as he let the horse pick its way down the far side of the hill and into another valley, rockier than the one he had left but still dotted with grazing cattle. Somebody took the time to ranch up here.

All day Slocum followed the rider's trail, until he came to a pleasant little valley that was more lush and inviting than the others he had seen. A chilly mountain breeze caused Slocum to shiver a little, but he didn't pull out his coat from his gear. He wanted to keep his arms free if he had to make a fast draw. There was no proof it was Jeter he had followed all day, but in his gut he knew he had the right sidewinder.

Movement in a cabin window drew him. As he neared, Slocum grew warier, but he didn't see a horse anywhere. He thought the barn might be some distance to the south, downhill some distance from the cabin. This was an odd arrangement, but the cabin had been built on sloping land. That might have been the only place with enough level land for such a structure as the barn without putting in considerable work.

He circled, found the barn, and looked inside for a well-ridden horse. To his surprise, he saw only a couple of goats and a sickly cow isolated in a stall. He finished his hasty search and saw no evidence of a horse anywhere. This made him a little easier going to the front of the cabin.

"Hello!" Slocum waited a decent amount of time, dismounted, and went to the door. Before he could knock, the door opened.

"Who are you?" the woman asked without so much as a "howdy."

"Just passing through, ma'am," Slocum said. He looked behind her into the cabin and saw no evidence that a man had been here in some time. It was done up in a frilly fashion, as if the woman decorated to suit herself and not to please a man. "I wondered if I might get some water? For me and my horse?"

"Go on," she said, pulling the door partly closed to keep him from seeing into the room. "Help yourself. There's a stream down below the barn yonder."

Slocum wasn't sure what made him ask the question that caused the woman to blanch.

"When did Jeter leave?"

"W-who?" The very way she stood, eyes wide in horror and her lower lip trembling, told Slocum the truth.

He yanked out his six-shooter and kicked open the door. Ready to shoot, he quickly scanned the room for trouble. No one but the woman was inside. He lowered his six-gun and then thrust it into his holster.

"You know Jeter, don't you? He comes here?"

"I don't know what you're talking about," she said with growing defiance. "Get out. Get your water and leave this property."

"Your property? Or is it Jeter's?"

"Who is this Les Jeter? I've never heard of him."

Slocum said nothing as realization dawned on the woman of what she had said. Slocum had never mentioned the outlaw's first name.

"Look, you don't want to tangle with him. He's a . . . killer."

"Reckon I know that," Slocum said. "What's he to you?"

"He . . . keeps me here. I can't get away without a horse."

"You could set out on foot," Slocum said.

"Where'd I go? I don't have any relatives. No friends. I've been here for over a year now and you're only the third person I've seen who wasn't Les. Sometimes, I think I'm going crazy." Tears welled in the woman's brown eyes and threatened to spill out. She caught up the edge of her apron and dabbed.

"Anywhere away from him is better than with him," Slocum said. He started to tell how Jeter had murdered the stagecoach driver and two passengers and left him for dead, but he held back on this story. He didn't even bother with the bank robbery and the deaths of the San Esteban deputy and several more, including all the employees of the bank. Such stories would add nothing to the situation.

"I suppose you're right, but I . . . I've been with him for almost ten years."

It was Slocum's turn to blink in surprise. The woman couldn't have been older than her early twenties.

"You related to him?"

"His w-wife. He forced me to marry him down in San Antonio. I didn't know any better and my ma and pa had just died. I was only fifteen."

"You've been with him ever since, so you know what he does."

"I know," the woman said, holding out her wrists to show the bruises. "But how can I leave him? Les said he'd track me to the ends of the earth if I ever tried leaving him. And I believe him. Oh, how I believe him!"

Slocum saw that there were victims of Jeter's evil other than those in graves. He wanted the man—bad. He wanted to settle the score with the outlaw, and he wanted his watch back. But the woman was at Jeter's mercy out here alone.

"You want to leave him?"

She blinked rapidly and the tears finally flowed down

her cheeks unabashed. She nodded, her brunette hair bobbing about. Some of the color Slocum had shocked out of her had returned to highlight her cheeks. He thought she was a sight prettier now than when he had first laid eyes on her.

"Y-you'd do that for me? Take me out of here?"

Slocum was torn, but knew he had no choice.

"I've only got one horse, but it's strong. We can both ride to San Esteban on it. From there, you'd be on your own. Do you have anything you'd want to take?"

The woman looked around and a wan smile came to her lips. She shook her head and said, "Not really. All this isn't mine. Well, it is, but it's Les's. What he wanted."

"You were a prisoner all this time?"

"I never thought of it that way. I thought it was how a wife was supposed to be. Les was gone a lot, but I never knew when he'd ride up and . . . want things from me. You know, what a husband wants from a wife. Sometimes he brought pretty things. Other times, he'd be shot up and I'd nurse him back to health. I thought that was all there was in the world."

"For some folks, you're right," Slocum said. Jeter had held her captive as surely as if he had put shackles on her. From the bruises on her wrists, he might do just that, although the woman had never come out and said that.

"My name's John Slocum," he said.

"Ruth. Ruth Jeter. Or I was Ruth Cameron before . . . before I got hitched to Les. Don't know what name's right to use."

"Don't go announcing yourself as Mrs. Jeter," Slocum advised. "Outside of this little valley are a whole lot of people willing to ventilate him."

"You look like you're familiar with using that six-shooter, Mr. Slocum."

He put his hand on the Peacemaker and thought of the times he had used it. They were legion.

"I don't let anyone steal from me. Jeter left me for dead after robbing me."

"You intend to k-kill him?"

Slocum knew the grim expression on his face answered the question.

"Can we go? I mean, right now? The sooner I leave here, the better I'll feel about everything. My life. My new life. What's San Esteban like?"

"We don't have to go right away," Slocum said. He was enough of a hunter to know decent bait when he saw it. If the rider on the ridge was Jeter, he might be snaking his way around, covering his tracks and coming home to his wife. Ruth would be perfect bait to lure the outlaw into a trap.

Ruth was no one's fool and saw what Slocum was thinking.

"He'll kill you, John. He'll flat out shoot you where you stand if he catches you here."

"He tried before. He won't be so lucky a second time. Does the prospect bother you that I intend to take him in? And if I can't, I'll gun him down?"

"Yes, no, oh, John, I don't know. This is all so confusing. What'll I do if I leave him? Everything I have in the world is here, what you see, nothing else."

"That should have occurred to you a long time back," Slocum said, not trying to sugarcoat his words. "A man who makes his way through life killing and robbing is going to end up on the wrong end of a rope eventually, if he's not shot down before the law gives him a trial."

"I never considered that," Ruth said in a low voice. "I was always watching for him and wondering when he would return. I don't know which I was more afraid of, never seeing him again or . . ."

"Seeing him again," Slocum finished for her.

She threw herself into his arms and hugged him tightly. He felt the hot tears she shed soaking through his shirt. When Ruth looked up, her brown eyes shone with tears, giving them a sparkling brilliance that captivated him. She closed those haunting eyes slowly and tipped her head back. As her ruby lips parted Slocum felt himself being drawn into something he knew was wrong. Ruth was married. But it was to a sidewinder who would end up dead. She was an attractive woman. Not as lovely as Amy Gerardo, but there was an earthiness to her that appealed greatly to Slocum.

He kissed her. Hard. She returned his passion with her own. Their bodies crushed together until he felt the throbbing of her heart as if it were his own. Her soft breasts mashed flat against the hardness of his chest until those breasts were the only things soft between them. Slocum responded powerfully to her.

"I want you, John. Please. Don't deny me," she said in a husky whisper he could hardly hear over the pounding in his ears.

He reached down, got his arm behind her legs, and lifted powerfully, sweeping her into his arms. Spinning around, he looked for a bed where they could continue. The small pallet in the corner of the room had to be where Ruth slept. It was hardly adequate.

"Outside," she said. "To the barn. The hay. It's so peaceful there and the hay's soft."

"Peaceful?" Slocum had to laugh. "You've got a sick cow there lowing and goats demanding to be set free."

He felt her stiffen in his arms.

"You've been there?"

"Looking around," he said. "I didn't know what I'd find."

"You found me," she said, melting against him again, her arms around his neck so she could pull herself closer and kiss him. Slocum carried her out into the cool air and downhill to the barn. He had grabbed a blanket as he swept out in a rush. He kicked open the barn door and found a pile of clean straw intended for the stall floors. Slocum spread the blanket on it and turned to find Ruth naked to the waist. She had unbuttoned her blouse and shucked it off, leaving her bare skin exposed to the cool night air. The temperature caused her nipples to harden into taut little red buttons he couldn't resist.

He bent and sucked first one and then the other into his mouth where he could toy with them. He pressed his tongue down hard, mashing the cherry button into the soft flesh beneath. Ruth groaned in pleasure at this oral assault. Slocum didn't stop with her breasts. Cupping them in his hands, forefinger and thumb tweaking each, he slid lower. His tongue pushed against the waistband of her skirt.

"Oh, let me get free, John. Free. Oh, yes, so nice, so very nice. He's never like this."

"What do you want?" Slocum asked.

"More. More of this. Ever so much more!"

He gave it to her when she released the ties holding her skirt up. It slithered over her flaring hips and then cascaded to the floor, leaving her entirely naked. Slocum pressed his face into the nut-brown nest between her thighs. He felt her begin to tremble as his tongue invaded her. Ruth opened her stance a little, but soon she sank bonelessly to the blanket he had spread out.

"I want you, John. I . . . I've never felt this excited before. Please, do—"

He cut off her words by applying himself to her most intimate flesh, licking and lapping, driving his tongue deep within her and wiggling it about, then slowly sliding up and down the insides of her thighs as he sought each and every spot on her body that aroused her. From the way she thrashed about, he was finding one after another.

Slowly, he worked his way up her body. Her legs spread wantonly for him. He fit neatly between them, his hardness going into the territory his tongue had already pioneered so successfully. She tensed, arched her back, and began rolling her hips around him. His manhood was trapped within a softly clutching, heated chamber. Her legs rose on either side of his body as he slipped forward even more. When he felt himself fully within her, he began rolling his hips.

Ruth gasped and went wild beneath him. Her upward thrusts ground their bodies together as she squeezed down all around him. Fingers clawing, the brunette half-rose from the blanket and kissed him fiercely.

Slocum began moving in ways he hadn't realized he could. In and out, spiraling as he went. His hips began to rock faster and faster as he returned the torrent of kisses she lavished on him.

"More," she gasped. Ruth fell back and her legs locked around his waist. He began more powerful thrusts, pinning her to the haystack. She reached up and began tweaking her own nipples. Eyes closed and her face a mask of ecstasy, the woman gasped, shuddered, and went limp.

This condition lasted only a few seconds. Slocum stroked over her breasts, down her sides, and cupped her buttocks, lifting them up so he could drive deeply into her at a new and more exciting angle. She had relaxed, and now he felt the tension returning to her. Ruth's breathing became ragged again as her passions mounted anew. He did all he could to tease every possible response from her willing, wanton body. She was strong and firm and he was hard and repeatedly vanishing into her wetness. The combinations of weak and strong, hard and soft brought her back to life under him. She gasped and moaned and began writhing about, impaled on his fleshy spike.

Slocum picked up the pace and slipped back and forth with increasing need. Deep within he felt the tides rising and tried to hold back. He enjoyed the sensations of making love to this woman. She wasn't the prettiest he had ever seen, but there was an attractive quality that appealed greatly to him.

He grunted, arched his back, and tried to bury himself fully in her molten core. He exploded and spilled his seed, then sank down atop her. Ruth's arms circled his body and held him close until he rolled off her to lie beside her.

"I've never felt anything like that before, John," she said in a low voice. "I didn't know. I never—"

"Quiet," Slocum said, sitting up.

"What's wrong?"

"Get dressed. Now!" Slocum hurried to obey his own command. He had heard the steady clop-clop of an approaching horse. From all that Ruth had said, it could be only one person.

Slocum wanted to capture Les Jeter if he could. And if he couldn't take the man alive, dead would suit him just fine too, as long as he got his watch back.

10

Slocum staggered when Ruth tackled him from behind. Her strong arms circled his shoulders and locked his hands to his sides. He shrugged and easily broke free.

"What's going on?" he demanded.

"You don't want to tangle with Les. Please, John. You can't. He's a killer. He . . . he does things you can't believe."

"I can believe," Slocum said grimly.

"I don't want to lose you. Not when I just found you," Ruth said, clinging to him fiercely. She buried her face in his chest and held him tight. "Let him look around. Hide here in the barn or maybe out back. He won't see you. Hide and let him go his way. There doesn't have to be anybody getting hurt."

"Except you," Slocum said, prying her hands away and holding out her arms to display the bruises. "He did that, didn't he?"

"He . . . he plays rough sometimes. He didn't mean anything by it."

"Do you love him?"

"I can't. Not after the way he's treated me. But he's a good provider so it's not that bad, especially when he is gone so much of the time."

"You know where he gets the money, don't you? He steals it, usually off dead men. He's got the town of San Esteban scared shitless. Nobody there will speak up against him for fear he'll ride in and destroy the entire town like he did the bank."

"Bank? Did he—?" From the expression on the woman's face, Slocum had to believe that she hadn't known the bank was robbed by her husband. He doubted Jeter shared much in the way of his activities as road agent and bank robber with her. And he would never tell his wife how many men he had killed unless it was to keep her in line.

"He robbed the bank after killing five or six men. I missed the exact count. Nobody knows how much he stole because he burned the bank down, with the president and all the employees in it. Your 'good provider' might be fetching you a couple thousand dollars."

"It's not worth so many lives."

"Those were only the ones *in* the bank," Slocum went on ruthlessly. "He killed the deputy and several others trying to rescue those he held hostage. For all the good it did them. The deputy's head was blown half off."

Ruth gasped and began to cry. Slocum reckoned she had to be a better actress than he gave her credit for to fake such shock and horror at what her husband had done.

"I didn't know any of this," she said in a weak, choked voice. "Not a bit of it. I thought I had talked him out of trying to rob the bank."

"You knew he was a road agent."

"Y-yes, but not that he killed all those people. The ones you said."

Slocum looked around the barn again for any trace of a horse or mule. It was a long walk for Ruth to leave this place without a mount. That had to be why Jeter kept her alone and without any means of escape.

"He's never gone for long, is he?"

"No," she said, looking up. More tears welled in her brown eyes, turning them to muddy pools. "Seldom more than a week and sometimes only a day or two."

"That keeps you from hiking out," Slocum said.

"H-he caught me once trying to get away," Ruth said. "Th-that's why I don't want you going up against him. He'll kill you and—"

"And you'll lose your ticket out of here?"

Ruth sniffed and nodded. "It's so selfish, I know, but I really don't want you hurt, John. That—what we just did—it's never been like that for me. I'm not lying."

"I know," Slocum said, gently pushing her away when she tried to cling to him again. "Stay out of the way. I'm taking your husband in, sitting upright or feet first. And truth to tell, it doesn't matter to me which it is."

"If you have to," Ruth said. She brushed a wild strand of brunette hair back from her eyes. She wiped her nose and then dabbed at her eyes. "Just don't go getting yourself k-killed."

"That's not something I intend to do," Slocum said, settling his gun belt around his waist. He drew his Peacemaker and opened the gate, spun the cylinder, and made sure he had six rounds ready to fire. He was ready to take on Les Jeter.

"I'll go back with the goats," Ruth said uncertainly.

"That's a good place," Slocum said, but his mind was

already on the fight. He pushed open the barn door a few inches and peered out. The sound of an approaching horse was gone. All sounds were gone. Slocum frowned. He might have been mistaken, but doubted it. And the chance he had heard another pilgrim traveling past was close to zero. Anyone seeing the cabin would stop by to say howdy, get some water and maybe food before riding on.

He slipped outside and looked around, then dashed to the cabin and dropped down beside the rain barrel. When he heard his horse neighing loudly, he cursed. Jeter had seen the horse and knew Ruth had a visitor. For the outlaw it wouldn't much matter who it was. Any caller was a threat to his hideout. And if he thought his wife had a secret lover, he would go crazy. Slocum didn't have to know any more about Jeter than what he already did to be certain of this.

Slocum backed away from the rain barrel and chanced a quick look behind the house. His horse jerked at its tether and tried to kick out to free itself. Slocum went to the horse and soothed it, but whatever had spooked it was still around. That had to be Les Jeter.

"Damnation," Slocum said when he realized Jeter wasn't in the cabin. The man's horse was nowhere to be seen. That could only mean the outlaw had ridden down lower on the hill and had come up from behind the barn. Throwing caution to the winds, Slocum sprinted for the barn and flung open the door in time to see Jeter pushing Ruth through a small window at the rear.

"Drop your iron!" Slocum shouted. He had his six-shooter out and aimed, but Jeter wasn't the surrendering kind. The outlaw brought up his six-gun and fired too accurately for Slocum's liking. One slug ripped through the brim of his hat and another made him wince as a hot line was traced across his cheek. Jeter was aiming for his head and a quick, certain kill.

Slocum reflexively ducked and fell into a stall. He came to his feet and thrust his six-shooter over the top, ready to shoot Jeter. The road agent had disappeared through the window behind his wife.

Slocum cursed as he made his way from stall to stall, wary of a trap. He poked his head out the window in time to see Jeter galloping away with Ruth in front of him on his horse. Gun raised, Slocum sighted and then lowered the Peacemaker. The range was too great and he might hit Ruth, in spite of the woman being in front of Jeter.

Not wasting a second, Slocum retraced his footsteps to the back of the cabin and swung into the saddle. The horse was glad to be free and away, but not so happy that it would gallop for Slocum. It had its pace and nothing he did made it go faster than a trot.

"They're getting away, you worthless hunk of horse meat!" raged Slocum. The horse ignored his curses and threats and kept plodding along, letting Jeter and Ruth get farther away by the minute.

Slocum knew how good Jeter was at hiding his tracks, but he had gotten onto the outlaw's trail too quickly this time for any such stunts. While his horse moved at its own molasses-slow pace, Slocum knew there was a bit of luck in his favor. Jeter had ridden hard and long from San Esteban, and now his tired horse carried almost twice the weight it had before. Slocum doubted Jeter would ever willingly give up his wife.

But he might kill her. If he couldn't have her, he'd want to make sure no one did. Slocum had no idea what the outlaw suspected about his wife and her unknown visitor. If Ruth was sharp and didn't get confused from fright, she would spin a tall tale about a bounty hunter or lawman come to arrest Jeter and how frightened she had been for him. If she hesitated an instant and Jeter became suspicious that she had slept with Slocum, a dead body would be drawing vultures and maggots before Slocum could find her.

"Come on, you refugee from a glue factory," Slocum said angrily, raking his spurs along the horse's flanks to get it moving faster. The horse protested noisily, but took the punishment rather than breaking into a gallop. In his day Slocum had seen his share of balky horses. Usually only mules acted this stubborn, but abusing the horse wasn't the way to overtake Jeter and Ruth. Slocum slackened his use of spurs and let the horse pick its way along the winding trail Jeter had taken.

Slocum rode more cautiously when he reached the edge of the valley and towering, sheer walls of rock. The outlaw might lay a trap anywhere along the way now that Slocum no longer had a clear view ahead. More than once he looked up, startled, when a stone dislodged and came tumbling down. His nervousness communicated to the horse. It increasingly shied at shadows or rabbits bolting across the trail.

Wishing for a better look ahead along the trail got him nowhere. He had to keep reminding himself Jeter knew the countryside like the back of his hand, and had probably figured out long since the best spots for ambushing anyone following him. Exhausted from the tension, Slocum gave his horse—and himself—a rest when they reached the top of a ridge. Ahead stretched a pass that wound about in such a way that Slocum saw only a quarter mile of trail. This would be a perfect spot for a dry-gulching.

Or would it?

Slocum looked more skeptically at the way the road rose up. Anyone following the trail would be exposed to gunfire from ahead, but the sniper would also be exposed because of the strange twist made just past the mouth of the pass. Taking his field glasses from his saddlebags, Slocum looked not at the pass but at the rugged area to the right of the pass and downslope from it. At first he saw nothing, then a sudden flash almost blinded him. It vanished as quickly as it appeared, but Slocum noted the spot and kept his binoculars trained on the distinctive rocks where he had seen it.

A slow smile came to his lips.

"Jeter, you egg-sucking dog, you were going to shoot me in the back if I went through the pass." Slocum caught a glimpse of Ruth as she struggled to get free of Jeter, then nothing. Waiting another five minutes didn't provide him with even a hint that the outlaw was lying in wait to kill him.

Slocum put away his field glasses and then pulled his rifle from the saddle scabbard. He jacked a round into the Winchester's chamber and set out on foot to deal with Jeter. The outlaw wouldn't expect an attack from his flank. Slocum wished he had the time to circle and come up on Jeter from behind, but the feeling that time was running out for Ruth drove him. Jeter wasn't the patient sort, and would begin to get antsy when Slocum didn't show up to get himself back-shot.

Making his way through the rocks, Slocum worked his way downslope, and then reached a rugged ravine leading over to where Jeter had pitched his camp.

"I swear, Les, nothing happened. He didn't touch me!"

"Shut up," the road agent growled. "I know men. He

might not have done nuthin' to you but he was thinkin' 'bout it. And I don't know if he ain't one of the posse on my tail."

"Posse? Why'd the law want you, Les? Tell me you haven't done anything wrong."

Slocum wished Ruth would shut up and let her husband do the talking. She was going to step over the line and reveal something she shouldn't. When that happened, Jeter would turn on her fast.

"What makes you think the law's got any part of this? It's a bunch of them owlhoots from San Esteban. I told you they didn't cotton much to me. They got it stuck in their craw that I know something about the bank bein' robbed."

"You didn't burn it down, did you?"

Slocum cursed and moved faster. Ruth had made a big blunder that Jeter wouldn't ignore. And he didn't.

"Why'd you say a thing like that? What's that son of a bitch tell you?"

"Les, nothing! I swear!"

Ruth gasped. Slocum couldn't see them, but guessed that Jeter was adding more bruises to the woman's arms.

"How'd you know about the bank?"

"Y-you said they were after you for robbing the bank. And you smell of smoke. Not cooking-fire smoke. This is a lot more acrid."

Slocum wasn't sure that explanation would do anything to Jeter's suspicions other than fan them. But it didn't matter now. He got to a spot where he had a clean shot at the outlaw. Ruth was hidden by rocks, but that only made the shot all the sweeter. Slocum could hit only Jeter and not his wife.

He lifted the Winchester to his shoulder, aimed, and

fired in one smooth action. The bullet missed Jeter by inches because the outlaw lurched forward to grab his wife. Jeter stumbled and went to his knees. Slocum got off a second shot. This one hit the man, but it only winged him. Slocum had hoped for a clean kill.

"Git over here, bitch!" Jeter scooted away on his knees, out of Slocum's line of right. A flurry of skirts and the woman wearing them appeared. For an instant Slocum caught sight of her. Jeter had her tightly and swung her about to use her as a shield.

Slocum rushed forward. As long as the outlaw fought with his wife, he wasn't going to shoot straight. Bouncing off first one rock and then the other, Slocum reached a level spot where he had a shot at Jeter again. It was a dangerous shot for Ruth. The outlaw held her in front of him, but Slocum was cool and his years as a sniper during the war stood him in good stead. He fired again.

Jeter let out a squawk and shoved Ruth forward, blocking another shot. When Ruth fell facedown on the ground, Slocum fired again. He cursed a blue streak and vaulted over the prone woman, only to hear a shot and feel sharp pain in his arm where Jeter's bullet narrowly missed doing serious harm.

Firing steadily at the outlaw, Slocum cut off any possible deadly reply. When the rifle magazine came up empty, he tossed it to Ruth and said, "Hang onto that. It's empty."

"John, please. Let him go!"

Slocum wasn't sure who she was worried more about, her husband or him. If she didn't care how she was treated, then her sympathies lay with Jeter. Slocum didn't wait to sort it all out or ask what she wanted. He drew his Peacemaker and went after the outlaw.

Jeter made no attempt to hide his trail. He couldn't. There wasn't time, and he was running for his life. Slocum pressed on and caught sight of Jeter worming his way between two closely spaced rocks. Slocum fired twice, bullets kicking off pieces of stone on either side of the fleeing man. He might have scratched Jeter, but nothing more.

"Give up, Jeter," Slocum called, looking around for a spot where he could gain the advantage of higher ground. The downslope gave him an angle, but the rocks were too close to one another for him to get a real shot at Jeter. He saw a boulder to the left of the trail and scrambled up it, dropped flat on the top, and waited for Jeter to reveal himself.

Nothing.

"Come on, you coward!" Slocum shouted. "You a yellow-belly? I'd never have thought you would run like a scalded dog. What's the matter, that woman of yours steal your balls?"

He felt a coldness descend on him when he realized that Jeter might be out of earshot. The silence was absolute. The gunfire had quieted the animals and even the wind, leaving behind an eerie calm. Slocum was sure he would have heard a flea moving across a rock—if there had been a flea moving. Jeter was long gone.

Slocum waited another few minutes, just to be sure. Patience would flush Jeter out if he was within a hundred yards. Slocum eventually gave up and slipped back off the rock. Jeter knew he had met his match and had started to run, and was probably still running.

Making his way back uphill, Slocum returned to the spot where Jeter had tried to ambush him. Ruth huddled in the vee made by two large boulders, clutching the rifle and shoving it in front of her as if she had a chicken stick and intended to whack a particularly aggressive rooster intent on pecking her.

"It's empty," Slocum said. "I told you that."

"I . . . I heard you before," she said. "Les might not have, though."

"You would never have bluffed him. He's too much of a hard case."

"I know," she said. Ruth struggled to stand and couldn't. She used the rifle as a crutch and still couldn't stand. "Help me, please. I'm stuck!"

Slocum had to laugh at her predicament. He grasped her work-hardened hands and pulled steadily, finally getting her free. She staggered forward into his arms. She felt good there, but Slocum knew this wasn't the time for such things when Jeter was on the loose.

"We got to get out of here," he said.

"You're letting him go? I thought—" A mixture of fear and hope mixed in her words.

"I want you out of danger," Slocum said. "You can stay at the farm."

"But Les might return!"

"He might," Slocum admitted, "but my guess is that he won't. He said something about a posse being on his trail. That means his own worthless hide is at risk the longer he stays in these parts."

"He's always talking about Mexico," Ruth said, but there was no conviction in her voice.

"He might cross the Rio Grande, but he won't stay there," Slocum said. "He's not had a chance to spend any of the loot from the robberies. That means he's hidden it around this area somewhere."

"The farm? He hid it there?"

"Most likely."

"Then he'll certainly go back, and I'll be there all alone!"

"Yep," Slocum said. He saw no way around that. He'd have to run Jeter to ground, or the outlaw could circle and return to the farm and his wife. It was a gamble Slocum made with Ruth's life, but he had no other choice. He was betting on his skill at tracking down Jeter fast, no matter how the outlaw tried to conceal his trail.

Slocum would hate to see the road agent kill Ruth, but that wouldn't happen if Slocum got him first.

11

Amy Gerardo snapped the reins and kept the buckboard on the road until she reached the sign telling her that the Rodriguez family lived at the end of a smaller lane. Cottonwoods dotted the countryside and undoubtedly hid the rancho—if it could even be called that. From what Amy had gleaned from her sources, this Paco Rodriquez wasn't the richest vaquero in West Texas or anywhere else. This brought a smile to her thin lips. Getting what she wanted from him would be that much easier. A few dollars and he would give her a precious artifact of the famed *bandido* Lester Jeter.

She glanced over her shoulder into the bed of the buckboard to be certain her bags were still there. Clothing she could do without if that bag had happened to bounce out on the rough road, but the other held her notebooks and research notes. Those would be added to when she found out the details of how Paco had come by Jeter's spurs.

She rounded a bend in the narrow lane and saw the

adobe hut ahead. A half-dozen children scurried about, some yelling for their mama. By the time Amy had pulled up in front of the adobe, a woman wearing an apron and a vexed expression had come to the door.

"What can I do for you?"

Amy liked it that the woman wasted no time and got down to business. She felt a curious need to dispense with pleasantries herself and be done with this hunt for another of Jeter's artifacts. Ambrose's approval was waiting for her. All she had to do was present the spurs to him and bask in his admiration.

"It is my understanding that Mr. Rodriquez has a pair of spurs that once belonged to a famous gunman. I would speak with him about purchase of those spurs."

Two of the children tugged at Señora Rodriguez's skirts. She shooed them away and stepped out into the bright sun. Holding up a hand to shade her eyes, she gave Amy the once-over, then nodded.

"It is so. He owns these spurs. You are the one who asked in the village?"

"I am, but I thought I was being discreet. It was my understanding the matter would not be discussed."

"Ha!" the stolid woman said, waving her hand in the air as if swatting flies. "Nothing is said that is not repeated a dozen times. What else is there to do here?"

Amy started to agree that the woman had a point. Seldom had she seen an area so blighted. An acequia carried water behind the house, but what it irrigated was a mystery. The cottonwoods flourished on the water, but nothing other than weeds were to be seen. There might be a field on the far side of the cottonwood grove, but what might be grown there was as much a mystery to her as how Jeter's spurs had ended up in a poor peon's possession.

"How did your husband come by them?"

"You ask him. He is in the field." The woman inclined her head in the direction of the irrigation canal. "You want a *muchacho* to show you?"

"I am sure I can find the way." Amy secured the reins and dropped to the ground. It was no surprise that the woman was several inches taller. Everyone was. That didn't deter her. She reached into the back of the buckboard and grasped the handle of the valise holding her notebooks and other items pertaining to the hunt for Jeter's life.

She nodded to the woman and set off, holding her skirts above the muddy ground the best she could. Before she had gone a dozen yards, it became apparent this was a fool's errand, and she let the hem drop and graze the weeds and occasionally soak up muddy water that stood in puddles. She kept moving, though, and eventually found a small bridge across the acequia. Looking around and not seeing Paco Rodriguez, she balanced carefully on the narrow board and crossed to the far side.

She had barely stepped onto drier, firmer ground when she saw Rodriguez sitting under a tree whittling. Amy went directly to him and stood over him, trying to look as important as possible to impress this peasant. It didn't work. He looked up at her and did nothing to conceal his contempt.

"What do you want?"

"Something you possess that my employer wishes for himself."

"You are the one they speak of in the village, no? The *alcalde* himself says you seek a certain pair of spurs, eh?"

"That is right," Amy said, vexed. The town mayor had been the one spreading her secret mission around. Ambrose had little faith or trust in the reliability of politicians. Reluctantly, Amy was coming around to agreeing with him, as she did on so many things.

"How much? How much will you give for these spurs I have found?"

"How did you come by them? They must be authenticated." She saw he didn't understand. "I must be sure they belonged to Jeter."

"How will you do this thing? How will you do this 'authenticate'?" Rodriguez let the new word curl around on his tongue like a sip of heady tequila. Amy was glad she had given him something new to do. To judge from the pile of shavings, his entire day had been spent whittling a piece of wood into a toothpick while his wife cooked and coped with a houseful of children.

She tapped her foot impatiently at the question.

"I must examine—look at them. There are marks and other things that will tell me they are legitimate."

"Legitimate?"

"The spurs," Amy insisted.

"They are hidden. Such valuable spurs, they must not be kept where anyone can find them." Paco Rodriguez looked around as if someone spied on them. Amy had seen no one other than his family in the area. Even the ride out from the village had been singularly lonesome, though she had the eerie feeling that someone had ridden just far enough behind her to remain out of sight.

She heaved a sigh of exasperation. To Rodriguez this was a game. To her it was serious business.

"Get the spurs, bring them here, let me look at them, then we'll talk about what they are worth."

"They are worth much. *Mucho dinero,*" he insisted.

She waved him away as his wife had done with her

small children. The gesture spoke to Rodriguez. He shot to his feet and hurried off, threading his way through the trees until he vanished, leaving Amy to stew. The things she did for Ambrose!

Rodriguez returned less than ten minutes later with a package wrapped in oilcloth. Amy was glad to see he was taking such care. Rust would diminish the value—and blood would enhance the importance for Ambrose. It would be even more important to establish whose blood spotted the silver spurs and place them in their proper spot in the events of Jeter's life. Provenance, Ambrose called it.

"May I?" Amy held out her hands. Rodriguez hesitantly passed it over to her. She knelt and laid the package on the ground in front of her. Carefully unwrapping the oilcloth revealed a single gleaming spur. She looked up at the man and said, "There's only one. I thought you had both spurs."

Rodriguez shook his head vigorously.

"No, no, only the one. It came to me through great misfortune."

Using her handkerchief to keep from putting a sullying fingerprint on the metal, Amy picked up the spur and examined it more closely. The single letter *J* had been scratched into the side. Her heart raced. Ambrose would be certain to put this in one of his special display cases!

"It's been scratched up," she said. "How'd that happen?"

Rodriguez shrugged eloquently. "This is how I got it. The scratch can be buffed out. I can do it if that makes you want to buy."

"That's all right," Amy said, trying to keep the enthusiasm out of her voice. If she seemed too eager, he would jack up the price to the point she might not be able to purchase it. Since Ambrose didn't know she was even here, she had to use her own money. For all his strong character traits and how much she admired him as a man, Ambrose Killian paid her frugally. Amy smiled crookedly. He wasn't frugal, he was a skinflint. But his parsimony made it possible for him to pursue his enthusiasms, such as collecting every artifact ever touched or used by Jeter.

"You will buy it?"

"I need to know everything about it," Amy said, laying the spur onto its cloth as if it were a religious relic. She rummaged about in her valise and took out a notebook. "Without the details, I cannot buy this. It might be from anyone."

"But the scratch, it looks like a *J*."

Amy looked sharply at Rodriguez. The man knew what he had, and she had to find out how he had obtained it. Since Jeter was still alive, it hadn't been a matter of robbing a corpse.

"Who gave it to you?"

"You know," the man said, looking crestfallen, "I did not get this thing myself. It was Bernardo who got it. He stole it from the man wearing it because he thought the spur was pure silver."

"It's nickel-plated iron," Amy said. "I've seen dozens of spurs just like it." She touched the sharp pointed tips on the wheel and imagined Jeter wearing it, raking the cruel Spanish rowel against his horse's side until he flew like the wind away from one of his brutal, bloody robberies.

"Bernardo did not know. The man who wore it claimed it was pure silver and worth much."

"Where?"

"Down by the river. The Rio Grande," Rodriguez said. "There is a cantina run by the *hijo* of Bernardo. Not so big, not so rich, but enough."

"By the Rio Grande," mused Amy. She made a note to investigate later. Such a place probably served as a halfway point for road agents making their way into Mexico to escape U.S. lawmen—and for *bandidos* fleeing the *rurales* and seeking refuge in Texas. Serving bad liquor would be less profitable than furnishing a hideout for criminals terrorizing both sides of the border.

"This is so," Rodriguez said. "He come, this gringo *bandido,* and got drunk. He had much money and boasted of his spurs. He put his boots on the table so all could see the fine leather—and the spurs."

"So Bernardo unfastened the spurs and stole them while Je—" Amy caught herself. She wanted Rodriguez to divulge the name of the former owner. It lent more proof that Jeter had been the wearer if the peon named him. "The spurs were taken off a gunman while his feet were resting on the cantina's table?"

"No, no, he drank much, this bad man. He passed out from too much pulque. Then is when Bernardo crept in like a snake, slithering over, and took this spur. He wanted both, but the gunman, he woke. Furious at losing his spur, he began shooting. The son of Bernardo was hit. Here!" Rodriguez pointed to his belly.

"So your friend Bernardo left his wounded son and brought you the spur?"

Rodriguez shrugged.

"What really happened, Paco?" she asked gently.

"Bernardo, he did leave. There was nothing to do for his *hijo*. He feared for his own life, so he ran and hid. The gunman was very angry. He shot many times, then left."

"What happened then?" Amy scribbled furiously to record every word Rodriguez said, even as she added her own annotation to the tale. Ambrose would eat this up!

"Bernardo come here, but he fears the gunman he will follow. So he hides the spur. It is pure silver, he knows. The gunman said so. He buried the spur and . . ."

"And you found it. You stole it from Bernardo?"

"I need money. Bernardo, he has a rich son. The cantina makes him rich."

"That isn't what you said before."

"He is richer than me," said Rodriguez. This justified his theft of the stolen spur. For Amy this was a believable explanation. She kept writing as Rodriguez went on. "He did not know I saw him hide this." He pointed at the spur.

"So you're selling it and not telling him?" She kept writing, her steel-nibbed pen dipping into her ink and scratching furiously on the notebook pages.

"I will share. If there is enough."

"Who was the gunman? Do you know his name?"

"Bernardo say it was Jeter, but I do not know this myself."

"The letter *J* is his initial?"

"*Jota*, the letter, yes, that is so. What will you give me for the spur?"

"I'm sorry, Paco," she said, closing her notebook and putting away her writing material in the valise. "It's just not worth much. It's not pure silver. See?" She spun the rowel until it squeaked. "Pure silver does not make such a sound. Nickel-plated steel does. This is an ordinary spur."

"But it was worn by this bad man."

"One dollar," Amy said firmly. "That's all I can offer for this." She forced herself to remain calm. Ambrose would pay a hundred dollars for such an artifact.

"No, no, not enough."

"Five dollars," she said, seeing Rodriguez weakening.

"Five dollars will buy a lot of pulque. Or tequila or whatever it is you want."

"Five, yes!" Rodriguez eagerly held out his calloused hand to be paid.

As Amy reached for her clutch purse to get the money, a loud screech startled her. She looked up to see an old man hobbling toward them, waving a three-foot-long tree branch like a club. Her eyes went wide, and then the gray-haired man let out a screech as he swung that would have caused an owl to cringe. The branch hit the tree trunk next to Rodriguez, causing him to jump away.

"What do you do, Bernardo?"

"I will kill you! You stole from me!"

The tree branch turned to splinters when Bernardo swung again and missed, hitting the trunk once more. Bernardo hobbled forward, his skeletal hands turned to claws. Rodriguez grappled with the old man and tumbled to the ground. Amy watched in fear, then hastily wrapped up the spur and tucked it away in her valise.

By this time Rodriguez had his hands wrapped around Bernardo's scrawny neck, choking the life from him.

"Stop, don't," Amy cried, but it was too late. Rodriguez sat astride the supine man, hands still pressing into Bernardo's windpipe. Panting, he looked up at Amy.

"I have killed my friend. I cannot stay here. I must go into Mexico. Give me money. More money! All you have!"

Amy was in shock and obeyed without thinking. She pulled a wad of greenbacks from her purse and shoved them in Rodriguez's direction. He grabbed them and got to his feet.

"Go. Run. You have seen nothing here. Run!"

Amy did, then slowed, turned, and looked back in time to see Rodriguez helping Bernardo to his feet. Both men were counting the money when Amy walked back slowly, fuming at how gullible she had been.

"Give me back my money," she said.

Both men looked up guiltily. Then Rodriguez sneered at her and shook his head vigorously.

"No," he said. "You do not deserve to have money while we have none."

"And you don't deserve to die over a few dollars," Amy said, drawing a derringer from her purse. She pointed it directly at Rodriguez's face. *"Adios, pendejo."*

"Wait! No, do not shoot," cried Bernardo. "Here. Here. Take it back. *Todo.* She will kill us, Paco. I see it in her face."

"You see what you want in the clouds, Bernardo. She will not—" Rodriguez stared at Amy and weighed her determination when she cocked the derringer. Her hand was steady and her gaze steely.

"Perhaps you are right, Bernardo," Rodriguez said uneasily. He held out the money, but Amy didn't take it.

"On the ground. Then you step back several paces. Not too many. I wouldn't want you to get out of range in case I have to kill you."

The men did as they were told. Amy scooped up all the money, then peeled off five dollar bills and dropped them to the ground.

"For the spur. Fair value." She backed away, derringer still leveled, then stopped. "Bernardo, was it a tall tale or was that what happened? How you got the spur?"

"It is true. We thought only to get more. When you did not pay it, we had prepared."

"Prepared your little drama," Amy finished for him. "The spur's for real? Jeter wore it?"

Both men nodded until Amy thought their heads would come unhinged and fall off. She made certain the spur was securely hidden in her valise as she backed away. She saw the two men dive on the scrip she had dropped like vultures seeing rotting carrion. Let them fight over the five dollars. They might actually kill one another for such a paltry sum. She didn't care because she had what she had come for. She hurried back to her buckboard, climbed up, and headed for the road.

"I might be small, but I'm mighty," she said to herself in satisfaction. She cast a quick glance back to the valise and the spur inside. Jeter had worn it. And Ambrose would be so pleased! She could hardly wait to see the look on his face when she presented the artifact to him and the riveting story that went along with it.

12

"Let me patch you up," Ruth Jeter said. "You're bleeding from a thousand gunshots and cuts."

"Not that many," Slocum said, checking his arms and torso. He had been grazed twice and had picked up more than his share of scratches as he made his way downhill after Jeter, but he was in no danger of bleeding to death.

"Please. It's all I can do."

"You're not holding me up so he can get away, are you?"

Slocum looked at the way she reacted. The thought hadn't occurred to her. That made him feel a mite better. She wasn't trying to get back with Jeter, at least as far as he could tell. Why she had stayed with Jeter for so long, no matter that he had kept her on foot and miles away from the nearest neighbor, bothered him. But he hadn't actually shackled her like a slave. Slocum wondered why Ruth hadn't summoned up the spunk to either leave Jeter or lay in wait for him and kill him. She knew how he was providing for her.

"That's good," he said when she finished tearing strips from her skirt and binding his minor wounds. "We ought to get on back to the house."

"You mean to leave me, don't you?"

"If I catch him, there won't be any reason for you to worry. Besides, the posse is out here somewhere hunting him. That's going to keep him on the move. He won't dare try to hole up at your place where they might surround him."

"He knows the Davis Mountains better than anyone in these parts," Ruth said. "He won't let them corner him or run him to ground."

"I've had a taste of how good a trailsman he is," Slocum said, flexing his arm and making certain the crude bandage didn't hinder his draw. He felt a touch of stiffness in his right arm, but it would never slow him if he came face-to-face with Jeter again.

"You intend to kill him, don't you?"

Slocum wasn't sure what he wanted to do with Jeter. After he got his watch back, it was possible he would turn him over to the posse or find a Texas Ranger to haul his ass back to San Antonio for trial. Jeter's killing spree had gone on too long to be ignored.

Slocum wasn't exactly pristine, but he had never killed someone like Jeter had just out of pure cussedness. During the war he had ridden with the bloodiest of them all, William Quantrill. After the Lawrence, Kansas, raid, Slocum had protested the way Quantrill had ordered every male in the town, age eight and up, shot down where they stood. Too many in Quantrill's Raiders had seen their own kin killed by the bluecoats for such a protest to go unnoticed. Bloody Bill Anderson had shot Slocum in the belly and left him to die. Slocum's recovery had been slow and painful, and by the time he was able to ride back to Slocum's Stand in Georgia, the war was over. The farm had been in the Slocum family since before the Revolutionary War, but a carpetbagger judge had taken a shine to it and claimed it for his own. No taxes had been paid during the war, he said, and he had both the law and a gunman to back up his decree.

He and the hired gun had ridden onto the farm, but only Slocum had ridden out at the end of the day. Two new graves had been dug near the springhouse. Burying them was more than they deserved, but Slocum had still done things the way they ought to be done then. No matter that he had had the right to kill the Reconstruction judge for what he was doing—it had been outright theft. But the authorities didn't see it that way.

Wanted posters with his likeness had dogged his steps ever since. No matter the crime, judge-killing seemed to be about the worst in the eyes of the law. This had kept Slocum moving on until he had come to like riding for the distant horizon and the freedom this afforded him. No ties. Free to do whatever he wanted.

But he was still bound to the past in one way. His brother Robert's watch was not going to remain in Les Jeter's pocket one tick longer than necessary.

"I'll kill him if he makes it necessary," Slocum answered Ruth. "What do you think about that?"

The woman looked troubled, and finally began to tear up again.

"He's about all I've ever known," she said. "Until you came along, I didn't know that I could feel the way I did when we—I mean when you and I—" She broke off in confusion. "You've made everything turn upside down."

"I've been accused of a lot worse on occasion,"

Slocum said, smiling. The way Ruth talked convinced him she wasn't likely to betray him to Jeter, even if she had the chance. He wouldn't fault her none if she had to do it to save her own hide, but she wouldn't go out of her way to betray him. Slocum felt it in his gut. Ruth was that kind of woman.

"I doubt that," she said, smiling a little shyly. Together they made their way back up the slope to where Slocum's horse cropped at tough grass growing from between the rocks. The horse turned a limpid brown eye toward him, as if complaining, but the animal didn't balk under Slocum and Ruth's combined weight as it returned to the cabin.

As they approached, Slocum kept a sharp eye out for any sign of Jeter.

"You have any idea where he might have hidden the loot from all the robberies?" Slocum asked. "He doesn't strike me as the sort of man to trust banks with his stash."

Ruth laughed harshly.

"He doesn't trust anyone. Ever. Not even me. That's why he never told me when he would return. Sometimes he would hint that he'd be gone a long time and return the same day. Other times I think he was in the hills around the farm, just watching to see what I would do. I asked about it once and he got furious."

"He hit you?" Slocum knew the answer by the set to the woman's body.

"You really think I'll be all right here by myself?"

"You'll be fine," Slocum said, hating himself for the plan taking form in his head. Using the woman as bait was the only surefire way of luring Jeter to where he could nab him. The loot had to be hidden nearby, but that wouldn't draw Jeter. Only Ruth would. Not because he loved the woman, Slocum guessed, but because he would never let anyone else have her. Slocum had to play on this possessiveness to get the outlaw in his sights.

Slocum helped Ruth dismount, then followed, glad to be out of the saddle for a few minutes. He turned and saw her staring at him with an expression he couldn't describe. She took a step toward him, parted her lips as if she wanted to say something—or to be kissed—and then turned away abruptly.

"I could use something to eat before I get back on his trail," Slocum said. "You have anything I might—"

"Yes," Ruth said hurriedly, glad to find a comfortable topic. "There's plenty. Les is a good provider. He never left me without food. Ever." She hurried up the steps, her skirt swaying as she moved. Slocum caught sight of one of her shapely ankles and a bit more. Her bare calf was exposed to his lusting gaze as she opened the door and a puff of wind came whipping up the valley. Caught between the box of the cabin's single room and the huge rush of wind, her skirt billowed up high. She gasped and pushed it down chastely. Slocum wasn't likely to see anything he hadn't already, but something about the way she responded so chastely told him in a different way that she wasn't likely to double-cross him with Jeter. She wanted a fresh start and saw Slocum as the way to get it.

If she had intended to sell him out, she would have blatantly exposed herself to him and tried to gull him into thinking with his balls and not his brain.

At least, that was what Slocum told himself as he climbed the steps, took a final look around for Jeter, and went inside where Ruth busied herself preparing something to eat. Before he knew it he was gobbling down a plate of fresh, crisp bacon and some fried potatoes. Ruth had added some greens that tasted a little like onions.

"I found that growing a ways off," she said. "Wild onion. At least it tastes a lot like onion," she explained.

"Good," Slocum said, wolfing it down. He chased it with a cup of coffee that was far better than anything he had ever boiled for himself out on the trail. "Very good," he said, wiping his lips and sitting back to look at her closely. She smiled shyly.

"I'm glad you liked it. I like pleasing you, John. It makes me feel . . ."

"Different?"

"Wanted," she said. "You don't act like I belong to you."

"You don't belong to anyone but yourself." Slocum was getting a little uneasy and pushed away from the table. "I have to find Jeter's trail before it gets too dark."

"But it'll be night in a couple hours. You can't hardly get back to the pass by then. Stay here tonight, John. With me."

"I will," he said. "Soon. But not tonight. Not now." He went around the table and kissed her lightly, then left before he actually thought any more about her invitation. He heard her sniffling, but she didn't break out in sobs as he had feared. He took his canteen off the saddle and filled it at the rain barrel, then corked it and reslung it over his saddle. It was time for him to end this chase.

He saw Ruth peering out from behind a curtain, but did not wave to her or even acknowledge that he saw her. If Jeter was watching, he wanted the outlaw to think his pursuer was intent on his trail. As he rode, Slocum hunted for the spot where he would camp and wait. Ruth had been right about the time it would take returning to the pass. If he had intended to track Jeter, that trip would have been necessary, but he had baited the trap. Now all he had to do was wait for the mouse to come sniffing after the cheese.

As twilight fell, Slocum left the trail he was following and went higher onto a ridge where he could look down on the cabin. He left his horse on the far side of the rise, took his rifle, and worked his way around to a cluster of rocks where he had a good view. A tiny white curl of smoke rose from the cabin chimney. He wondered if Ruth was only burning some wood to stay warm against the gathering chill, or if she was cooking something else. Something special. For him.

As those thoughts crossed his mind, others pushed them away. Jeter was a cold-blooded killer and would turn on Ruth in a flash if he thought she was no longer faithful. That she was married to the outlaw bothered Slocum enough that he worked to make it all right in his head. A married woman shouldn't be with a man who wasn't her husband—and a gentleman wouldn't even ask. Slocum was long past being a Southern gentleman, but remnants of the social code remained to nettle him.

"She was too young to get married," Slocum decided. "Jeter offered her a life and she took it. Hell, for all I know, Jeter killed her entire family just to be with her."

This thought assuaged some of his uneasiness over what they had done in the barn and what was going through his mind right now. He knew Ruth lusted after him too, from the way she had acted when they got back to the cabin. Her offer for him to stay the night had included sharing her bed. There was no mistaking that.

And there was no mistaking the solitary rider coming down the valley from a direction where Jeter might have escaped after the shoot-out back at the pass. Slocum stood and squinted trying to get a better view of the rider, then turned his head to the side and looked at the man out of the corner of his eye. He had found his night vision was better this way.

"Jeter," he said under his breath. He recognized the way the man rode. He could smell him. Slocum's hand tightened on his rifle as he pulled it up to his shoulder and slowly followed the rider's progress down toward the cabin where Ruth waited.

Slocum lowered the rifle when the rider suddenly halted and looked around. Slocum knew Jeter couldn't see him, but the man had some uncanny sense that warned of danger. Frozen as he was, he became virtually invisible. Slocum didn't want to shoot, give away his position, and miss his target. He had lured Jeter back. He had to take full advantage of it or he would have one hell of a hard trail to follow.

The rider shifted about and rode directly for Slocum's position in the rocks. Seeing this, Slocum faded back into shadow. Maybe Jeter had his loot hidden in these very rocks! Slocum had picked the area for its concealment. Jeter might already have found a spot to bury his loot.

A dozen things flashed through Slocum's mind in that moment. The money had been stolen and the stagecoach company had survived. Nobody would miss what had already been taken from them. If Jeter revealed his treasure trove and Slocum killed him—he had given up on the idea that he would ever take Jeter alive—the stolen money would make a mighty fine poke for him to travel on.

Maybe some of it could go back to the San Esteban bank. Those folks had been hit doubly hard, losing the bank and its employees as well as whatever money they had deposited there. Then Slocum shoved the mercenary thoughts of taking the money aside. If he didn't handle this right, he would be the dead one and Jeter would spend the rest of his days telling time using Robert's watch.

The rider came closer, and Slocum knew his instincts had been accurate. Les Jeter rode with his hand resting on his six-shooter, but did not draw. The outlaw passed within a dozen yards of where Slocum crouched in the rocks, and never twigged to the rifle or the man behind it.

Jeter passed from sight and dropped to the ground. Slocum heard boot soles scraping against rough rock as he climbed. Sinking down farther and making sure his rifle barrel was hidden, Slocum pressed close to cold rock when Jeter got to the boulder farther up the hill. Chancing a quick glimpse at the outlaw convinced Slocum that Jeter was as anxious about approaching the cabin as Slocum had been about leaving Ruth alone there. But Jeter had more to lose.

Slocum slid a little more around the rock and sighted along the barrel, his sights aligned perfectly. He could shoot the outlaw down. Or he could do what he foolishly did.

"Surrender, Jeter!" he shouted. "I've got you covered!"

Jeter did what Slocum would have. He threw himself to the side and let gravity help him escape. Slocum fired, missed, cursed, and got to his feet to go after his quarry. And this almost cost him his life. Jeter hadn't run, he had gone to ground and whipped out his six-gun.

Slocum saw foot-long tongues of orange flame leap from Jeter's pistol. He returned fire, the more powerful rifle roaring as he fired one round after another to drive Jeter back and to ruin his aim. Slocum heard two more slugs whine past, and then Jeter's six-shooter either hit an empty chamber or he had a misfire.

Slocum had choices. He could retreat and regroup before Jeter could get off another round. Or he could attack, trusting that the outlaw's six-gun was empty or jammed.

With a rebel yell torn from his lungs, Slocum swarmed up and over the rock where Jeter was. He caught the road agent by surprise. Jeter had the side gate of his six-shooter open as he tried to eject the balky round. Slocum fired at the outlaw and knocked him back. To his surprise, Slocum saw that the outlaw wasn't hurt by the slug that had caught him in the belly.

Slocum had no time to lever in another round. He kept up his attack and hit Jeter like a load of falling bricks. The pair of them toppled to the ground and rolled over and over, vying for advantage. A sudden pain in Slocum's back distracted him. He had speared himself on a particularly sharp shard of rock.

Jeter grabbed the rifle and wrenched it free from Slocum's grip.

"You're not going to win," Slocum grated out. Rather than try to grab the rifle back, he kicked hard. This drove the stone deeper into his back, but again he caught Jeter by surprise. The toe of Slocum's boot knocked the rifle out of the outlaw's grip. A second kick swept the man's feet from under him.

Slocum tried to get on top and failed. They rolled over again, this time Jeter coming out with the advantage of wrapping his fingers around Slocum's corded neck.

Slocum felt the air shut off. The world spun and then began to turn black. Only one thought came to him that helped.

"My watch," he grated out. A surge of anger gave him the power to lift Jeter bodily from him and throw the outlaw downhill. For a moment Slocum gasped for breath, then rolled to his hands and knees and went for his Peacemaker. His hand was stopped by Jeter's powerful grip on his wrist. The outlaw had hit the ground and come to his feet, reversed his path, and returned.

"You won't die, damn you. You been screwin' my wife?"

"Yes," Slocum got out. "And she likes me better than you."

He had hoped to anger Jeter enough to force the man into a mistake. Nothing of the sort happened. A truth flashed through Slocum's mind at this instant. Jeter felt nothing for Ruth other than as a possession. There was no love, no feeling other than obsession—and this summed up everything the outlaw did.

"You don't even want the money, do you? Where is it hidden?" Slocum got the words out before Jeter brought his knee up into his groin. The darkness he had experienced before when Jeter was strangling him now turned to bright, spinning spots. Slocum weakened as pain assailed him. Jeter forced him back, then down to his knees.

Slocum tried to get his pistol from its holster, but Jeter beat him to it. The outlaw grabbed the six-shooter and swung it hard. His aim was a little off and the barrel only grazed the side of Slocum's head, but it was enough to knock him flat onto his back.

He stared up into the panting, fierce face of Les Jeter.

"Die, you son of a bitch."

Jeter aimed Slocum's own six-shooter at him. His finger drew back slowly, and Slocum waited to die.

13

Amy Gerardo was exhausted from her trip and kept looking over her shoulder at the valise with the spur and her notes about it. As tired as she was from her nonstop trip after purchasing the spur from Rodriguez, she was buoyed by the thrill Ambrose would get when he saw what she brought him. He had been hunting futilely for such an artifact for months, and her chance eavesdropping had put her on the right path to get it.

Heaving a sigh, she pulled up in front of the door leading into the hacienda. She grabbed the valise, leaving her clothing behind. This was important. Amy went to the door and rattled the latch, but it was locked on the inside. Stepping back, she called out to the servants to let her in. It would be too much to expect that Ambrose himself would come to the gate.

"Where are you?" she fretted. No servants. This worried her. Had something happened while she was gone? "Ambrose! Mr. Killian!" she cried. "Are you all right?"

No answer.

Clutching her bag, she went around the house. The hacienda had been built in the Spanish style and had reminded her of a fortress more than a home. The central courtyard was surrounded by the house, built in a large square with few windows on the outer wall and the rooms and windows opening onto the central area. She had admired the garden there, and the fountain always delighted. It was her personal refuge—hers and Ambrose's. Sitting with him, listening to his exciting stories of an eventful life, thinking how she could help him . . . and more. Amy hardly admitted it to herself, but she fancied herself the perfect match for him. He was just too much of a gentleman to make a pass at her, as much as she wanted it.

Circling the house, she came to a rear gate leading to a small area just outside the kitchen.

"Hello!"

She heard movement inside and called again. This time the locking bar was removed from the gate. It opened to reveal the cook.

"Consuela," Amy said, glad to see the elderly woman. "Is anything wrong? The front gate was barred. Is Ambrose—Mr. Killian—safe?" The old woman gave her a sour expression and inclined her head toward the kitchen door. Amy hurried inside, fearing the worst.

She stopped dead in her tracks and stared.

"Mr. Killian, are you all right?"

Ambrose turned and glared at her. He had bandoliers slung across both shoulders, forming an X over his broad chest. Six-shooters hung at his sides, ready for use. He had dressed in rough denims and high boots, as if he intended to hike out in the desert. But the look on his face chilled her. She had never seen him look so ferocious.

"I am furious. Word has just arrived that I missed him. I missed a golden opportunity!"

"What are you talking about?"

"You silly bitch, I missed Jeter! He shot up the bank in San Esteban and then burned it down. I missed it all. I could have been there instead of sitting here and polishing that damned black powder pistol of his."

"But you couldn't know . . ."

"I pay good money for people to alert me of possible robberies, and not a one of them knew of the bank robbery. It was a daring robbery. Pure Lester Jeter. He walked in during business hours, shot everyone inside, shot up half the town, then burned the bank to the ground to escape. And several in the crowd gathered outside saw him leave. They didn't know they were watching the most cunning outlaw in all of Texas. In the entire goddamn West!" Killian slammed his hand again a heavy wood door and sent it swinging hard against the wall. Bits of plaster broke off and adobe dust filled the air in the kitchen.

"He's cunning," Amy said. "He wouldn't let anyone in San Esteban know what he intended to do. It's not their fault."

"Not their fault!" roared Killian. "What do you know? Of course it is their fault. Whose else could it be?"

Amy swallowed hard and stepped up, opening her valise to take out the spur.

"I located this. It was a spur—one of a pair—that Jeter wore. It was taken from him while he was drunk. Down by the Rio Grande at a cantina trafficking in outlaws from both Mexico and Texas."

She held it up, only to have it swept from her grip with a pass of Killian's hand. The spur crashed into the wall and produced its own small damage. Amy stared at the broken plaster. The hole in the wall it left might have come from a bullet. The sharp Spanish rowel had done its worst, but hardly matched what Ambrose had done.

"Don't be foolish. No one takes a spur off a man like Jeter, not unless he's dead. And he's not dead. Oh, no, he's not dead. Far from it! He's robbing the damned bank in San Esteban!" Killian stormed from the room, leaving Amy to stare at the spot he had vacated. She wasn't sure what to do. She wanted to soothe him and she wanted to kill him. How dare he dismiss her effort in such a fashion!

She picked up the spur and put it into her bag. She would tell him the details later after he had calmed down. At the moment, she was glad she had paid only five dollars, and that in scrip, for the spur. That Rodriguez and Bernardo had tried to swindle her was beyond question. That didn't mean the spur hadn't once adorned Jeter's boot or that any part of their story had been a lie. She wanted to believe it for Ambrose's benefit, but right now she had other matters to attend to.

"Ambrose? Ambrose?" She hesitantly followed him through several rooms and into his trophy room. He stood, arms crossed on his chest, glaring at the artifacts of Jeter's criminal career.

"Ambrose," Amy said softly. She laid a hand on his shoulder. He jerked away and spun to face her.

"Don't touch me," he snapped.

"I don't like to see you like this. You have done so much so well. Look around you. You've produced a complete picture of a man who has done his best to remain in shadow. You've found out more about Jeter than the lawmen who have chased after him for so long. Why, some of them don't even know when he commits a robbery. He is a mystery to so many of them, including the Texas Rangers."

She saw that he was being mollified. She kept up her compliments and wheedled him out of his foul mood. When she thought it was time, she brought out the spur again and handed it to him.

"I was careful, sir. I detailed everything about this spur's provenance." She was pleased that she had learned that word from him.

"Let me see it." Ambrose snatched the spur from her hand and turned it over several times, then snorted in contempt. "It's not Jeter's. It couldn't be. Someone has scratched his initial into the spur to make it seem that he was the owner. He would never do such a thing. Look around. Look carefully, Miss Gerardo. Is there *anything* else marked with his initial? No! Jeter is not a man to advertise himself in such a crass fashion."

"You're saying this isn't his spur?"

"Of course not. And that cock-and-bull story of someone taking it off him while he was drunk? It never happened. Not only would Jeter never brag about how great a road agent he was, he would never get drunk. Not once in all my research about him have I found one instance where he became so drunk that he lost control in any way."

"But—"

"The man is about control, Miss Gerardo. He fears losing control. Everything around him must be under his thumb, his personal domination. Anything less and he becomes violent."

"That sounds like you." Amy put her hand over her mouth in horror. The words had slipped out before she could check them.

"It does, doesn't it?" Killian said reasonably. "Perhaps this shared trait is what draws me to him. He is the arch-villain. I document him. He is ruthless in killing. I am ruthless in finding everything about him I can. That's what galls me so about not knowing he was going to rob the San Esteban bank. So close! I was so close and I missed my chance."

"Would you have killed him?" Amy eyed the bandoliers of ammunition and the twin six-guns hanging at his hips.

"It would have been murder," Killian said. "He is a blindingly fast gunman, and his aim is that of a dead-eye. If I ever have the chance, I will have to shoot him in the back. Otherwise, he will kill me."

"You'd murder him?" This stunned Amy. She had never before realized how completely involved Ambrose was in his pursuit of the outlaw.

The look on his face chilled her even more. It wasn't cruel, it was beatific.

"I want to go to San Esteban right away. Prepare to join me."

"But I just—" Amy cut off her protest about being near exhaustion after finding and fetching the spur at such great risk to her own life. Ambrose had it firmly fixed in his head that they ought to investigate the bank robbery. "Very well," she said, turning to go to her quarters. She had some clean clothing she could pack, replacing the dirty dresses from the trip down to the Rio Grande and back. It was difficult work keeping up with Ambrose Killian, but she thought it was worth it.

"Arrange for rooms," Killian ordered. "I'll see to the ruins of the bank."

"Very well, sir," she said, starting to drive to the only decent hotel in San Esteban. From all Amy could tell, it was the only hotel. This wasn't the crossroads of West Texas by any means, and probably the only visitors who needed rooms were those there when the stagecoach laid over for the night.

"Wait. Get the rooms later. You should accompany me and take notes. I'll want a full report on this crime from all the witnesses. Chasing them down later might prove difficult, if not impossible."

"Are you sure?" Amy tried to keep the testy tone out of her words and failed. Ambrose looked at her with his piercing gaze.

"Do you have something else to do, Miss Gerardo?"

"No, sir. It's just been a long trip, and after I returned from the Rio Grande cantina I didn't have any time to rest." She saw that he was already focused elsewhere, hailing a man with a badge pinned to his chest. She heaved a sigh and climbed down from the buckboard, her short legs aching—as well as other unmentionable portions of her anatomy. She fished around in her valise and got her notebook and a pencil, since she would have no opportunity to continually dip ink from her inkpot. She could transcribe the notes into a more permanent form later, after she had a room in the hotel.

"This gent's the new town marshal," Ambrose said, not turning to her. "He's going to tell me what happened."

"The old marshal, he caught wind of what happened here and never came back from ridin' circuit. Sent word with a cowboy comin' to town. Nobody else wanted the job, so I took it."

"Why's that?" asked Amy, curious. "If the job proved too dangerous for your predecessor, why did you take it?"

The man scratched his head and looked at her.

"You're real purty, ma'am, but I don't much unnerstand what you mean."

"Never mind her, my good man," Ambrose said, dismissing Amy's sensible question. "What can you tell me about Jeter and his raid on the bank? Do you know where he got off to after he cleaned out the vault?"

"Well, we ain't sure he cleaned it out. Mighta burned down with it."

"You have the body? Can I photograph it?"

"Don't know, 'bout that, mister."

"Ambrose Killian, pleased to make your acquaintance. And you are?"

"The new marshal," the man said, frowning. "I tole you that already."

"He meant what's your name," Amy explained.

"They promised me thirty dollars a month to be marshal," the man said, looking more confused than ever.

"Yes, and I'll give you that much here and now if you'll tell me what you know of the bank robbery and the burning of the building and Jeter."

"Eaton. Sid Eaton."

"What?" It was Ambrose's turn to look confused.

"That's his name, sir," Amy said.

"You'll let me photograph all the bodies?" Ambrose said to Eaton. "And you can identify them for me?"

"Reckon so. I lived here in San Esteban fer purty near a year now and know everyone. Anybody I don't know's likely to be the robber."

"You've heard of Les Jeter?"

"Course I have. That was the name the stage depot agent kept screamin' at the top of his lungs. Not that ole Sanford knows squat."

"Will you form a posse and go after the bank robber?" Amy asked.

"He burnt up in the building, I tole you." Marshal Eaton looked increasingly confused with the pair of them questioning him. Amy looked to her employer and saw how irritated Ambrose was becoming too. She applied her pencil to her notebook and resolutely shut her mouth. It was better if Ambrose asked the questions, even if they were not likely to generate decent answers from the simpleminded marshal.

"Miss Gerardo, fetch my photographic equipment. Bring it over to the bank." Ambrose sniffed and made a face at the acrid smell still hanging over the town like some angry pall.

Amy closed her notebook and hurried back to the buckboard, gathered the tripod and camera, and dragged them to the front of where the bank had stood. The adobe walls were intact, but anything that had been made of wood was gone. The vigas holding the roof had burned through early on and had caused the roof to collapse into the bank itself, adding more fuel to the fire. In some places the already kiln-fired adobe had become so hot that it caused the bricks to turn brittle and crack. In spots the straw used to hold the mud bricks together had ignited and destroyed the bricks entirely. She couldn't imagine how hot that fire must have been.

"The photographic plates, girl. Get them! I can't do a thing without them."

"Sorry, sir," she said contritely, returning to the buckboard and hefting the large metal case holding the photographic plates. She struggled under the weight until the marshal saw her and offered to help.

"She can get it. You're answering my questions," Ambrose told him.

"But that's a powerful heavy load fer such a small woman."

"She's strong and determined. Set up the camera for me, Miss Gerardo. Now, Marshal Eaton, the bodies. Have you pulled them from the ruins?"

"Got 'em over there. Five of 'em."

Ambrose snapped his fingers at Amy and pointed to the spot where he wanted the camera tripod placed. He walked to the bodies and gingerly poked about on the charred carcasses.

"Which one can't you identify?"

"That one, the one you're pokin'," Marshal Eaton said. "Them others, well, that's the teller, them two's the guards, and the one with the fancy vest, or what's left of it, he was the bank president. Real fine fella too. Loaned me money when I needed it."

"I'm sure," Ambrose said, dropping to his knees and further examining the corpse. He drew out a slender knife and cut through the charred clothing, then recoiled.

"Ready for the first picture, sir," Amy said.

"That won't be necessary. This is not Jeter."

"How kin you tell that?" Marshal Eaton peered over Ambrose's shoulder curiously.

"This is a woman, you dolt!"

"Cain't tell from the clothes."

"I can't say one way or the other myself, sir," Amy piped up. She wasn't defending the marshal as much as observing that the degree of destruction was almost total. Casual examination would not reveal even this most basic of differences.

"The clothing is almost totally destroyed, I admit," said Ambrose. "She must have received the full brunt of the fire when the roof collapsed. Her skull is crushed and there might have been kerosene spilled on her. But cutting away the layers of scorched cloth reveals, uh, womanly attributes not entirely erased by the intense fire." Ambrose bent lower and sniffed, then gagged. "I can't tell. The smell of her burned flesh is . . . overpowering."

"Do you want me to take the pictures, sir?"

"No, of course not."

"It's all ready," Amy said.

"I don't want pictures at all! Why waste expensive silver bromide plates on these . . . citizens. I want pictures of Jeter!"

"He ain't here," Marshal Eaton said. "You tole me that one there was a woman and—"

"I know that," Ambrose snapped. "This is why I'm not shooting any pictures. Put the camera back, Miss Gerardo."

"You sure it was this Jeter fella what robbed the bank?"

"And got away with it," Ambrose said grimly.

"He a fellow 'bout this tall?" asked a man who had watched the gruesome examination. "Pleasant fellow? The one up in the valley?"

"You know him?" Ambrose turned and stared.

"Took me a while, but I remembered I seen him in town once before, over at the store gettin' supplies. He mentioned in passin' how he was settled down with his missus up in Limpia Valley. Real nice stretch of land. Other folks was up there, he said, but they passed on and he took it over."

"Passed on?" Ambrose took three steps until he was in the man's face.

"That's what he said. Happens around here, what with Injuns and all. We get our share of them Meskin *bandidos* crossin' the Rio Grande too. They want nothing but to lie low until the Meskin law's not breathin' down their necks, then they sneak back across the border. But they's evil. Nasty cusses."

"Did he give a name? The man in the store?"

"Nope, and I didn't ask. Didn't seem important. Ain't seen him since either, not till right after the robbery carryin' that bag over his shoulder."

"Limpia Valley," Ambrose said, his eyes shining brightly. "Jeter could be holed up there."

"Then I reckon I got to get me a posse and go after him," Marshal Eaton said, surprising Amy greatly with his initiative. "Might be a reward on his head. Have to ask ole Sanford 'bout that."

"The Texas Rangers would dearly love to see you apprehend this outlaw," Ambrose assured the marshal.

"Do tell. Then I kin git me a dozen or so men whipped up to a frenzy. You'd be surprised at the folks what lost money in the bank robbery. They'd do most anything to git a shot at the gent who stole their life savings."

The marshal strutted off, bowlegs pumping quickly, as he headed for the nearest saloon to rustle up a posse.

"You joinin' in the fun, mister?"

Ambrose looked at the man. "No, I think you and I ought to set a spell and talk over everything you know about this Limpia Valley and its residents. Or former residents. Might their names have been Jeter?"

Amy sucked in her breath. There had been unconfirmed rumors that Jeter had killed his own parents. The deaths up in the valley might tie in with that—and prove to be a fact.

"Miss Gerardo, a moment." Ambrose took her by the elbow and steered her away from the man, who peered at the camera and then at the bodies. "After you store the camera equipment, prepare for the . . . end result."

"The one you mentioned earlier?" Amy's eyes were wide with amazement. "We're that close to catching Jeter?"

"I think so. We remain in San Esteban because if the posse does not capture him but he is flushed from his lair, he will likely come here as he flees."

"He might go into Mexico," Amy said.

"I don't think so. If Marshal Eaton and his men are successful in driving Jeter from his sanctuary, he will want revenge. I know the man intimately well. He will return here and burn the entire town to the ground. If that happens, I will be prepared to face him. And if the marshal is successful in capturing him, they will return here for the trial. Ergo, there is no cause for us to stir." Ambrose turned and looked at the man still poking about the camera. "Especially since there are events and details about Jeter to add to our store begging to be annotated here."

"Yes, sir, I'll get on it right away."

"And rooms, Miss Gerardo, get us rooms." With that Ambrose hurried back to steer the man away from the camera toward the restaurant. Amy's belly growled. She wished Ambrose had offered her some food too, but that could wait.

She gathered up the photographic equipment and lugged it to the buckboard, stored it securely, then took a deep breath. She knew what had to be done next.

She went directly to the undertaker to order a fancy coffin for Lester Jeter. Whatever happened, the outlaw would end up being planted in the cemetery at the edge of San Esteban, and Ambrose wanted him to be sent off in a style befitting a legend.

14

"Les, no, don't!"

Jeter's attention strayed from killing Slocum for an instant. This was all the time it took Slocum to grab a rock and fling it clumsily at the outlaw. Jeter was torn between Ruth struggling toward him, coming up the hillside, and Slocum.

"You slut!" Jeter swung his six-shooter around and fired at his wife. "You bedded him!"

This was the last thing he got out before Slocum slugged him with another rock, driving him to the ground. Fists flying, Slocum took out his frustration and anger on the fallen man until Ruth grabbed him and pulled him away.

"Please, John, don't. You'll kill him!"

"Get out of here," Slocum said harshly. "Why'd you come up here?"

"I saw him coming for me, then he headed away. I had to find out why."

"You wanted to know where he hid the money he's taken from all the robberies, wasn't that it?"

"No, no, I worried he was after you. That's the truth, John."

"I want my watch back."

"What watch?" Ruth looked confused. Slocum had no time for her. He grabbed her upper arms and physically lifted her off the ground and set her behind him. Then his heart almost exploded. Jeter was nowhere to be seen.

"You decoyed me away," Slocum said accusingly.

"No, John, I don't want him. I want to be free of him. I kept him from killing you. Tell me that's not what happened."

"You distracted him," Slocum admitted. He moved to keep her behind him when he saw a glint of starlight off his Peacemaker. Jeter had dropped it as he made his escape. With a quick move, Slocum scooped up his six-gun and checked it. He took the time to reload. Facing Jeter again might require all six rounds.

"John, you can't go after him. He's a killer."

"And I'm not?" The expression on his face froze the woman. She pushed away from him and stared. Her mouth opened, then closed. She took a deep breath to get her wits about her before trying to put her thoughts into words again.

"I see that, John. But you're not like him."

"You don't know," he said. "Get on back to the house."

"You'll have to kill him, John. Otherwise, he's going to kill me."

"Then we both have a reason for me to get after him." Slocum angrily slammed his six-shooter back into his holster. How Jeter had disappeared like an Apache was a tribute to the outlaw's skills. That kept Slocum from bulling after him and falling into a trap, but he stood a better chance of keeping out of an ambush himself if he pressed Jeter. Hard. Keep him on the move and the road agent wouldn't have the chance to do anything but high-tail it across the border into Mexico.

"I'll be waiting for you," Ruth said in a choked voice. She turned and stumbled back down the hill.

Slocum fought down the urge to take her in his arms. Better that she get the hell away so he could listen for Jeter. Slocum turned slowly, using his ears more than his eyes. The faint natural night sounds came to him, but he heard nothing to put him onto Jeter's trail. He estimated where Jeter had left his horse and made his way there cautiously.

He took a deep sniff of the cold air and caught the scent of fresh horse flop. Working his way through the rocks, he came to a level area where Jeter had left his horse. The steaming pile confirmed how recently the outlaw had been here. Dropping to hands and knees, Slocum looked closely at the rock and patches of dirt, found where Jeter had entered and the direction he had gone when he left. How he had gotten his horse away so quickly without making any noise was yet another tribute to his skills.

Slocum might have been up against a more skilled man, but he couldn't remember when. Getting to his feet, he got a sighting on the stars to establish a direction, then went to get his own mount. As he worked his way out from the rocks to a more level ridgeline, he looked down into the valley and thought he saw a dark figure resolutely moving toward the cabin with its curl of white smoke going heavenward. If he didn't pursue Jeter, the outlaw would return.

Keeping him away from Ruth became a bigger obligation. There was no doubt in Slocum's mind that Jeter would kill her if he got a chance. And it wasn't likely to be an easy death. Slocum was on the trail of a man who thought nothing of killing everyone in a bank and then burning it down.

He sawed at the reins and got his horse headed in the direction he had determined by sighting in on the stars. It would be a long night catching up with Jeter.

Slocum dozed, his chin dropping to his chest. He jerked awake and reached for his six-shooter when he heard something moving. He had been on the trail for three days, and was no closer to running Jeter to ground now than when he had started. Turning slowly, he faced the direction of the sound that had roused him. Slocum slumped. It was only a curious marmot. Slocum relaxed and tried to convince himself not to jump at shadows, but he knew if he dropped his guard for an instant, Jeter would kill him. They had played cat and mouse since the chase had started—and Slocum wasn't sure which was the quarry and which was the prey.

Not six hours ago, he had ridden into a ravine, only to have a large boulder tumble down almost crushing him. He had avoided death, but worried that Jeter had been responsible. Rocks fell in the mountains all the time, but why such a large once should come crashing down when he rode below it was a poser. He had expected Jeter to follow up with a rain of bullets, but they hadn't come. Was Jeter playing with him, or had it been an accident of nature?

Questioning such things was driving him crazy. He had to end this fast or he would be jumping at every noise and bolting at every shadow like a skittish colt.

Slocum settled down and let his mind drift until he felt a calm wash over him. He wasn't usually this jumpy, but Jeter brought together a lot of his worst nightmares. The man looked enough like Bloody Bill Anderson to bring back memories of getting shot in the gut and spending long, painful months recuperating. But it went beyond that. He worried about Ruth, and he wanted his watch back. Worst of all, Slocum feared he had met his match when it came to skill on the trail—and outright meanness.

His mind drifted like the thin clouds masking the stars as he worked over the problem facing him. He'd had the right idea when he had gone into the rocks above Jeter's house back in the valley. Let the outlaw come to him rather than trying to find him in territory the man knew intimately well. Slocum had found himself turned around more than once, and had only found Jeter's trail because of a healthy dose of luck.

If he would chase his own tail endlessly, he had to find another way of catching Jeter. Baiting the trap had worked once. Slocum turned over this notion in his head and decided it would work again. While more dangerous, it would work because Jeter would never see this coming. He was too confident and full of himself.

Slocum stared into his guttering fire until only embers remained, then nodded off again, the plan forming. When he awoke in the morning, he was stiff from sitting up all night, but felt good for all of that. He knew what had to be done. After tending his horse and eating a cold breakfast, he mounted and rode slowly along his back trail, as if giving up the hunt. The back of his neck itched, and he was certain that every small sound was going to precede the whistle of a bullet digging its way into his spine.

By midday, he found a small stream and camped there.

Leaving his horse, he scouted the area thoroughly, finding only two spots where Jeter might try to ambush him from. Slocum worked to make one spot less attractive, and then concentrated on the other to be sure Jeter had a good view—almost—into the camp. As the sun sank, Slocum began to work more frantically to get a dummy made. He stuffed his spare shirt with dried grass and found a rock about the size of his head. Spreading his bedroll and positioning the dummy, he built the fire far enough away to cast only long shadows.

He was ready for Jeter. If only the outlaw would come to finish the job he had started.

Slocum slipped into the countryside, staying low and finally flopping behind a mound of dirt where he could watch the location he hoped Jeter would be drawn to most. He dozed fitfully, uncomfortably, then came awake a little after midnight. Slocum wiped the sleep from his eyes, checked the stars above, and got his bearings.

The shadow moving dropped down in exactly the spot where Slocum had anticipated. From the vague outline he made out Jeter kneeling, rifle raised and sighting in on the dummy covered with the blanket in Slocum's campsite. Slocum slowly pulled out his six-shooter, aimed, then drew back the trigger and was momentarily blinded by the muzzle flash.

"Gotcha," he cried, scrambling to his feet and rushing forward. His bullet had lodged squarely in the middle of the shadowy body. As Slocum approached, he saw movement and fired twice more. Then he was on top of—what?

Slocum kicked out and sent a hat flying. But the body where he had plowed three bullets was similar to the dummy he had made. The rifle was real. Slocum scooped it up and stared at it. He couldn't identify it as Jeter's, but whose would it be? He kicked out again and sent the innards of the dummy flying to reveal a small branch and a rope attached. Jeter had been at the other end of the rope, tugging away to keep the dummy erect.

Slocum swung about and froze.

"You're a dead man if you move," Jeter said coldly. "I don't rightly know why I shouldn't cut you down where you stand fer all you've done to me and mine."

"Are you going to talk me to death, Jeter?"

"Ought to. That'd be crueler than putting a bullet through you," the outlaw said. "I just wanted you to know how much I admire the way you kept on my trail. Ain't more 'n one or two men in all of Texas who could have tracked like you did."

Slocum had figured out where Jeter was hiding. He was crouched behind a lightning-struck stump of a cottonwood. Getting off a shot that would do any damage wasn't possible. Slocum's goose was cooked.

"I reckon I ought to change that to 'admired' you since you're a dead man fer what you did to my wife."

"Do you even know her name, Jeter?"

"What?"

Slocum knew he had struck at the heart of the outlaw's vanity. Otherwise, he would have been dead by now. Playing for time gave him added seconds to find a way of getting out of the ambush that had turned sour on him.

"You neglect her. You keep her like a slave. You ever own a slave, Jeter? Before you married one?"

"You son of a bitch!"

The first shot missed Slocum. He was ducking and moving when he spoke, knowing what Jeter's response would be. He had goaded the outlaw into losing his composure—and his aim. The bullet went wide. Slocum spun around and began firing steadily in Jeter's direction. He missed with every shot, but drove the outlaw back.

Slocum had tried attacking before and had never made it work. He might have been crazy then, but now he was furious, at himself, and at Jeter for being better than he was at tracking and trapping. For all the work Slocum had put into laying his trap, Jeter had outdone him in only a few minutes.

Getting to the log, Slocum launched himself blindly into the air. His fingers closed on cloth. He clawed his way up, being dragged along as Jeter tried to escape. This time Slocum weighed down his quarry and brought Jeter crashing to the ground. The outlaw's lungs let out a whoosh as he hit a rock and lay limp.

Slocum slugged him. Again. He started to hit him a third time and crush his skull, but hesitated. He knew he ought to kill Jeter now that he had the chance, but killing an unconscious man wasn't his way.

"Get on over," Slocum grunted, rolling Jeter onto his back. He grabbed the outlaw's six-shooter and thrust it into his own gun belt. Then he took a double handful of shirt and pulled Jeter up to a sitting position. With a grunt, Slocum hefted the road agent over his shoulder and staggered toward his camp in triumph.

He had finally caught the son of a bitch!

15

He couldn't get free of him. Les Jeter had tried yet another tactic to throw his tracker off, but didn't have much hope. Ever since the man had laid the trap above the house, he had been like flypaper sticking to Jeter's trail.

"If I can't get rid of you, then I'd better think on some way to kill you," Jeter said. And that suited him well. The son of a bitch had been fooling with his woman. She was Jeter's property and should have been off-limits to anyone else, especially some ugly galoot who was just passing through.

"Or *was* he just passin' through?" Jeter wondered aloud. There was more than a drifter's feeling to the man. The drifter had fought Jeter well at the barn, and had followed when he had taken Ruth with him. Most men would have quit then and there, but not Jeter's flypaper. He had followed and caught Jeter off guard, taking Ruth back to the cabin with him.

That had infuriated Jeter, but he had been cautious approaching the cabin that night. The place had looked peaceable enough, so he had ridden to where he had hidden most of the loot he had accumulated over the past few months of holdups. Locking horns with the man in a clever ambush had almost been the last thing Jeter had done.

He would have ended it all except for the way Ruth had butted in and saved the man.

"Bitch," Jeter snarled. "Bitch and her mangy cur sniffin' all around." He'd had the drop on the man, and then the world had turned upside down. He had barely escaped. And for the past couple days he had done everything he had ever learned, and even some tricks he had only thought up on the spur of the moment, to get free. Nothing had worked.

"Flypaper. Goddamn flypaper," Jeter grumbled. But he was not a man to let adversity get him down. He needed a few hours lead on the man dogging him so diligently so he could lay his trap. Jeter wasn't sure what that would be yet, but he would find something that would work since the man's luck had to run out. And only luck had let him be such a pain in the ass this far.

Jeter worked his way up the side of a hill, not content with the lay of the land but knowing this was the best he was likely to find in this stretch of the Davis Mountains. He was glad he had spent so much time scouting. Such careful preparation was playing off in spades now. A little bait down below would slow his tracker; then he could gun him down when he dismounted to study the spoor.

"Ain't elegant, but it'll do," Jeter decided. He scuffed up the ground, kicked over a few rocks, and then let his stallion dance away onto a rocky patch where his trail wouldn't be immediately obvious. From here he wended his way higher until he reached a spot where his horse would be hidden and he had a decent downhill shot. Those were always tricky, but Jeter knew he was up to it, especially this time. The son of a bitch had been screwing his wife. His only regret was not letting him suffer a mite before he died.

Jeter pulled out his rifle and lay in wait. A slow smile curled his lips when he saw the shadowy outline of a rider coming down the trail.

"Closer, get a little closer so I won't miss." But Jeter fell silent when his flypaper drew rein, then reversed course and disappeared into the inky night.

"What's he tryin' to do? Gull me into thinkin' he ain't interested in me anymore?" Jeter spat. He looked above his hiding spot to be sure nobody could circle and get above him to shoot him in the back the way he had intended to do to the man on his trail. He had been too careful, and his flypaper was giving up.

"Time to go huntin' on my own. He's not gettin' away with anything." Jeter grinned at the notion of killing the man on his trail, then returning to the cabin and spending the night with Ruth. It had been a while since he hadn't been thinking of the next job or looking over his shoulder, watching as the clumsy attempts to arrest him had played out. Yes, it would be real good what he would do to Ruth for the entire livelong night.

He settled his rifle back in its sheath, then mounted. Turning his stallion back downhill proved difficult in the dark, but the horse was surefooted and did not disappoint him. What did bother him was how he lost the trail of his personal flypaper when he got to the last spot where he had seen the man. Jeter got down and studied the trail before coming to the conclusion he had to be more careful than usual. He had a sense of danger, and it screamed at him right about now.

"He wants me to rush after him," Jeter decided, patting his stallion's neck to keep the horse quiet. "I'll wait him out. He's plottin' something bad fer me. It's not gonna work."

He slept the sleep of the righteous, and was up early and in the saddle. It didn't take long to find the ineptly concealed tracks, as if the man who had followed him so closely had forgotten all his skill when it came to hiding his own trail. It took until midnight the next night to see what devilment had been thought up to catch him. Again Jeter had to admit there was a combination of cleverness along with outright bad planning.

"So you want me to think you're still in camp, eh? Where are you?" Jeter prowled about, discovered how unsuitable another section of the terrain was for sneaking up on the campsite, and knew immediately he was being maneuvered into a trap. "You're about the best I ever came up against, I'll give you that. It's gonna be that much more of a pleasure killin' you." Jeter turned dour thinking of the man with Ruth and her enjoying it. He might have to kill her too after his night with her, after he dispatched this annoyance.

That would make him real sad, Ruth dying because of what she had done, but life was full of sorrow.

He rummaged about in his saddlebags and found an old shirt. It took Jeter a few minutes to stuff it with leaves and twigs and another few to find a branch for stiffness and to look like a rifle, and a fist-sized rock. Using a short section of rope, he rigged the shirt, his hat atop it, so it would pop up when he pulled the rope. The branch caught against the rock and held shirt and hat in place. But he had to use his own rifle since there wasn't any way the crooked branch would fool anybody. That didn't matter much. He would be close enough to use his six-shooter. He went a few paces uphill, found an old stump, and settled down behind it to wait.

It wasn't long before Jeter heard a soft hissing sound—leather boot soles gliding across rock.

"You are good, you cayuse," Jeter said under his breath. He had heard Indians make more noise as they moved. But neither the Indians nor this piece of flypaper realized how acute Jeter's hearing was or how much he thought through every move.

Everything happened fast. He saw a flash of starlight against metal and yanked on the rope, causing the shirt with the rifle attached to pop up. An immediate gunshot rang out, dazzling Jeter since he had been staring directly at the spot where the reflection had caught his attention.

"Gotcha," the man cried, rushing out like he had before. Jeter thought the man was a glutton for punishment, but that only made it easier. And it made it even sweeter when the man realized how he had been duped into believing his trap had worked, only find a hat and shirt stuffed with weeds.

"You're a dead man if you move," Jeter cried in triumph. He had the man silhouetted against the night sky and couldn't miss. "I don't rightly know why I shouldn't cut you down where you stand fer all you've done to me and mine."

"Are you going to talk me to death, Jeter?"

"Ought to. That'd be crueler than putting a bullet through you. I just wanted you to know how much I admire the way you kept on my trail. Ain't more 'n one or two men in all of Texas who could have tracked like you did." Jeter chuckled, knowing how completely he had trapped this one.

"I reckon I ought to change that to 'admired' you since you're a dead man fer what you did to my wife," Jeter added.

"Do you even know her name, Jeter?"

"What?" This rocked Jeter. It mirrored something Ruth had said not too long ago about how he didn't know her because he was always gone. The dumb slut should have known he did all the robbing for her. They were going to be rich and go off to Mexico and live in style in a fancy hacienda with servants. And all because he was risking his life to keep her and please her and guarantee that she would be able to lead a life of luxury like nobody in her damn family had ever believed possible.

"You neglect her. You keep her like a slave. You ever own a slave, Jeter? Before you married one?"

"You son of a bitch!"

Jeter wasn't even sure what happened. One instant he had the lying bastard in his sights, the next he was jerking his six-gun around and firing wildly into the night.

Then he was put on the defensive when a fusillade came his way. Jeter scrambled back, caught his heel, and sat heavily. He tried to get his pistol up and firing, but was off balance. And then he had his hands full of a powerful, angry man ready to rip out his throat with his bare teeth. Jeter caught at the hands reaching for him, twisted away, and tried to roll and run, only to trip and fall heavily. A rock jammed itself hard into his chest and breath painfully gusted from his lungs, leaving him vainly gasping for air.

Jeter felt the hard fist landing repeatedly and then,

clutching at sharp rocks all around him on the ground and not finding escape, he passed out.

The sun was warm on his face. This brought Jeter awake faster than cold water dashed into his face could have. He sat bolt upright and almost fell from his horse. He fought to keep his balance, then discovered his hands were tightly bound behind his back. Turning slightly, he saw that he couldn't fall off his horse.

He was securely tied into the saddle.

"Welcome back to the land of the living."

"I'll cut your liver out and eat it for lunch," Jeter snarled. He had never been caught like this before and it didn't set well with him. Straining against the ropes holding his wrists only produced a sluggish flow of blood. He had been tied up expertly. There wasn't any way he could hope to get free of those bonds by struggling.

"More likely, I'll cut out yours and feed it to you," the man said.

"Who are you?" Jeter had to ask, and found it hard to keep a hint of admiration from his voice. He had met his match after all these years. It was hard to believe it was some West Texas drifter. The man rode straight as a ramrod in the saddle, strands of lank black hair poking out from under the dusty Stetson pulled down to the tops of his ears. There wasn't a trace of fat on his body—only whipcord muscle. But he was like a hundred other cowboys Jeter had seen—and killed.

He was like them all except for the cold green eyes. Jeter had seen eyes like that before, every time he looked in a mirror.

"Name's Slocum, as if that matters."

"Slocum," Jeter said, turning the name over and then spitting it out as if it burned his tongue. "That the name you want on your tombstone?"

"For a man who's all trussed up, you've got a powerful lot of boastfulness left in you. Maybe I ought to pound some more out of you."

"There's nothing you can do . . ." Jeter's words trailed off when Slocum reached into his vest pocket and pulled out a watch. He held it up so the sunlight caught its gold case, flashing like a lighthouse beacon as it spun on its chain. Jeter felt as if he had been stripped naked. The son of a bitch had stolen his watch!

"It's mine, Jeter," Slocum said coldly, responding to the expression on his face. "You should never have taken it from me."

"The stagecoach robbery," Jeter said. "I remember now. You were the galoot I thought was dead beside the road."

"Before you murdered the other two passengers and driver," Slocum said.

"I didn't murder them. It was self-defense. They tried to shoot me."

"You were robbing the stage. What'd you expect them to do?"

"What they did. Die!"

Slocum made a big deal of sticking the watch back into his pocket. Jeter watched with narrowed eyes. He'd enjoy taking the watch back off Slocum's dead body. It'd be a matter of time. It didn't matter that Slocum had Jeter's six-shooter thrust into his belt and had him all tied up like a Christmas goose. This was a challenge, nothing more. And Lester Jeter was up to it.

He shifted uneasily in the saddle, wondering what torment Slocum had inflicted on him. Then he settled down when he realized what it was. Flopping around on the ground had cut up his chest something fierce. It looked as if he had been the loser in a vicious knife fight the way his shirt was all sliced up and caked with blood. But being on the ground had done something more to him—for him.

A sharp piece of flint had embedded itself in his left buttock. As he bounced in the saddle, it sent jabs of pain up and down his leg. A sharp edge also protruded the barest amount from his flesh. Straining until it felt as if he would dislocate his shoulder, Jeter began dragging the ropes around his wrists across the razor-edge. Every movement caused new pain to shoot into his leg as he pressed the flint deeper into his own flesh, but he could withstand the pain in return for getting free—and getting revenge.

"Why'd you do it?" he grated out, trying to cover his furious work on the ropes. "Reward? Is there a reward out for me?"

"Don't know and don't care. When I told the station agent in San Esteban about the robbery, he wasn't even sure of your name. You've been real good covering your trail."

"I killed them all so they couldn't identify me."

"That why you burned down the bank?"

"I had to. They forced me to do it if I wanted to get away."

"The cornered rat," Slocum said. "You'd do anything to escape with the money you took from the vault."

"You'd have done the same thing. Don't try to lie to me or yourself," Jeter said, feeling a few strands break away due to his efforts. With the progress came new pain all through his left leg. He gritted his teeth against it and kept sawing. "You got the look of a road agent. And don't tell me you never kilt a man."

"What I am doesn't matter as much as you being my prisoner."

"I'll pay you. I'll give you money to let me go. I got a whole mountain of money hid."

"Must be around the cabin back in the valley," Slocum said. "That's why you headed for it after I saved Ruth."

"Saved her? How could you save her from her own damn husband! You kidnapped her. You raped her and kidnapped her and—"

"Don't stop," Slocum said, laughing now. "I like seeing you get all het up. Your face is turning red about like it'll look when you're dancing in midair with a rope around your filthy neck."

"I'll—" Jeter almost laughed when he felt the final strand of rope cut free from his wrists. He forced himself to keep his hands clenched together so he wouldn't reveal his hard-won freedom. He rubbed them together the best he could to get the circulation back, then clutched at the piece of flint buried in his ass. His fingers were too slippery with his own blood to get it out.

"You'll do nothing but stand trial," Slocum said with some satisfaction.

"You want Ruth. That's all you're after. You want to steal away my wife."

"What she does is her business. I'm not in the market for a woman."

"Yeah, that 'cuz you like little boys?"

Jeter almost shouted in triumph when Slocum slowed and rode closer.

"You looking to get your face shoved in?" Slocum asked.

It was Slocum's face that got smashed in. Jeter swung his fist around in a powerful roundhouse punch that caught a cheek and opened a cut. But dishing out punishment to Slocum wasn't what he was after. As he struck, Jeter leaned over and grabbed the handle of his six-shooter shoved into the man's belt. He whipped it free, cocked, and fired.

He would have killed Slocum if both horses hadn't reared. Jeter's stallion rocked back on its hind legs and kicked out as he fired. Slocum's horse took the round in the back of its head and fell, dead.

Jeter fired a second time, but he couldn't control his rearing horse too well. By the time he got the powerful horse under control, he saw there was no big hurry. Slocum was pinned under the deadweight of his horse, struggling to get free.

"Good-bye, Slocum. Burn in hell!"

The hammer fell on an empty chamber.

16

"I have all the notes I need," Ambrose Killian said happily. "Whether I ought to take photographs of the townspeople is a matter I need to consider further. The plates are so expensive and developing them is a tedious and somewhat dangerous process best done back at my hacienda rather than here in some improperly appointed room."

"I can help," Amy said. She smoothed the wrinkles in her skirt as she sat primly across from Ambrose in the hotel lobby, such as it was. The hotel was only a two-story clapboard structure that whistled when the wind blew. She tried to ignore the little mounds of sand in the corners of the sitting room that had escaped the cleaning woman's attention, if there even was a cleaning woman. The only staff she had seen were the bored clerk and a handyman who had passed out from too much liquor. Once there had also been a kitchen staff, but the clerk had informed them when Amy had arranged for the rooms that the kitchen was shut down. If they wanted food, they had to go to the restaurant beyond the Prancing Pony Drinking Emporium down the street.

Amy was familiar with the place, having taken John Slocum there when she interviewed him. She tried not to sigh as she thought of the man. He was so commanding, but he was nothing like Ambrose. Her eyes worked up from her examination of the lobby floor and fixed on her employer. Ambrose was caught in throes of excitement over the nearness of Jeter's capture. It made him seem so boyish in his enthusiasm, though he retained his manly bearing.

"There's no need. I will shoot the pictures I need when they apprehend Jeter. How long's it been since the posse left to track him down?"

"Two days," she said. "You mustn't be too anxious," she said. Staying with Ambrose was exciting for her, even if they had separate rooms—and beds.

"How can I avoid being excited?" he asked. "My life is wrapped up in that rapscallion. If I can call such a cold-blooded murderer that."

"It does seem more in line with a mischievous school-boy rather than a man who kills and robs the way Jeter does."

"Never mind that. He'll be brought to heel soon. The town finally got its dander up."

"The posse looked less than . . . reliable," Amy said, choosing her words carefully. For all the excitement Ambrose showed for the posse going after Jeter, she held only a wary regard for them. They had made certain their saddlebags were filled with bottles of liquor supplied by Luke, the barkeep at the Drunk Camel Saloon. "For medicinal purposes," Marshal Eaton had said, but Amy worried they were heading for trouble if they drank too heavily and actually found Jeter. The man would enjoy killing the posse one by one, especially if they were too drunk to fight.

While she didn't wish any of the temporary lawmen to be killed, such a massacre would only enhance Jeter's reputation and make Ambrose's quest for artifacts and details the more important. What pleased Ambrose pleased her.

If only he would knock on her door at night and invite himself into her room. She would not mind if he called her into his and they—

"Miss Gerardo! Pay attention."

"Sorry, sir," she said. "I was going over . . . details in my mind. To be sure everything is ready."

"That's all well and good, but I need the notes transcribed as quickly as possible so I might check them to see if I have omitted anything. Now is the time to add those pertinent details, while events are fresh in the townspeople's minds and they haven't scattered to the four winds. You know how it is with these small-town residents. They'll be off to find their fortunes elsewhere as soon as the railroad takes away their stagecoach route."

"I understand, sir. Should I see if the undertaker is ready?"

"We can go now."

"Good!" Amy jumped to her feet, then realized such unseemly eagerness would only put her in a bad light. "I'm ready, sir."

"You arranged for decent work? Not some cheap pine box?"

"The very finest available. The undertaker, a man named O'Dell, assured me he is a first-rate carpenter and able to make any coffin, from the plainest to the most ornate."

"While I have a moment, let's talk to this O'Dell. I need to be certain."

"I've checked it all myself." Amy was pained that Ambrose didn't care that she had attended to the details personally. Worse, he thought her incompetent to arrange for the coffin to be constructed in a suitable fashion befitting an outlaw of Jeter's stature. He had to see for himself. She trailed him out into the hot afternoon and across the street to the undertaker's parlor.

O'Dell rose and moved around his large wooden desk, hands clasped together in front him and looking like a ghost. His pale face bespoke little time in the sun, and the odors rising from his clothing did more than hint at the fluids used in his profession.

"You are Mr. Killian. I am pleased to be doing business with you, sir," O'Dell said in his curiously squeaky voice. Amy was fascinated by the way the man's Adam's apple bobbed in his scrawny throat as he talked. She imagined an ugly albino bird pecking its large curved beak down for grain and then clucking as it swallowed.

"That desk," Ambrose said curtly. "Where'd it come from?"

"Why, I built it myself. Although San Esteban can be a violent place, there have been rather long stretches when no one dies. I make furniture then and sell it. If you've been in the Drunk Camel Saloon, you might have noticed another example of my work. The bar was lovingly crafted, I assure you."

"Yes, yes," Ambrose said, dismissing this information. "Show me the coffin I've purchased for Jeter."

"This way, sir." O'Dell bowed slightly and held open black silk curtains leading to the back room. "I have roughed it out, and will do the exterior carving and finishing in a day or two. Would you like something more done on the interior?"

"Hmm, nicely done," Ambrose said, walking around the coffin on a worktable in the middle of the room. He ran his hand over the padded satin interior. "No, the inside is adequate. I see you have roughed in the exterior curlicues already. Good, very good. But I need to see the viewing room."

"This way, sir," O'Dell said, holding the curtains for both Ambrose and Amy. As she pressed past O'Dell, she caught the faint scent of lavender water and embalming fluid. It caused her stomach to clench and her nose to drip. She took her handkerchief and dabbed discreetly. She hastened after Ambrose through an arched doorway on the far side of the office leading into the viewing room.

"Everything is as you specified," O'Dell said, sounding more cheerful now as he strode up the narrow aisle, pews on either side. "The departed will lie in repose surrounded by what wildflowers we can find when the moment is at hand. This time of year poses a problem. If you wait until fall, there are brilliant flowers throughout the Davis Mountains."

"Where can I set up the camera tripod? It requires at least eight feet distance." Ambrose paced around, studying angles and tinkering with the lamps strategically placed at the sides of the room.

Amy saw that her employer couldn't care less about flowers and other more delicate observances. All that mattered to him were decent photos of Lester Evan Jeter—taken as soon as possible.

"On the dias, to the side," O'Dell said. "Miss Gerardo has measured and approved the location."

Amy shuddered when he mentioned her by name and looked at her. She wondered if he wanted her sexually from the way he fixed his button eyes on her—or if he was only mentally measuring her for a coffin. The notion that both were possible made her shudder again, in spite of the closeness of the room.

"Excellent, excellent. You're doing a fine job, Mr. O'Dell."

"The reception, if that is the proper term, has been arranged at the restaurant. There will be facilities for more than twenty people. If you desire more room, it might be necessary to go to the Drunk Camel and ask if that establishment might be rented. We might consider it a wake, in the Irish fashion. I doubt many will mourn, but many might be drawn to a celebration of this nature."

"The saloon?" Killian frowned as he considered the merits of such a venue for the wake. "That might be best. Twenty sounds so limiting."

"Sir, I don't know if it would be appropriate for me to go to a saloon, even when reserved for this particular affair," she said.

"What's that? Oh, don't worry, Miss Gerardo. If you don't feel up to it, I am sure your services wouldn't be needed. They no doubt have pretty waiter girls who can serve the libations."

"But I've supplied so many pieces of his life. The spur—"

"We've been over that, Miss Gerardo," he said sharply. "The spur was not a legitimate object d' Jeter."

O'Dell eyed them like a vulture waiting for its meal to die.

"Sorry, sir," she said contritely, but angry fire still burned within. She had risked her life to retrieve that spur. She had done everything possible to make certain it was a legitimate artifact, and Ambrose had discarded it out of hand. Worse, he'd derided her for the effort. Amy wondered if it would matter if she took Ambrose to speak directly with Paco Rodriguez and his crazy friend Bernardo.

"How many people do you expect to attend this special . . . service?" O'Dell asked. He folded his hands in front of his belly again and leaned forward, making him look even more like a buzzard with his hooked nose. His black eyes shone liquidly.

"We'll invite the entire town. And why not? After the trial and execution, everyone will be relieved that such a violent man no longer preys on them. Why not have a party for everyone?"

"At the saloon, sir? The women—"

"The women can go make a quilt to commemorate the occasion. Or go to the church for a social. I don't care. What's important is the pageantry. And how many pictures I can take. May I inquire about the cemetery, Mr. O'Dell?"

"All prepared, though it seemed a little premature to dig the grave. The wind fills the hole quickly enough, making it necessary to redig the grave site if it stands open longer than a week or two."

"I'm sure," Ambrose said, a distant look on his face.

"What of the tombstone, sir?" Amy asked. "Have you considered what sentiments to put on it?"

" 'Here lies the most dangerous outlaw in Texas history' sounds like a decent epitaph."

"That would require more than a simple tombstone like those on other graves," O'Dell said. "For such an extensive message to eternity, you would need something more like a monument. Perhaps that is what you have in mind?"

"What's a little more expense?" Ambrose said airily. "Of course. A large monument towering above the grave. Make certain it mentions my part in its erection. I'll let you know the exact wording."

"It will require shipment of granite slabs from Austin," O'Dell said. "Freighting such heavy slabs here might take a few weeks, even if I ordered them today."

"Do it. Miss Gerardo will take care of your monetary needs for this too. Down payment now, the balance on completion."

"Very good," O'Dell said, rubbing his hands together like a miser contemplating his gold. Amy realized that this might well be the same for the undertaker. Never in his career would he have such an opportunity to rake in tons of money.

"I'll see to the saloon," said Ambrose. "I can use the opportunity to wet my whistle."

"But, sir, I shouldn't go into the saloon. It's not a fitting place."

"I didn't ask you to accompany me, Miss Gerardo. What's gotten into you?"

"The excitement, sir," she said. "I hoped we could go back to the hotel. You and me. We could . . . discuss the unresolved details." Her heart beat faster at the thought of returning to the hotel with Ambrose, going to his room, having him undress her slowly, and then—

"Later, my dear. There'll be plenty of time later. Now, I'll have a few shots of whiskey and speak with the owner about rentals. No one in West Texas, from San Antonio to El Paso, will ever forget the trial, execution, and celebration of that prince of thieves, Lester Jeter!"

Ambrose left abruptly, going down the street to the saloon. Amy looked uneasily at O'Dell, then bade him good-bye and returned to the hotel and her room.

Alone.

17

Slocum went ass-over-teakettle when the single shot killed his horse. The reliable old nag put its head down and somersaulted, taking Slocum with it. He hit the ground hard. The impact jarred him so much, he lay dazed and only vaguely aware of the horse's massive body pinning his leg to the ground. He blinked through the pain and stared up at Jeter.

The outlaw had his six-shooter aimed directly at Slocum's face. Slocum reached for the pistol that had been thrust into his belt, and discovered it was missing. This brought him around, struggling hard to get out from under the deadweight holding him to the ground.

"Good-bye, Slocum. Burn in hell!"

The outlaw's six-shooter misfired. Slocum fumbled to get his own six-gun out, but it was under his body, grinding into his left hip. As he fought to get it out, Jeter rode over. He was still securely tied to the saddle, but had somehow freed his hands. In a flash Slocum saw a multitude of things. The outlaw's hands were bloody from the ropes and a stream of blood ran down his left leg, soaking his pants, and turning his saddle a gory red.

And Slocum saw the road agent swinging his pistol. Ducking fast, he got out of the way so the gun barrel only knocked off his hat and not his head. Slocum kept trying to get his own gun free, but couldn't. His left leg was turning cold from lack of circulation, and if he didn't get it free quickly, he might as well cut it off. There was no pain, but the immense weight of the horse was slowly killing his leg.

As Jeter intended to kill him.

"You're the luckiest son of a bitch I ever seen, Slocum," Jeter called. The outlaw rode closer and swung again, missing Slocum's head again. Being tied into the saddle limited how far he could lean, and again saved Slocum a busted head.

Slocum felt his strength fading fast. He should have killed Jeter when he had the chance. Only some misguided notion of getting the man to San Esteban for trial had stayed him. Had he wanted Ruth to know the full extent of her husband's evil ways? Or had he wanted to prove to Jeter—and himself—that he was the better man? Nothing mattered now.

Slocum reached for the knife sheathed in his right boot top, but his fingers were inches shy of it.

"Damn you, Slocum, you aren't gettin' away with this." Jeter furiously tore at the ropes holding him to the saddle and managed to pull free. He left blood-soaked strands behind as he jumped to the ground. He almost collapsed as his weight bore down on his left leg. Slocum saw the outlaw was in almost as bad a shape as *he* was. Whatever had injured his hip still caused a steady flow of blood.

Slocum doubted Jeter would bleed to death before he killed his helpless foe.

Jeter fell to his knees and scooted over to Slocum. His bloody hands batted Slocum's away as he dived down to the vest pocket holding the watch. Jeter pulled it free and let it spin, as Slocum had, to torment him.

"Got it, Slocum, got it back. And it's gonna stay mine this time. No way you're gettin' it back!"

Jeter swung again with his pistol. Slocum caught it in both hands and tried to wrench it free. If the fight hadn't been so deadly serious, Slocum would have laughed. Neither of them could have fought a kitten and won. Jeter realized the same thing, and fell backward out of Slocum's reach.

"Enough of this. You're gonna pay for everything you've done, you kidnappin', rapin' owlhoot!" Jeter began fumbling at his gun belt to pull free a cartridge to reload. His hands had turned to nerveless lumps.

Slocum pushed and shoved and worked to get to his own six-shooter. And then his luck rushed back to save him.

Jeter had dropped a second cartridge when he looked up, head turning slowly. His nostrils flared like a horse ready to rear and flail out with its hooves.

"You're a dead man, Slocum. And I'll be the one sendin' you to hell!" Jeter forced himself to his feet, put his fingers to his mouth, and whistled. His powerful stallion came trotting up. Painfully swinging into the saddle, Jeter bent low and brought his horse to a quick trot, disappearing from sight in seconds.

Slocum kept fighting the deadweight on top of him, to no avail. He sagged back, caught his breath, and started working again. Then he heard what Jeter, with his keener hearing, already had. Hoofbeats.

"Here, I'm over here!" Slocum shouted until he was hoarse. He almost cried when he saw five men gallop up. The lead rider wore a marshal's badge pinned on his coat.

"Got yerself a tad of a problem, don't ya?" the marshal said, pushing back his hat and looking at Slocum's dilemma. "How'd you come to shoot yer own horse? Heard the shot and came to investigate."

"Jeter did it—the man who robbed the San Esteban bank."

"Now ain't that coincidence," the marshal said. "He's just the owlhoot we're lookin' for. Got good evidence agin him too. Which way'd he go?"

"Get me out from under here," Slocum said. "I'll be more 'n happy to show you."

"He ain't the one we're lookin' for, is he, Marshal Eaton?" asked a rider alongside the lawman.

"Don't look nuthin' like him. You heard that Killian fella. He gave a real good description, after askin' round town 'bout those who seen Jeter runnin' from the bank."

"Get me out from under this pile of horse meat!"

"What? Yeah, 'spect we'd better do just that." Eaton took the lariat off his saddle and tossed it to the man who wasn't sure if Slocum was the outlaw they were hunting. "Loop that around the horse's neck so's I kin pull it off. You stay down there, boy, and help him out from under. What's your name?"

"Slocum."

"You help Mr. Slocum if'n he cain't wiggle free on his own. Saw a man crushed to death when a horse fell on him. Ugly sight. Blood and bones pokin' out." The marshal shook his head sadly. "Didn't even want to touch him to bury him, but there wasn't no choice."

The rope was fastened around the dead horse, then to

Eaton's saddle horn. The pulling began in earnest. Slocum saw that Eaton's horse had been trained for such things, making Eaton more of a cowboy than a lawman. As the weight lifted from Slocum's leg, he didn't care if Eaton was the devil incarnate. The relief he felt was almost enough to make him pass out. The deputy on the ground grabbed Slocum under the arms and tugged him free.

"You stand up on your own?"

"I can, Marshal. Thanks," Slocum said. "You Marshal Benbow?"

" 'fraid not. Marshal Benbow got wind of Jeter and his doin's and kept on ridin'. He didn't have a bunch of friends to help him track the varmint down like I do."

"What's the reward?" Slocum knew this was the only way more than one or two men could be glued together into a posse.

"We each get thirty dollars for lookin'. Twice that if we catch Jeter."

"Is Killian putting up the reward?"

"Surely is," the youngster next to Slocum said. "He's a real civic-minded fella."

"Time's a'wastin'," Eaton said pompously. "Which way'd he go? You sure it was Jeter and not some other lawless element?"

"It was Jeter," Slocum assured him. He pointed in the direction Jeter had taken. "He shot my horse, stole my watch, and rode off before he could finish the job of killing me. You pulled my fat out of the fire, Marshal."

"That's my job," Eaton said even more self-importantly. He puffed himself up, let out an earsplitting whistle, and yelled, "We got the trail, men! This way!"

Slocum looked at his dead horse and shook his head.

Without even the slow-moving but steady mount under him, he had no chance of catching Jeter. He wanted personal satisfaction for all the outlaw had done to him, but having the posse catch him was about as good. But Slocum had seen firsthand how expert Jeter was at hiding his trail. He didn't have much of a head start, but these cowboys weren't what Slocum would call accomplished trailsmen. They would lose Jeter the first time he rode across a rocky patch.

"You know these mountains?" Slocum asked.

"What's that?" Eaton waved some more to draw the attention of the rest of his posse. Seven more men slowly rode toward the marshal. "I only been in West Texas a couple months. Worked a ranch down south. Heard they might need hands up here. Didn't. I was gettin' set to go back to Beeville when I got myself appointed marshal of San Esteban. Never thought I'd be wearin' a badge." Eaton ran his finger around the circular badge.

"I can track him. He's good, damned good, and you'll likely lose him. Jeter's memorized every single rock in the Davis Mountains."

"You tryin' to horn in on our reward money?" demanded the young man who had helped Slocum out from under the dead horse.

"Keep the money," Slocum said, forcing himself to keep a lid on his boiling anger. "I want my watch—and to see Jeter brought to trial."

"You don't want no money?"

Slocum's cold look caused the boy to wilt like a delicate flower in a blue norther.

"You can't keep up with us on foot," Eaton observed. "You could ride double with Billy there."

Slocum looked at the youngster and then his strawberry roan. The horse was strong enough to carry the pair of them, but not fast and not all that far. He would have to make good on his claims about tracking Jeter within a day or the horse would simply give out under him and Billy.

"Let me get my saddlebags," he said, pulling them free from the dead horse. "Let's go. Time's not on our side as long as Jeter is riding."

"Dunno if the horse kin stand our weight and your saddlebags too," Billy said, looking skeptical about sharing his horse with anyone. Slocum understood. He also knew that they had to quit quibbling and get after Jeter right away.

"I'd buy the roan from you, but I don't have that kind of money," Slocum said. "Jeter's taken about everything of value I have."

"Real mean son of a buck," Billy agreed. "Well, I reckon we kin both get on there. But your saddle's gotta stay here."

Slocum had already decided that. His few remaining possessions were stowed in his saddlebags. He took a few minutes, got out spare ammo, and made sure the cartridges were stuck into the loops along his gun belt. In a fight with Jeter, he would need every single round.

"Let's ride," he said. Billy mounted, and Slocum swung up behind.

"Don't you go gettin' too fancy with them hands of yers," Billy said a little nervously. Then he hiccuped, and Slocum smelled the booze on the young man's breath. When the roan trotted after Eaton and the rest of the posse, Slocum heard sloshing coming from Billy's saddlebags.

"Going after a dangerous man like Jeter's not something you do half-drunk," Slocum said. "You need Dutch courage?"

"Aw, quit funnin' me," Billy said. "Thass another reason I joined up. Luke at the Drunk Camel gave us all a couple bottles of his prime whiskey. The reward's nice, don't get me wrong, but free booze? How kin anyone pass up that?"

Slocum said nothing. He hadn't realized the rest of the posse was all likkered up too. They were more dangerous to each other in a gunfight than they would be to Jeter. If the outlaw figured that out, he would rack up another half-dozen murders and let the rest of the posse shoot one another.

"Where are we headin', Slocum?" called the marshal. "We got ourselves a Y canyon comin' up real soon. Left or right?"

Slocum saw that the split in the canyon was the kind of thing Jeter would relish. A less experienced lawman would split his posse, making it easier to kill whichever half came after Jeter. Looking down at the ground, Slocum saw the muddled tracks Jeter had left intentionally, but there had to be something the road agent had done that wasn't quite as intentional. He was only a short distance ahead and didn't have the luxury of hours to lay a fake trail.

Jumping down, Slocum walked alongside Billy.

"Keep a ways back, will you? I don't want the trail muddled up more than necessary."

"Hell, Slocum, there's no way you can track him across *that*!" Billy pointed to the rocky stretch extending from the mouth of one canyon halfway across the other. "No horse is gonna leave hoofprints on solid rock."

Slocum studied the ground and had to agree. Whether Jeter had turned lucky or had known of this spot and then come here directly wasn't something Slocum wanted to ponder. Jeter had given them two choices.

"We can split up," suggested Eaton.

"No! That's what he wants. Half your men would be riding into an ambush. That means Jeter's not up to taking you all on."

"All of us? Hell, man, even with six in each party, he's up against a damn army!" Eaton looked around, and the men with him cheered. Slocum saw a couple of them raising almost empty pint bottles in salute to their courage and skill.

"Yeah, let's split up and go after him. The ones what get to that snake in the grass first gets *all* the reward!" someone shouted.

Slocum saw this was an increasingly popular decision because the men were too drunk to realize the full impact of what they were up against. Soused, they saw only the reward Killian had offered and a single outlaw on the run. If they thought about it, they would remember a dozen or more murders during the past weeks, the deadly robberies, including their town bank being burned down, and Jeter's ability to keep from even being seen until recently.

With a deliberate step, Slocum paced across the rocky flat and saw shiny marks left by a horseshoe. Dropping to his belly, he caught the sunlight just right off one scratch, and decided which way Jeter had traveled when he left it. But not a dozen feet away was another, going in the opposite direction. Slocum considered the spacing, then turned and went to the right canyon.

"Anyone know where this goes?"

"You think that's the one he took, Slocum?" Marshal Eaton asked.

"Could be. He went to a little trouble to make it look as if he had gone the other, but he's rushed and can't do his usual good job of hiding his tracks."

"What'd you think, Luke?"

The drunkest of the lot, the barkeep at the Drunk Camel, finished off his bottle before answering with a belch and a slurred, "Could be. But then my nose says he went the other way. What say we split up and devil take the hindmost!"

"Devil take Les Jeter!" went up the cheer.

"You sure he took the right fork, Slocum?" Billy looked uneasily at Luke and the marshal as they broke out fresh bottles and began passing them around.

Slocum considerd the young man for a moment, then said, "You finally figured out if you're drunk and meet up with him, you're also dead?"

"Something like that, I reckon," Billy said. "But if they go the way Luke says, and they're wrong, that means you and me'll be fightin' him all by our lonesome."

Slocum nodded glumly. He had cautioned them not to divide their force. Now he was the one who was inclined to do just that since they were heading in the wrong direction.

"Marshal," Slocum called out. "Why don't we take a break and talk this over? He went that way down the right canyon, not down the left fork." Slocum felt as sure of this as he had anything in his life. "You wanted me along as scout. This is the way I read the signs."

"Might be he's in cahoots with Jeter," Luke said loudly. "Might be he wants us to head in the wrong direction so's his friend can escape."

Slocum went over to the drunken bartender, looked up at the big man, then grabbed a handful of shirt and pulled him off his horse.

"I don't know if it's the drink that's making you stupid or if you're that way sober too, but I want him caught. I want him dead." Slocum held the drunk up enough so he stood on tiptoe, then shoved him back and turned to face the rest of the posse. "Anybody doubt me?"

"Don't go gettin' your dander up, Slocum," the marshal said. "We're just as convinced as you 'bout how good it would be to bring Jeter to justice."

"Good?" Slocum spun on the marshal. "Good? He's going to kill every last one of you if you don't keep an eye peeled for him and his traps. He's about the best I've ever seen, and I've seen a bunch."

Luke regained some of his composure. "What he's sayin' is true. Let's camp, get some grub, then figger what to do after we got full bellies."

"And I got another near-full bottle," piped up another. This produced a round of laughter that made Slocum ball his fists. But there was no stopping the men as they sat around their campfire and diluted their poisonous coffee with healthy slugs of whiskey.

As they drank and ate their trail rations, Slocum made a more complete circuit of the area and came to the same conclusion he had before. The right canyon. Jeter had made an obvious start into the left, then gone to the right.

"How do you know he didn't leave that trace to the right to confuse you, then actually go the way he seemed to go at first?" Billy asked.

"Time," Slocum said. "And he thought I was dead or left behind. The only reason he would be that subtle is if he knew I was after him." Slocum fell silent. Was he out-guessing himself? He decided he wasn't. Jeter's contempt for most trackers would convince him they would follow the obvious trail. If there had been time, Jeter wouldn't have left any trace at all, making it seem that he had disappeared into thin air.

Slocum stared up the right canyon, noted how close to sundown it was, and knew they were riding into a trap. Jeter couldn't run forever. He would make his stand, take out as many of the drunken posse as he could, then slip away in the confusion. That was what the outlaw would do because that's what Slocum would do in his boots.

18

"I dunno, Slocum, this is mighty risky, ain't it?" Marshal Eaton looked around nervously. He took the pint bottle Luke passed him without even noticing who was passing it around. He took a big swig and handed it back mechanically.

"It's even riskier not going after him. Let a man like Jeter have enough of a start on you and he'll disappear like a puff of smoke in a Texas tornado."

"Mighty fine image, that one," said Luke. The barkeep belched, wiped his lips, and silently held the bottle out for Slocum. Slocum declined with a brusque shake of his head. "Other than losin' all that reward money Killian offered, we'd be better off if Jeter did vanish like that. Who ever sees the puff of smoke again when the wind takes it away?"

"The smell lingers," Slocum snapped. "You have to get him."

"You just got a bug up your ass, Slocum," Luke said.

"It's not like that," Billy said, taking Slocum's part.

"He's right. We gotta find him fast. Who wants to spend the rest of their days out here in the mountains chasin' our own tails?"

"It's not so bad," said Eaton. "If we was back in town, we'd have chores to do. Out here, we kin just ride and enjoy the scenery."

Slocum almost drew his six-shooter and shot the lawman to put him out of his misery. How could any man be that stupid and not hurt all the time?

"We don't even know if this here canyon's the right path. It looked like the other one was the right way to go," Luke went on. "And the marshal's right. It's real peaceful out here. I don't like dealin' with all you drunks when I have to be behind the bar at the saloon. Or that asshole who's my boss. Wait till he finds out I gave y'all so much booze! Out here now, it's quiet and the stars are twinklin' just right."

"He'll kill every last one of you," Slocum said coldly. "That's what he does, and he's damned good at it. It wasn't until that bank robbery went south on him that any of you even saw his face."

"He showed up at the general store. You said so," Marshal Eaton said.

"He might have been a rancher and nothing else. He kept low and you never knew who was doing all the robbing until I came along."

"You been shamed by him once too often, Slocum? Is that what's eatin' at your soul?" Luke tipped up the pint bottle and drained it, then tossed it away, clumsily drew, and fired at it. The sound echoed through the still night like a cannon shot. Others in the posse went for their six-guns, not having seen Luke toss the bottle.

"Relax, boys," Luke drawled. "I was just practicin' what I'll do when I git Jeter in my gun sights."

"You think that shot'll warn him we're comin'?" Billy asked Slocum.

"He knew we were on his trail," Slocum said, "but he might have thought his decoy back at the juncture had worked. He knows different now." Slocum looked up the dark canyon and saw yucca stalks bending stiffly in the wind whipping down its length. The gunshot would have brought Jeter up like a coyote getting the scent of a chicken.

"I can get him now. He thinks you'll camp all night," Slocum said, coming to a swift decision. "I'll go after him."

"That's my horse," Billy said. "I'm not lettin' you go nowhere without me."

"You'll get yourself killed," Slocum said harshly.

"Then he won't be shootin' at you, will he? That'll let you plug him and end this."

Slocum stared at the young man's face, hidden in shadows formed by the dancing campfire, then laughed. He slapped Billy on the shoulder.

"You got spunk," Slocum said. "Not a bit of brains, but you've got spunk. Saddle up and let's go."

"Where you headin', Slocum? You and the boy? The two of you like each other than much?"

Slocum stopped, turned slowly, and squared off in front of the barkeep. Luke looked up from the rock where he sat and turned visibly paler. His hand shook as he drained the bottle Eaton had handed him, and then set it down with preposterous care.

"You want to repeat that to my face?" Slocum asked in a voice level and more frightening than if he had shouted.

"I didn't mean nuthin' by it, Slocum."

"You don't mean much on any score, do you?"

"Slocum, be careful," Billy said. "He carries a hideout gun in his coat pocket."

"What're you goin' on about, Billy? You and yer lover."

That was the last Luke spoke. Slocum drew with lightning speed and slammed the long barrel of his Peacemaker across Luke's mouth. Teeth shattered and blood from a split lip spewed forth. The barkeep's head snapped back, and he fell heavily. There was a crunch as his head collided with a big rock behind him.

"He's out cold."

"He got lucky," Slocum said. "If he was still awake, he'd have to draw. Then he'd be dead."

"He was drunk, Slocum," the marshal said uneasily. "He didn't mean nuthin' by his joshin' of you and the boy."

"This 'boy' is the only man here," Slocum said. "Him and me're going after Jeter and we'll get him. Dead. Alive. One way or the other we'll stop him while you're sitting around a fire, warming your fat asses, and getting drunk."

Slocum was fed up with Eaton and his fair-weather posse. If they had gotten into a real gunfight, the ones that didn't turn tail and run would have been dead. He swung into the saddle, and this time Billy didn't say anything about riding behind on his own horse. They rode away from the posse and were swallowed by the darkness within yards. The dry air sucked at the moisture in Slocum's eyes and mouth and made his skin crawl, but he was away from the clowns trying to make an act of their bravery.

"He'll shoot you in the back, Slocum," Billy said. "Luke's real mean."

"I'm meaner. He won't say a word when we bring back Jeter," Slocum said.

"We got to find him first. You're prob'ly right that he's a real ghost. I heard tell of a couple bounty hunters who had come through a month back lookin' fer any road agent they could find to claim the reward. It musta been Jeter they followed. One came back. The other was kilt in his bedroll. Somebody snuck into their camp, slit his throat, and left his partner sleepin' sweet as any babe in its mama's arms."

Slocum had to admit this sounded like something Jeter would do, just for the hell of it. He was all about showing the world how he was better than anyone else.

"Finding him might not be as hard as it seems," Slocum said, thinking on the matter as they rode slowly deeper into the canyon. "Jeter isn't likely to have gone too much farther, wanting to sit and eavesdrop on what's going on in camp."

"He's watchin' us now?"

"Quit shaking so much," Slocum said. Billy trembled so hard it was spooking the horse. "He might not be that close, but he can see what's going on around the campfire. That'd put him above us, on one side of the canyon or the other."

"That'd trap him. He'd have to climb down or keep goin' on up to the rim. Ain't likely he's got a trail for his horse to follow, not around here."

Slocum agreed. The sheer walls sloped away farther on, but in this section of the mountains, the canyon walls were rugged and perfect for a snoop—but not his horse.

"That side," Slocum said, pointing left. "It's a mite

closer to where the posse's camped and looks to have good places to spy."

"I kin almost feel him movin' around, watchin' us, linin' up that rifle of his, and gettin' ready to shoot."

"Quit spooking yourself," Slocum said. He sat straighter in the saddle when he heard a horse nickering. He elbowed Billy and pointed off to the base of the wall where a small rock crevice afforded the perfect place to corral a horse while scaling the heights above the canyon.

"His horse. That's what's makin' that noise, ain't it, Mr. Slocum?"

"I'll go check." Slocum got his leg up and over the roan's head and slipped to the ground, making only a slight scuffing sound when he hit. He drew his six-shooter and advanced slowly. If Jeter was here, he wanted to get him with the first bullet, but he thought only the powerful black stallion the outlaw rode would be in the crevice.

Slocum wasn't sure if he was happy or vexed that he was right. The horse pawed at the sparse grass growing in the rocky nook, but Jeter was nowhere to be seen. Making sure he wasn't falling into a trap, Slocum slowly circled the horse and saw that the only way in or out was through the notch in the rocks. He turned his attention upward. While it was hardly a grand staircase, he made out distinct steps a man could follow in the dark without undue trouble.

He returned to where Billy nervously fingered his six-gun.

"Y-you find him, Mr. Slocum?"

"He's up there," Slocum said, looking up into the inky expanse of rock. He made out a few scrubby trees clinging tenaciously to the canyon rim outlined against the cold stars and night sky.

"What do you want to do? Should we go up and git him?" Billy's teeth were chattering now.

"I'll go after him. You have to head back to the camp and tell the marshal I've found him."

"You don't want me backin' you up?" The young man sounded both outraged and relieved.

"You will be backing me up," Slocum said. "By fetching the posse. It might take more firepower than I've got to bring him down. If I can pin him down, the more rifles down here pointing up the better."

"You ain't gonna try takin' him by your lonesome, are you? That'd be plumb foolish."

"Get the marshal and the rest of the posse. Be quiet about it, though. I don't want him knowing we've found his hiding place."

"Yes, sir, Mr. Slocum. Right away!"

"Quiet now," Slocum cautioned.

He saw the young man ride off, intent on doing as he was told. Slocum heaved a deep sigh, then turned to begin the climb. He had led Billy to believe he wasn't going to tangle with Jeter until the posse arrived. Nothing was further from Slocum's mind. Eaton and the others were probably drunker than skunks by now. Luke would either have one whale of a headache or still be unconscious. Slocum hoped it was the latter. He had no idea if the barkeep would "accidentally" shoot him in the back, but the idea would undoubtedly occur to a man who had been humiliated so thoroughly. Slocum knew he had made an enemy in Luke and didn't much care. Drunk or sober, the man had to learn to watch his tongue.

Slocum slipped past the stallion, taking a moment to soothe the high-strung horse. It was a real beauty. Slocum could see how, astride such a powerful horse, Jeter outlegged any pursuer. Coupled with his knowledge of the Davis Mountains, he was uncatchable.

Until tonight.

The stony staircase led Slocum back and forth up the face of the cliff. As he started climbing, the steps were broad, if low. This forced him to shuffle a mite, and only pick up his boot for a few inches at a time. But as the steps went higher, the risers became more exaggerated and the width narrower until Slocum was forced to cling to the rock with his fingers as he made his way along.

Once he looked down, and was startled to see he was already forty feet above the tiny niche where the horse stared up impassively at him. He wasn't afraid of heights, but worried about what lay above him. A dozen other schemes for catching Jeter flashed through his head. He could have taken the outlaw's horse and forced him to flee on foot. That carried a double dose of bad luck for Jeter. Not only would he have lost a horse, he would have been humiliated that Slocum was the one taking it. That would have kept him coming back—on foot—at Slocum until hell froze over.

Slocum could have done that, but he felt it was too late to backtrack now. He was more than halfway up the face of the cliff. To retreat now would be risky. If Jeter's attention strayed from the posse's camp for an instant, he would see a human fly stuck to the side of the cliff and do something about it. A few rocks would send Slocum tumbling to his death four stories below.

Or Slocum could have waited for him at the base. Stake out the horse, keep a drawn six-gun trained on the spot where Jeter had to descend. Once he had the drop on the road agent, he could do as he pleased. Cut him down or force him to surrender after a few well-placed slugs in the man's legs. Slocum realized he would have liked to see Jeter crawl, just a little, after all he had endured at the outlaw's hands. He kept edging along the increasingly narrow stone path, face inward and fingers working to cling to the rock like a spider.

Slocum expected to keep going like this for some distance. He stumbled and fell forward when the rock face opened to a long, wide ledge running away from the face. The mountain itself had been split open, and gave plenty of room for a man to pitch his bedroll and watch the entire canyon floor.

Slocum spilled forward, off balance and unable to go for his six-shooter. But Jeter was also startled. He turned, slipped, and almost tumbled off the rocky platform. Both men scrambled to regain their balance and get into position.

"Slocum," Jeter hissed, seeing who had found him once more. "Won't you ever die? I hoped you was dead, but then again, I hoped you wasn't!"

Slocum wasted no time speaking. He dug his toes into the rock, found purchase, and launched himself. Jeter was trying to pull out his six-shooter, but Slocum knew better than to draw. His arms were too close to the rock face and he might even drop his six-gun. He crashed into Jeter and sent the man staggering. Jeter let out a shriek, and almost pitched over the brink to the canyon below.

Slocum did nothing to save him. Jeter did it on his own, twisting at the last instant and grabbing a rock outcrop and swinging around. Slocum kicked viciously and tried to take Jeter's legs out from under him. That would leave the man dangling, arms circling the rock needle. But Slocum missed and kicked the rock. The jolt went all the way up into his hip and forced a cry of pain from his lips. His left leg wasn't quite recovered from being crushed under his dead horse.

He tried to ignore the pain, but failed. Jeter swung around and came at him, bony fists swinging hard. The two fought like titans on the narrow ledge. Somewhere in the midst of their fight, Slocum got his feet tangled in Jeter's bedroll and sat down heavily. The outlaw swarmed on top of him, forcing him flat. Jeter caught him in a schoolboy pin, his knees pressing Slocum's shoulders down hard.

Jeter's face was only inches from Slocum's as he sneered and said, "I got you now, Slocum. You're gonna die. I wish it could be slow and painful, but you're a slippery one."

"You still trying to talk me to death, Jeter? You must have killed dozens of men that way, the ones you didn't shoot in the back." Slocum hoped to anger Jeter again, to get him mad enough to make a mistake. That had worked once. Not now.

"Die, Slocum, die."

Jeter's fingers clamped around Slocum's neck and began squeezing the life from his body. Slocum fought to get his arms up to strike at Jeter, to claw his eyes, to force him away. The man's bony knees held him down too securely. Slocum kicked and tried to roll Jeter off. The solid rock cliff face prevented it in one direction, and his left leg was too weak to give much impetus the other—the direction that would have taken Jeter over the ledge.

But Slocum's groping fingers found the knife sheathed at the top of his boot. Clumsily he drew the knife and knew he had only one chance. In spite of tensing his neck muscles and fighting, Slocum realized Jeter was too strong for him. His air was cut off. The blood to his head was restricted. A heavy roaring in his ears would have warned him of approaching death, even if the world collapsing into a long dark tunnel hadn't.

He thrust with the knife.

For an instant he didn't think he had done anything. He tried to stab again, but the blade slipped from his fingers. Slocum frantically grabbed, but his fingers had turned slippery and slid off the hilt.

Then Jeter let out a grunt and toppled to one side. Slocum should have followed him, gone after him, and strangled him the way Jeter had been strangling him, but the air refused to come to his lungs. He tried to sit up, but all the strength had fled from his body. His hand reaching for his six-shooter couldn't even lift off the cold stone ledge.

Slocum blacked out.

19

Pain lanced through Jeter's side, causing him to lose his grip on Slocum's neck. He fell to the side, then screeched like a hoot owl when he started to tumble over the side of the ledge. His fingers grabbed, slipped, and then he plunged away, kicking and screaming as he went. Only pure chance saved him. He hit the stone stairway in the side of the mountain, and managed to grab on long enough to slow his fall.

Panting harshly, Jeter skidded a few feet lower and then stopped, legs still dangling over the side of the ledge but body and arms firmly across the staircase. He felt his left leg tingling from the hunk of flint embedded in his ass, but the pain arrowing throughout his body came from the knife wound. Carefully wiggling forward, he flopped onto the stone pathway and winced as he reached down to touch the new wound.

"Damnation," he muttered. "The son of a bitch left his knife in me." Jeter grasped the bloody handle and gingerly pulled. Every inch was acid agony, but he finally extracted the blade and cast it away from him as if its touch were something vile. He looked back up the side of the rocky face and tried to guess how long it would take for him to return to his former hiding place. He had Slocum to kill once and for all.

As he tried to stand, weakness washed through him like a tidal wave. Wavering, dizzying, Jeter sat down hard and fought to keep from passing out. He was tough. He could go on. He could climb up the stone steps and kill Slocum.

"Like hell I can," he muttered. He had stayed alive this long knowing what he could do and what he couldn't. If he tried to finish off that piece of human flypaper, he would die before he reached him. Slocum had to wait for another day. Right now, Jeter had to get to his horse and ride like the wind out of here.

"Downhill's easier," he told himself. And for a spell it was. He slid on his rump over the stone, marveling at the ease. Then it came to him that he was bleeding so much that his rear lubricated the rock. Jeter slowed his descent, worried off his shirt, and tried to examine the wound between his ribs. Slocum hadn't been in any position to really drive in the knife blade, but he had done a fair amount of damage. Just touching the gash made Jeter woozy. A few quick rips had his shirt torn into strips long enough to wrap around his chest. The rest of the shirt he pressed against the wound before he cinched himself up. The act of self-doctoring made him violently ill to his stomach. He retched, but he had eaten damn little in the past few days.

"You owe me a meal, Slocum," he grated out. "How about I eat your damned liver?" Wiping his lips, Jeter sat for a few more minutes garnering his strength. Then with a supreme effort, he heaved himself to his feet and lurched down the increasingly broad stone steps to where his horse was still corralled. He had expected Slocum to steal the horse, and was surprised to find the stallion where he had left it.

"Whoa, boy, down. Don't rear up like that," Jeter said as he neared the horse. The scent of blood spooked the horse. It took him several minutes, both because of the horse's fright at the blood and because of his own weakness, to get into the saddle. When he did, he sagged forward and hung on for dear life.

"Get me outta here. Anywhere you want. You got your head," Jeter said to the huge black horse. The stallion got through the narrow neck of the nook and out onto the canyon floor.

For a moment Jeter got turned around, and didn't realize that the horse was carrying him toward the posse's campsite. When he snapped out of his lethargy, he sawed at the reins and turned the horse's head.

"Other way, boy, other way. Go fast." The horse tried to buck him off, but Jeter was expecting it. The stallion didn't like it when he sawed on the reins like that. But he had no other choice. To have been carried smack dab into the middle of the posse was a death sentence, even if they were mostly drunk and many had passed out.

Jeter fumbled to find his six-shooter, and was content when he discovered it securely in his holster. He couldn't remember much about the descent from his aerie on the mountainside, but as he passed the point directly below, he looked up almost expecting to see Slocum aiming a rifle at him. But that was ridiculous. He wasn't sure, but thought he had broken the son of a bitch's neck. Jeter stared at his hands. They were cut and bleeding, but some of that blood came from bandaging himself. The rest came from the scuffle.

A final glance over his shoulder. Still no Slocum beckoning him to return to finish their fight.

"Killed him," Jeter said, getting dizzy and almost falling from his horse. "Swatted the fly on my flypaper."

He wobbled and held on tight, then sat straighter when he heard something he couldn't immediately identify. He sucked in a great deep breath and gagged when the pain in his side got to be too much. Jeter took a gentle bend in the canyon and cast a look over his left shoulder, and uttered a string of curses when he saw the source of the curious noise. The echoes trapped by the canyon walls had disguised the sound of a dozen horses—all on his trail. He had thought the posse was drunk on their asses and no threat. He couldn't have been more wrong.

Jeter slowed his horse, and then halted to be certain the sound was that of the posse. He heard muffled voices as they drunkenly argued. One came through clarion clear, though.

"He took his horse and went that way, Marshal Eaton."

"I heard you the first time, Billy. You put a lot of trust in Slocum. Where's he off to?"

"It don't matter, Marshal. Nuthin' does but arrestin' Jeter. That's what Slocum said 'fore he sent me back to fetch y'all."

"Flypaper," Jeter muttered. "Even when he's dead I can't shake him." He brought his horse to a slow walk, hoping no sound reached back to the disorganized posse. If he kept moving and they didn't spot him, he would get away scot-free. They were too drunk to keep up pursuit of a ghost for very long.

"Stay out of sight," Jeter repeated to himself until he believed he could do it. A smile crossed his face and joy momentarily blotted out the pain when he saw the far end of the canyon. Another branch. Without Slocum to steer them in the proper direction, he could lose them all here. Or half, if they chose to split their forces. With the proper choice, he could even take on all of them. The western canyon was rugged, but the one going off to the southeast afforded better spots for ambush. That was the one he would take.

A few shots and they'd hightail it all the way back to San Esteban with stories of being up against the fiercest *bandido* in all of Texas!

Jeter was approaching the juncture when he realized that the posse was getting closer. Too close for him to lay a false trail, even if he could. Jeter's head spun, and he felt as if his body would split into sections. His left leg might fall off, but that would be all right. His chest filled with liquid fire every time he sucked in a breath. Clinging to the hope of eluding the posse, he turned into the rockier canyon. The other would have given him more chance to ambush them. Jeter was in such bad condition now he wasn't sure he could hold a six-shooter without it shaking too much to aim properly.

"There he is!" went up the cry behind him. He had tried to make his choice of paths and not have them spot him. Considering their condition, the members of the posse might have argued an hour or until they passed out from too much booze. But they didn't argue. The one who was sober—Billy—had spotted him.

Jeter gave the stallion its head, letting the powerful horse run through the jumble of rocks, finding the surest path, getting him away from the law. This was the first time the horse had ever been given such freedom. Usually its rider was in complete control, but not tonight.

"Get me home," he said, clinging to the horse's neck.

The stallion failed him.

It took a turn into a narrow canyon that proved to be a dead end. The horse reared and pawed at the air when Jeter jerked hard on the reins. So little time before the posse caught up. So little time. No time at all.

Jeter went for his six-shooter when he saw four of the posse arrayed in a fan behind him. All of them had their rifles trained on him. Drunk or sober, good marksman or bad, there was no way the four would miss if they opened fire. And behind them crowded the rest of the jeering, shouting lawmen.

"I surrender," Jeter said, hands going up into the air. He knew it was a mistake, but he was too pain-racked to fight. The new town marshal would arrest him, patch him up, and go through a mockery of a trial. Somewhere along the way a deputy or the marshal himself would slip up and Jeter would be free again.

He was smarter than the lot of them put together. Eventually, he would ride out of San Esteban and most of them wouldn't.

"Don't shoot, boys," Marshal Eaton called. "We got him fair 'n square."

"What now, Marshal?" asked the youngster. Jeter fought to keep the young man in focus. This had to be Billy, the one Slocum had put on his tail. Jeter might clear leather and cut him down if he got lucky. But that would mean the others would kill him. No sense dying now. He could escape the town jail and then eliminate every member of the posse, one by one. Might be, he would save

Billy for the last since he owed him the most. Watching the callow youth's face as he begged for mercy and didn't get it would be a memory that might keep Jeter warm for months afterward.

"You got me. No need to get itchy trigger fingers." Jeter almost fell from the saddle.

"It's a trick, be careful," Eaton warned his men.

"No trick, Marshal," Billy said, riding closer. "There's not a patch of clothes anywhere on his body that's not soaked in blood. He's a complete mess."

The others rode closer to look at him as if he were a circus elephant, or one of those damned camels they had tried at Fort Davis years back and that the Drunk Camel was named for.

"What happened to you?" asked Eaton.

"You should see Slocum," Jeter got out. He grinned through bloody lips and looked like a death's skull. He got a thrill out of seeing the reaction a simple smile produced. When he got back in the saddle and went after these men, they would do more than recoil in horror. They would shit their britches before he pulled the trigger and ended their miserable lives.

"He don't look like he'd make it back to town, Marshal," Billy said. "What we gonna do 'bout that?"

"Yeah, what you gonna do?" Jeter laughed and then spat blood.

The marshal pushed back his hat and scratched his chin as he stared hard at Jeter. It took him a few seconds before he said, "Must be an oak tree around here somewhere."

"What?" Jeter didn't understand what the man meant. "What are you sayin'?"

"You won't live to stand trial so I reckon we gotta hang you now. Saves the citizens of San Esteban the trouble of gettin' a judge down from Fort Davis and goin' through the charade of a convenin' a jury."

"I can ride," Jeter said, his heart feeling as if it would explode in his chest when he realized what the marshal intended to do. "I can make it alive."

"Which of you men knows how to tie a hangman's knot?"

Jeter tried to escape, but there were too many of them and he was as weak as a kitten from loss of blood. They took him to a nearby oak with the strong limb at just the right height, then settled the knotted rope around his neck. Les Jeter had a curse on his lips as he flopped off his horse and died, kicking.

20

Amy Gerardo came awake, her hand on the derringer under her pillow. She lay in the hard bed a moment longer, then rose and went to the hotel room door. From outside came the strange, rhythmical sound again. Clutching her derringer, she unlocked the door and peered into the hallway. The threadbare carpeting stretched toward the rear of the hotel and a stairway down to the alley. Empty.

Sucking in her breath, she opened the door a little farther and chanced a quick peek in the other direction, toward the stairway leading to the lobby. The noise became a distinctive creaking sound as boards gave way under a heavy weight. Someone was coming up the stairs.

She knew it had to be close to dawn, but this was a strange time for anyone to be in the hallway—if their intent was legal. Cocking the derringer, she lifted it as a head slowly appeared above the top of the stairway. Then she lowered it hastily and hid it in the folds of her nightgown when she saw Ambrose Killian.

The man had a distracted look and stared directly at

her without seeing her. Amy felt a surge of irritation at this. She was in her nightgown! He should have reacted in some way! At least he could have averted his eyes and mumbled an apology. Or he could have come to her, taken her in his arms, kissed her, then pressed her back into the hotel room and—

"Ambrose?" she called, uneasy at the way her thoughts were taking her. "Are you all right? You look so . . . distant."

"Hmm? Oh, Miss Gerardo. What are you doing out in the hallway?"

"Come in, quickly, Ambrose," she said, moving to let him into her room. Her heart beat so fast it caused her breast to pulse and the frilly lace of her nightgown to ripple as if some unseen breeze disturbed it. Amy worked to find a spot to hide her pistol. Explaining why she had gone into the hallway to greet him with a gun would be too confusing at this time of the night.

To her delight, Ambrose brushed past her, his arm pressing for the briefest instant into her breasts. Then he seated himself in the single straight-backed wood chair in the corner of the room by the wardrobe. He kept both feet flat on the floor and his hands folded in his lap, as if he were an obedient schoolboy.

"Why are you wandering around like this, Ambrose?"

"You shouldn't open the door without some way of protecting yourself, Miss Gerardo," he said in his distracted tone. "I should buy you a small-caliber pistol and teach you to use it in self-defense."

"I heard a noise in the hallway," Amy said, sitting on the edge of the bed. She drew up her nightgown a little to expose her ankles, then her bare calves. Ambrose didn't pay any attention. She put the derringer down on the beside table. His eyebrows rose slightly, but he did not comment on the pistol. He was too consumed by something else.

"I had a strange feeling," he said.

"I have one too," she said, her breath coming faster now and a flush rising to her cheeks. "Right now."

"Amazing," Ambrose said. He stood, and she thought he was coming to her. Instead he went to the window and pushed back the curtains to stare into the dark street running through the feeble heart of San Esteban. "I was sound asleep and this odd feeling of loss hit me like a brick. Something was suddenly gone."

"Gone?" Amy sprawled back on the bed, her legs now wantonly bare as she pulled up her nightgown.

"It was as if I had lost an arm or an old friend or—Jeter." He turned and stared at her without seeing her. "I think Jeter is dead. Did you sense that too?"

"No."

"It can't be. I had arranged for a judge to come up from San Antonio. A jury would be easily rounded up. There would have been a sentence, an execution, and I would take pictures of Jeter on the gallows and you would record every word uttered at the trial. I had it all planned so completely."

"And his coffin," she said, remembering the elaborately carved box O'Dell had made. The undertaker was a true artisan, skilled and quick.

"Yes, yes!" cried Ambrose. "I intended to use that photograph as a cover for my memoirs of him. *The Fall of a Titan: The Outlaw's Deadly Life* I was going to call it."

"A nice title," Amy said, pursing her lips. She tipped her head back and parted her lips slightly. "Come closer, Ambrose, and tell me all about it."

He ignored her and began pacing. She recognized the cadence now as the one that had awakened her. Only this time Ambrose Killian was pacing about her room, not about the lobby below, with the clicking periodicity of a metronome. He bent forward, hands clasped behind his back, as he moved around the room. His gaze was fixed on the floor, not on her. Amy wondered what she had to do to attract his attention. She reached up and untied the top satin bow on her nightgown, showing the upper parts of her fine, firm breasts.

"Could it be so? You said you felt something too. Is he dead? Could those buffoons actually have murdered him?"

"The marshal and his posse?"

"Who else? I worried that they might chase him off with their blundering about, but what if they did find him and gunned him down? A vital chapter—more!—in my book will be gone. I must prepare for any eventuality. What if he is no more?"

"Come, sit down, Ambrose. We can think of something." Amy patted the bed, but he took no notice.

"We can still have the funeral, of course. And pictures of the body. I need those."

"You might be worrying over nothing," she said. "A nightmare, nothing more. You have no proof anything's happened to Jeter. Why, he might have killed everyone in the posse. Think what a chapter in your book that will make."

"But he must be brought in for trial."

"Perhaps Mr. Slocum will capture him," Amy said. The sudden mention of John Slocum slipped from her lips and had a curious effect on her. She was already damp in the nether regions, thinking of what it would be like to lie with Ambrose. He was so close. But Slocum was so uncouth and brutal. Not like the far more cultured and educated Ambrose Killian.

"I did not think too highly of him when you told me about him, but perhaps you are right. There might be a core of steel under that filthy exterior, but who would win in such a match? Jeter or Slocum?" Ambrose kept pacing, then stopped suddenly in front of her door. For a heart-stopping instant she thought he was going to lock the door and come to her. Instead, he opened the door and spun into the hallway, talking to her as he went.

"That might make a far better chapter. Maybe the posse didn't even find Jeter. It must have been Slocum. Man against man, drifter versus vicious outlaw. Who will win? Who will be triumphant? Yes, if Jeter is dead, this will make a perfect chapter between description of his crimes and pictures of his funeral. I must see that Slocum is given a huge reward. His type appreciates such a gesture."

"Ambrose!" Amy called to a shut door. She heard his footsteps fade out as he entered his room across the hall. The creaking of the floorboards did not cease, though. She knew he was pacing to and fro in his room, hands clutched behind his back as he worked out a new chapter for his damned book.

Amy threw herself facedown on the bed and wanted to cry, but the tears wouldn't come.

21

There wasn't a joint or muscle in Slocum's body that didn't hurt like fire. He rolled, reached out, and felt nothing but thin air and came instantly alert. He opened his eyes to a forty-foot drop. His heart leaped into his throat, then slowly descended to its proper place as he carefully inched away from the precipice. Once safe, Slocum sat up and examined himself. He had come by all the aches and pains honestly. He was covered with scratches and deep cuts that turned him into a bloody mess, but he was able to stand. At first he was nauseous, and then he held down his gorge long enough to get used to the sensations rippling away at him.

"Jeter!"

The name was almost ripped from his throat. He looked around, then examined the puddle of blood on the stony ledge. He hadn't lost this much blood—Jeter had. Slocum reached down to his boot top and found the empty sheath there.

"I knifed him," Slocum said, memories flooding back

now. He had driven his blade into the outlaw's side while Jeter was squeezing the life from him. Slocum gingerly touched his neck and winced. The bruises there were tender and throbbed with a vitality of their own. But he was alive and Jeter wasn't. He couldn't have lived. Slocum went to the edge and looked down into the darkness below, trying to make out where Jeter's body must have fallen.

His heart leaped back into his throat when he realized Jeter's stallion was missing. Slocum wasted no time getting down the stone staircase to the small corral. He saw patches of blood all the way down, and marveled that Jeter was able to walk. But the horse was gone and the evidence made it look as if Jeter had been the one riding away.

"Damnation, what's it take to kill that son of a bitch?" Slocum drew his six-shooter and checked the cylinder. Fully loaded. He shouldn't have tangled with the outlaw in a hand-to-hand fight. Find him, wait for him to turn his back, and shoot him. That was what he should have done.

Slocum followed the horse tracks to the floor of the canyon, saw the turn to the right and the sudden reversal. There was no reason for Jeter to have headed directly toward the posse's camp unless he had become confused. That made Slocum think the outlaw was in worse shape than ever before. This was the best chance he had of catching him and getting him back to San Esteban for trial.

As he walked, following the obvious trail, Slocum saw other hoofprints on the ground. He sucked in his breath. Marshal Eaton and the rest of the posse must have come after Jeter when Billy went to fetch them. In a way, this surprised Slocum. He hadn't thought the marshal had enough command of the men riding with him to muster them all in the middle of the night after their drunken debauchery. It was almost idle speculation on Slocum's part when he pictured Luke riding along with them. The barkeep had been knocked out and in no condition to stand, much less ride.

"Might be Luke's horse is still back at the camp," Slocum thought aloud. He could catch up with the posse faster if he rode. But backtracking would waste another hour. He needed to keep moving, to find Jeter and settle accounts with him before the posse found him.

And he knew they couldn't find their own hats if they were squarely atop their heads.

By sunup he smelled fire. Slocum walked a little faster in spite of being footsore and more exhausted than he could remember being. The fight with Jeter had taken the starch out of him, and only the thought of facing Jeter again kept him putting one foot in front of the other. Every time Jeter's leering face flashed through his brain, he reached over and touched the cold butt of his Peacemaker. Six rounds might not be enough when he caught up with the road agent.

The odor of cooking meat made his belly growl and his mouth water. Slocum heard the men laughing and joking long before he actually spotted them or their fire. The posse made no attempt to hide their position or keep their voices down. Slocum reckoned that was due to working hard all night long on the prodigious amount of booze they had packed in their saddlebags.

"Mr. Slocum!" Billy jumped to his feet, stared at Slocum for an instant, and then rushed forward to embrace him in a bear hug. "I thought you was dead!"

"Takes more than Les Jeter to do me in," Slocum said.

He looked around at the men. They all had shit-eating grins on their faces.

"Have somethin' to eat. We got plenty. I shot a couple rabbits and we made some biscuits and—"

"Where's Jeter?"

Billy's eyes went wide and he started to speak, but no words came out of his mouth, no matter how much his lips moved.

"He met his Maker, that's where he is," Marshal Eaton said, coming over. "You look a fright. Truth is, you look worse 'n Jeter and he's dead."

"You shot it out with him?"

"Not exactly," Eaton said, looking uneasy.

"He surrendered, Mr. Slocum. He surrendered and they hung him." Billy looked aggrieved at this.

"We saved the taxpayers of Jeff Davis County a few dollars, that's all," the marshal said. "Why bother with a trial when he was in such sad shape he wasn't likely to survive the ride back to San Esteban?"

"You hung him without a trial?" Slocum didn't know whether to be outraged at being cheated or to laugh.

"I tole them it wasn't the right thing to do," Billy said.

"He'll grow some fur round them balls of his one day," Eaton said, glaring at Billy. "We done what we had to. He was dyin' from his wounds."

"So you hung him before he could die?"

"Something like that. Justice was done."

"Is this here knife yours, Mr. Slocum?" Billy fumbled around in his bedroll and pulled out Slocum's knife. "I found it at the base of the cliff. That's what caused him to be so weak and all, I reckon."

"But he had other wounds. A nasty one in his ass," said another of the posse. "Don't know how he rode with that one. Soaked his entire leg in blood, just like that knife wound in his side did to his shirt."

Slocum took the knife and slid it into his boot sheath. "Where is he?"

"Still strung up 'bout a quarter mile that way," the marshal said, pointing. "None of us had the heart to cut him down. Seemed fittin' fer all the men he killed to let him swing in the wind till the crows finished with him."

"I have to find him," Slocum said. He turned to go, but Billy stopped him, his hand strong and sure on Slocum's quaking arm.

"Ain't nuthin' you kin do for him, Mr. Slocum. He's *dead*."

"There's nothing I want to do *for* him," Slocum snapped. "There's plenty I want to do *to* him. He stole my watch and I'm going to get it back."

"This one?" Marshal Eaton fumbled in his side coat pocket and pulled out Slocum's watch. "If you claim it's yours, I'm not gonna argue. Any of you boys?" A sea of shaking heads answered the lawman. He handed over the glittering gold watch.

Slocum took it as if it were the most precious item in the world. And for him it was. His brother Robert lived as long as the watch ticked away. He tucked it into his own pocket, where it had ridden since the war. It felt good.

"Thank you," Slocum said. Heads turned toward him. They all heard the sincerity in his voice.

"Uh, you walked from back there, Slocum?" The marshal jerked his thumb over his shoulder in the direction of the canyon where Slocum had fought Jeter.

"My horse is dead. You know that, Marshal. Jeter shot it out from under me."

"You want another horse to replace that one?"

"Who got killed?" Slocum looked around the camp, counting and trying to remember the men's faces. Everyone, including Luke, was here. Luke's head was bandaged and he stared off into space as if he was thinking hard.

"Not Luke, but he's in a bad way. I had a cousin who got kicked in the head by a mule who acted like him. Luke might not be right in the head again," Eaton said almost gleefully. Slocum guessed most of the posse felt about Luke the way *he* had.

"If everyone is still all right, then what horse are you offering me, Marshal?"

"One nobody wants," Billy said. "The one Jeter was ridin' when he was hung."

"He's right, Slocum. Not that we're superstitious or anything, but none of us wants to ride a hangin' horse."

Slocum heard Jeter's stallion neighing loudly from the rude corral they had made some distance away. He had admired the horse's vitality and heart. It seemed only fair that he take it since Jeter had killed his.

Slocum didn't even care that a man had died astride it, a rope around his neck. If anything, that made receiving the horse all the more attractive.

22

"Mr. Killian, here they come!" Amy Gerardo leaned out the hotel window and looked around the edge of the building and down the dusty street. She saw the sunlight glinting on the marshal's badge and nearly a dozen men trailing behind.

"Successful? Do they have Jeter?" Ambrose pushed past her, and she didn't mind the feel of his body warmly pressing into hers. She just wished he noticed it as acutely as she did. He was oblivious to all but the posse returning from their manhunt. "I've got to get down and see. Hurry, girl, hurry. Bring your notebook. We'll need notes! And I should get my camera too. There's a man in a litter. That must be Jeter. They wounded him and brought him back."

Amy wondered if any tornado had ever whirled through Texas faster than Ambrose just did as he left her room and rummaged about in his own across the hall, getting his camera and fresh photographic plates. She picked up her notebook and a pencil, then closed the door behind her. As quickly as she moved, Ambrose was faster. He was already down the stairs and outside.

She followed at a more sedate pace, wondering what the future would bring now that Ambrose's obsession with Jeter was about at an end. The outlaw would rob no more. His trial couldn't possibly last longer than a few minutes after being so expertly orchestrated by Ambrose.

The heat crushed her like a hammer smashing a fly. Amy let out a tiny sigh and squinted against the sun as she went into the street to stand behind Ambrose and hear his conversation with Marshal Eaton. The lawman looked as if he had been pulled through a knothole backward, but so did the rest of the posse. Their chase must have been long and difficult. Amy smiled. This would please Ambrose and give him yet another chapter in his book.

"Is he badly injured, Marshal?" Ambrose edged around the lawman's horse and stood on tiptoe to peer at the man sprawled on the litter. "He's hardly moving."

"Oh, he's alive. He's a tough one," Eaton said. "We got to get him on over to the doc's office."

"What happened?"

"Well, he hit his head and—"

"Go on, tell him what really happened, Marshal," said an angry young man.

Amy looked at her list of names of those in the posse. She leaned forward and whispered to Ambrose, "His name's Billy Cassidy."

"Is there a fact Mr. Cassidy knows that you don't, Marshal? Or are you trying to hide something?"

"It's a mite embarrassin', that's all. Slocum swung and hit him when he called him a, well, let's say he called him somethin' no man wants to hear."

"Slocum was with the posse?" Amy perked up.

"Yup. He drew that Peacemaker of his faster 'n I ever seen a man move; then he swung the barrel and caught Luke across the cheek with it. He fell back and—"

"Luke? You mean Jeter, don't you?" Ambrose looked shocked.

"No, no, Luke, the barkeep from the Drunk Camel. He brought along too much tarantula juice and was drunk. He deserved what he got, but he hit his head on a rock when he fell and ain't been right since that."

"Luke? What about Jeter!" Ambrose rushed around and stared down at the litter. Amy pressed close behind and saw the man with a ruined mouth and a bloody patch on the back of his head larger than a silver dollar. Although Luke's eyes were open, they stared like he was blind.

"Well, I suppose I oughta tell you 'bout that, Mr. Killian," said the marshal, dismounting and swinging his reins around a hitching post. "Like you wanted, we caught him."

"Where is he?" Ambrose was turning frantic as he went from one posse member to the next looking for Les Jeter. "He's not here!"

"Of course he ain't, Mr. Killian. He was so banged up when we caught him, we knew he'd never make it back alive, so we hung him."

Ambrose Killian stared at the lawman as if he had sprouted horns.

"You did what?"

"Hung the son of a bitch, just like we'd of done after a trial here in town. Only, Jeter'd never have made it back so—"

"Where? Where'd you hang him?"

"From an oak tree. Real sturdy one too."

"I don't care about the kind of tree, you idiot! Where's Jeter now?"

"Still swingin' in the wind, I suppose, 'less the coyotes and buzzards got to him." Marshal Eaton looked increasingly angry at Killian. "I don't like the tone you're takin', Mr. Killian. You tryin' to back out on payin' that reward you put up?"

"I wanted Jeter!" Ambrose screamed so loudly that Amy went to him and tugged at his sleeve.

"Sir, please, you're making a scene. The marshal's getting mad too. There's no telling what he'll do if he—"

"I want the goddamn body!"

"You settle down there, Mr. Killian," said the marshal. "You're raisin' too much of a ruckus. I wouldn't want to fine you fer disturbin' the peace."

"I want the body!"

Amy took a firm hold on her employer's arm, in spite of him trying to pull free, and steered him back in the direction of the hotel. She spoke quietly and rapidly to him.

"We can find out where the body is. This isn't a loss, Mr. Killian, it's a boon. Think of the drama in the situation."

"I wanted a trial."

"But you heard the marshal. Jeter's body is still out there. You can take pictures. And Mr. Slocum had a part. He would make a fine hero pitted against the evil Lester Jeter."

"*I'm* the damned hero, not this Slocum."

Amy saw that Ambrose was settling down and recovering his usual good nature, although very slowly as the reality of missing out on the outlaw's trial sank in. She motioned to Billy Cassidy to come over since the young man stood uneasily a few yards away, paying more than a fair share of attention to Ambrose's temper tantrum.

"Ma'am, Mr. Killian," Billy said. "I heard what you said to the marshal."

"So?" Ambrose was turning petulant now. Amy found she wasn't too inclined to like this aspect of his character that had not been revealed to her before, but she knew how to coax him back to his usual good nature.

"I think Billy wants to tell us he can take us to where Jeter was hanged. Isn't that it?"

"Oh, sure, ma'am, that's easy enough. But I wanted to say that the marshal, well, he don't spread around the praise too much. I think the reward's blindin' him to the fact that we'd never have caught Jeter if it hadn't been for Mr. Slocum. Him and me, we lit out of camp on our own and tracked Jeter. Mr. Slocum had a right good idea where that son of a gun might be. And he was. I went to fetch the rest of the posse from camp and Mr. Slocum tangled with him all by his lonesome."

"Is Mr. Slocum all right?" Amy found herself asking with a touch of real concern.

"Oh, yes, ma'am, he's right as rain. Well, he got banged up a mite, but he's not hurt. Fact is, he got Jeter's watch and took his horse as reward."

"Jeter's watch? His horse? Slocum has them? Which one's Slocum again?" Ambrose craned his neck around, but most of the men had gone into the Drunk Camel. With Luke at the doctor's office getting patched up, nobody was tending the bar, and the posse all deserved a drink or two on the house.

"Where are Jeter's belongings? Other than the watch and horse?"

Amy saw how her employer perked up like a hunting dog who had finally scented a bird.

"Don't know for sure. Could be Mr. Slocum took 'em back to Jeter's widow."

"Jeter was married?" Ambrose rubbed his hands together. "I had heard hints of it, from down south, but there were no courthouse records and I never found a minister or priest who claimed to have married Jeter and anyone. But there were always rumors."

"Don't know the details, but Mr. Slocum seemed to. He said he'd go tell the missus that she ought to be wearin' widow's weeds."

"Where?"

"As I said, Mr. Killian, I don't know for certain sure, but I kin take you out to the oak where they hung Jeter."

"Miss Gerardo, get a buckboard. Have it provisioned for—how long will the trip take?"

Billy rubbed his almost clean chin and said, "Took us less than two days to ride home, but we was takin' it easy 'cuz of Luke's head bein' all stove in like it is. In a buckboard, prob'ly take you as long in a wagon as it did us."

"Get provisions for a week, Miss Gerardo. Load my camera and plenty of photographic plates. No, no! All of them! Don't hold any in reserve. I must be certain I have the pictures of Jeter hanging from that oak tree."

"Ma'am, I kin help you, if you like," Billy offered.

"She can handle such minor details, son. That's what I pay her to do. You and I must talk. Give me all the details. Everything you know and what you suspect about this Slocum fellow. And don't scrimp on the details surrounding Jeter's hanging. I want to know it all!"

Ambrose put his arm around Billy and steered him toward the saloon to get him drunk. Amy took a step after them, wishing Ambrose was leading her off. Then, crestfallen at being neglected like this, she turned and went to the livery stables to arrange for the buckboard, team, and whatever supplies they would require on their trip to see the culmination of Ambrose Killian's obsession.

23

Slocum stared at the cabin nestled between the ravine that hid the barn, the low hills where he had started Jeter on his run for freedom, and the lush green grass that was so at odds with most of the West Texas desert down around San Esteban and Fort Davis, and saw none of it. As if his eyes could pierce walls, he saw Ruth inside the cabin, sitting at the lone table, doing some small task. Sewing? Maybe she was fixing a meal. That would set well with Slocum about now. He hadn't had anything to eat since leaving the oak tree where Jeter's body still swung slowly in the hot Texas wind. How would she react to knowing that her husband was dead?

She had tried to stop Jeter from killing Slocum earlier, but that didn't mean she would take the news well. In spite of this uncertainty, Slocum knew he had to tell her since it was only right. Ruth had to move on with her life, and doing it free of Jeter was going to be a boon.

Slocum turned and stared hard at the hills where he had spied on Ruth and the cabin, using her as bait to draw

Jeter back. Somewhere in that rocky expanse Jeter had hidden the loot from all his robberies. It might be a considerable pile of money or it might be a few odd dollars. Slocum just didn't know. Ruth ought to have it. If that seemed a way to go after he told her of Jeter's unsightly death, he might suggest they hunt for the outlaw's ill-gotten gains. He ought to get something for his trouble, but Ruth deserved it more.

Patting the stallion, he knew riding this horse was likely to be better reward than anything else he might get from Jeter's life as a road agent.

He urged the horse onward. Sensing it was about home, the horse broke into a trot and took him to the cabin far sooner than he anticipated. Before he could dismount, Ruth came out, wiping flour off her hands. She had been cooking.

"John? Is he—?"

"He's dead," Slocum said, seeing no reason to beat around the bush. From her stricken expression, she knew the answer already. Why delay it longer than necessary since her feelings were going to be the same no matter what he said or did?

"I had a dream a couple nights ago. It was a sad dream, but not frightening. I saw Les being killed. The posse got him?"

"I tried to take him alive, but he was quite a fighter."

"There was a ledge," she said. "High up on the side of a mountain and you two fought and he got away. Then the posse closed in."

"They hung him," Slocum said.

"I didn't dream that part. J-just that he was dead." Ruth turned abruptly and dashed into the cabin. Slocum had done his duty and told her. He could leave Jeter's few belongings on the porch and ride away. He could have done that, but he didn't.

Slocum swung his leg over the saddle horn and dropped to the ground. The impact caused his legs to buckle slightly. He was still weak from his fight with Jeter, and might take a few more days to recuperate. Fishing around in his saddlebags, he got the few items of Jeter's that the posse had left. Clumsily carrying them, he went up the steps and stopped just outside the door. Ruth sat at the table he had seen so clearly, face buried in her hands, sobbing hard. She looked up, wiped her eyes, and sniffed.

"I'm sorry, John. I didn't even like him, but he was my husband. That sounds strange, I know, but it's the way it was."

"I have his belongings," Slocum said. "Some of them at least. Where should I put them?"

"There. On that box is fine. I don't know what I'll do with them. His gun? That horrid six-gun must have killed dozens of men. He never bragged on it to me, but I knew he was proud of gunning them all down. It was the way Les was."

"I should go. If there's anything—"

"John," she said, staring at him. Her brown eyes still brimmed with tears, but the firmness of her chin and the set to her body told him her grieving was about over. Almost.

"You don't have any way to get into town," he said. "I'd forgotten. I'll ride in and fetch back a buggy. Or if you want to take along any of this, I should get a wagon."

"There's not much I want from here, John. There're only bad memories, memories of days and nights waiting anxiously for Les and not having him return. Then he would suddenly appear when I was about to give up hope

I'd ever see him again." She sniffled a little more. "How could I want him to come back to me and at the same time to die and never darken my door again? It doesn't make sense."

"No, it doesn't," Slocum said, going over and pulling out a chair to sit across from her at the table.

"You've seen a lot of dying, haven't you, John? I see it in your face." Ruth reached out and placed feverish fingers on his cheek. Without taking her hand from his face, she stood and moved around the table. A quick sweep of her arm sent the plate and other settings flying. She sat on the table and hiked up her skirts. "I need you, John. I need you more than I ever thought it was possible to need a man."

Slocum said nothing. He had seen this reaction before too. A woman needed a connection with life when faced with death. He had seen it in men too—he had felt it himself.

His hands pushed up her skirts, slowly revealing her bare legs. They were trim and white and warm. Slowly he spread those legs and exposed the nut-colored nest between her thighs. He bent forward and kissed gently, then dragged his tongue the length of those trembling pink flaps. A shudder passed through Ruth's body. She leaned back on the table, supporting her weight on her arms. Her head lolled back and her chest heaved in reaction to his mouth moving up and down her nether lips. When his tongue entered her, she lifted her rump off the table and tried to grind herself into his face.

Slocum's hands went under the woman's buttocks and clutched at them, holding her firmly in place as he kissed and licked and sucked at her juices. The trembling became a shudder that rattled the woman's teeth, but Slocum never slowed in his oral assault.

"More, John, I want more than your sweet mouth." Ruth sank back to lie on the table. She hiked her feet up to the top edges and held them wantonly wide. "I want you inside me, John, all the way. I *need* you!"

Slocum said nothing as he kissed higher, pushing unwanted clothing out of the way as he went. He got to the woman's belly. His tongue dipped briefly into the deep well of her navel and then slithered upward. She worked frantically to open her blouse. By the time he reached her breasts, they were bare and shaking, the red cherry tips hard with need. He suckled first at one and then the other, but as nice as this was, Ruth wanted something more.

So did he.

Her fingers reached around clumsily and worked at his fly. She got one button undone before Slocum stood upright and finished the job. He let his jeans drop as he stepped closer to the table. He grabbed a double handful of assflesh and pulled her toward him. The purpled tip of his manhood rubbed across her gash. Then he sank into her until his crotch pressed intimately into hers.

Ruth cried out once. Then she was silent. Her eyes were screwed tightly shut and her face had become a mask. Then she bit her lower lip and began to move. Her hands reached out to grip Slocum's forearms. Her hips began to gyrate, slowly at first, and then with wilder, wider movements. All Slocum had to do was stand there, erect and hidden within her, to get the full benefit of her desires.

He felt the tightness of her channel as she squeezed down moistly all around him. And he loved the sensation of her inner muscles flexing as he gripped her buttocks. Lifting her up allowed him to inch into her even more. This small movement was enough to bring a cry of stark desire to the woman's lips.

"More, move, oh, oh!"

She tensed again and threatened to rob Slocum of all his control. He withdrew, then slowly entered her once more. This time there was a liquid sound that worked on his senses and sent ice-pick jabs of delight down into his own loins. He moved slowly, but was doomed to speed up until the friction between their flesh was more than he could stand.

He thrust fiercely, gripped her ass tightly, and then withdrew slowly. The pressures mounted within him, causing him to ache with need. He began stroking with a more rhythmic motion, and this sent him soaring. The liquid fire within spilled out. His cries mingled with hers as she once more tensed with the ultimate release of the sexual tensions locked within her.

Slocum stroked until he began to melt within her, then bent forward and lightly kissed her. Brown eyes fluttered open and a smile came to her lips.

"That was what I needed, John. You did it so well too."

"We both needed release from our ghosts," he said. He started to straighten, but her arms circled his neck and brought his face back to hers. They kissed for some time, and only then did she release him.

"You taste good," she said.

"So do you." He ran his fingers over her belly and worked lower. His middle finger slid once more into her and wiggled about.

"Oh, nice, so nice," she cooed, "but later. Not now. There's so much to do, to think about and do, oh." She caught his wrist and held it to keep him from moving away. “Don’t stop. We can talk about what to do later. Right now I want more of this.” She stroked up and down his arm. “And this.” Her fingers lightly tapped his flaccid organ.

“You’ll have to coax me,” he said.

She did.

24

"Can't be more 'n another few minutes," Billy said, looking around. No matter how he studied the countryside, though, Amy noticed that the young man's eyes always returned to her. She preened a little to get him to move along, maybe pushing out her chest a bit more than she would have normally. She was a small woman, but that only accentuated the size of her breasts—and she knew it.

Amy turned in the hard seat to look out of the corner of her eye at Ambrose. She wished he knew it. He drove the wagon like a man insane, hitting bumps in the road hard enough to rattle her teeth. After a pair of days of this Amy wished she had stayed in San Esteban, no matter that she was out here alone with Ambrose.

Alone with Billy Cassidy and Ambrose, she amended. The one man looked at her like she wished the other would. She sagged a little on the hardwood seat.

"What's wrong, Miss Gerardo?" Ambrose snapped the reins and kept the team pulling hard up a slight incline. "We'll be there soon. Our guide says so."

"He might be lost or taking us in circles," she said wearily. That much was true. She didn't put it past Billy to get them lost so he could spend a little extra time gawking at her.

"There's no way he could have us driving in circles. These canyons don't allow it."

"There, there it is. The tree!" Billy stood in his stirrups and pointed ahead.

Amy had ridden along with Ambrose enough to instinctively grab on as he whipped the team to even greater speed. She was jostled and tossed about, but it was over quickly enough. Ambrose yanked back on the reins and simply stared. She put up her hand to shield her eyes from the bright sun, and saw it.

Him. It. Jeter swung slowly in the wind, hands bound behind his back, a knotted rope around his neck.

"They did hang him," Ambrose said in a voice almost too low for Amy to hear. "Sons of bitches! I wanted him alive to stand trial."

"You want I should cut him down, Mr. Killian?" shouted Billy.

"No! I want photos first. I want everything recorded for posterity."

"That one of your kin, Mr. Killian?"

"What? Never mind. Let me have a few minutes with him to pay my respects."

"What then, Ambrose?" Amy hardly realized she had used his first name addressing him. He was so excited that he paid her no heed. "How will you celebrate?" She could send Billy off on a wild-goose chase if Ambrose really wanted to celebrate.

"There'll be no celebration, not yet, Miss Gerardo," Ambrose said. "Set up the tripod over there. I want to get as much light on the body as I can for the first shot. We are losing the sun rapidly because the sun sets behind the hills so quickly. If too much is in shadow, it will not photograph well."

Amy did as she was told, dutifully moving the camera around, occasionally reaching out to stop Jeter from swinging too much. She wished she had gloves. Touching the outlaw's corpse was distasteful since it had begun to decay. Not even the carrion-eaters were interested in pecking away at the body now. It was all she could do to even look at it. Crows had pecked out the eyes and other soft tissue. Coyotes had jumped up and nipped away at the legs, and general putrescence made the rest of the body too ugly for her to bear. If anything, though, Ambrose was in his element.

More than an hour later, he took the last photograph and had her begin the tedious process of stowing the camera and the cases holding the exposed plates.

"Help me cut him down," he called to Billy.

"Well, all right, sir, if that's what you want. Mind if I ask what you're gonna do with the body?"

"Take him back to town for burial. The undertaker's got a fancy coffin all ready for him."

"More pictures, huh?"

"That's right. And I'll want to take one of you with the body laid out in the coffin. You can stand over him, pistols crossed on your chest."

"I didn't do that much. It was all Mr. Slocum's doing. Well, gettin' Jeter to run was. Capturin' him wasn't much of a chore. He was all cut up and had bled so much he was weak as a kitten."

"You're too modest," Amy said, grinning weakly. "I'm sure you did more than you're letting on."

"Well, I did help tie the noose," Billy said. "But it was Marshal Eaton that put it round his neck. Some of the men argued over whether we ought to set fire to the horse's tail to make it run. The arguin' got so bad, the marshal just whacked the stallion on the rump and there was a dull cracking sound and it was all over."

"How . . . colorful," Amy said, a little sick to her stomach.

"There, be careful," ordered Ambrose. "Don't break off anything. I want his body intact."

"He's surely heavy fer a man what's been dead for a week almost," Billy said, wrestling with the body.

"And I want the rope. I want every inch of it, and don't disturb the knot."

Billy did as he was told while Amy and Ambrose watched. She saw a strange light come into Ambrose's eyes, and didn't like it.

"We ought to get on the road back to town as soon as possible," she said. Her heart sank when she heard his answer.

"Slocum left with Jeter's belongings."

"To take them to Jeter's widow, yup, that's right," said Billy, dusting off his hands as he joined them. "Got the body all trussed up so it won't bounce out of your wagon."

"Can you follow a trail?" Ambrose asked.

"Me? I know a little, I s'ppose. I could never have tracked Jeter. He was too good. Even Mr. Slocum had trouble, and he's 'bout the best I ever seen."

"Track Slocum, will you? Track him to Mrs. Jeter's place. I'll pay you an extra five dollars."

Amy saw the way Billy looked from Ambrose to her. A smile split his face. The young man would have paid five dollars to spend another couple days on the trail with her. She wished Ambrose had seen that. It might give him ideas.

"You got yerself a deal, Mr. Killian." Billy thrust out his hand. Ambrose shook it without the slightest sign of distaste at what the young man had just been doing.

"Never knew this place existed," Billy said. "Real purty, ain't it? A man could make a decent life for himself here."

"And for his family," Ambrose Killian said. "That cabin's got smoke coming from the chimney. Somebody lives here."

"Could it be Mr. Slocum?" Amy asked. "Billy said the tracks led directly here, no hesitation, no wrong turns."

"That might just mean he's been here before, ma'am," said Billy.

"He's right. He might have come this way hunting for Jeter," Ambrose said. Amy saw the gleam in his eyes again. He had been so despondent after learning that the posse had hanged Jeter, but now a new mission had come to him. Collecting all the artifacts left by the dead Jeter could take years.

"Shall we hurry?" Amy looked over her shoulder into the wagon bed. The corpse was turning noxious in the summer sun, in spite of the canvas shroud they had wrapped Jeter's body in.

"I agree. Let's go!" Ambrose snapped the reins and bounced and banged across the grassy area just behind the cabin. Amy wondered at the large number of rocks until she noticed the nearness of the rocky knob poking up not that far off. Then again, Ambrose had a knack for hitting every single rock, no matter how well buried.

They pulled up in front of the cabin. Before Ambrose could secure the reins a woman came out. Amy sniffed at the sight of the woman. Definitely not the sort of woman a man like Slocum would care for, she decided. That meant this was Jeter's woman. His wife, if Ambrose's sources were accurate, and Amy had no reason to think they were not. Ambrose was nothing if not thorough when it came to finding out details about Jeter's life.

"Mrs. Jeter?" Ambrose hopped down without offering to help Amy and went up the steps, hand on the brim of his hat. Amy wondered if he would take his hat off to this woman. He did.

"Can I help you down, ma'am?" Billy stood at the side of the wagon, looking up at her like a puppy dog.

"Thank you, Billy," she said, letting him take her hand to help her jump to the ground. She landed, turned her ankle, and felt his hands grab her around her trim waist, supporting her and keeping her from making a complete fool of herself.

"Careful," Billy said, grinning. "It's a long way down from up there."

"For me, it is," Amy said, smiling weakly. He didn't immediately remove his hands from her waist, forcing her to disengage him. "Thank you."

"My pleasure, ma'am," he said.

Amy hurried around the wagon and climbed the steps to stand beside Ambrose. He had already done the introductions and didn't bother introducing her to Mrs. Jeter. Amy wasn't sure if this was a good thing. It was impolite, but she had no desire to know or be known by this plain-looking woman.

"May I call you Ruth?" asked Ambrose. "I know this

is forward of me, but after so many years following your husband's career, I feel I know you well."

"If you like," Ruth Jeter said, a tiny smile curling the corners of her mouth. "Would you like to come inside?"

"Of course I would. I need to speak to you of important matters."

"It's about Les, isn't it? I already know. He's dead." Ruth's face turned impassive. "The posse hung him. Mr. Slocum came by to let me know."

"Slocum, eh?" Ambrose made it sound as if this were the first he had heard. "You know him well, this Mr. Slocum?"

"Not that well," Ruth said, and Amy perked up. The woman was lying. Why, she couldn't say. "He came through hunting Les a week or so back, then left this morning. He . . . he promised to get a wagon so I could move my belongings into San Esteban."

"How kind of him," Amy said with more than a hint of sarcasm. "What will you do there?"

"Move on, most likely. I don't have much in the way of family. And I've been out here so long, all my friends have drifted away."

"How sad," Amy said. She got an irritated look from Ambrose and she quieted down. Why Ruth Jeter's tale of woe affected her this way, she couldn't say.

"It's my understanding that Slocum had all your husband's belongings. The ones not taken by the marshal and the posse. I would like to examine them, if I could."

"Why?" Ruth looked puzzled.

"I am an historian," Ambrose said. This was the first time Amy had heard him use such a term to describe his collecting hobby. "I intend to document every stage in your late husband's life. Of course, I would pay you for any of the belongings that would play a significant part in this documentation."

"I don't understand," Ruth said, "but what Mr. Slocum brought's over on the table. It's Les's gun and holster, a few other items. Nothing much."

"His hat," Ambrose said, pouncing on the items like a hungry cougar on fresh meat. He held it up and ran his fingers over the dusty brim. "And his six-shooter, of course. And the belt. It has seen better days, hasn't it?" He slid the six-gun in and out of the holster a few times. Amy saw how well-worn the holster was and how quickly the pistol slid free.

"Not a great deal worth much," Ruth said. "That sums up my life with Les, I suppose."

"I'll need to interview you at length," Ambrose said. "But later, since you are going to San Esteban. Will you stay there long?"

"I don't know. Honestly, I do not."

"I see. Yes, there'll be time for us to talk. I have so many questions about your late husband." Ambrose coughed, cleared his throat, and rested his hand on the table holding the hat, six-gun, and other items. "I am interested in these things for my research. What price would you place on them?"

"Price? I don't know. I hadn't thought to even take them with me."

"Fifty dollars," Ambrose blurted out. Amy saw the shock on Ruth Jeter's face at such a princely sum for something she would have discarded. "Fifty now and that much more if you have other items of his for sale."

"You can look around. I don't know what there might be, but you're welcome to it."

Ambrose gestured to Amy to box up the six-shooter and the rest, as if Ruth Jeter might change her mind. Amy obeyed, hefting the gun and wondering how many men it had killed. Too many. She looked at how Ambrose was seated at the table, his hand on Ruth's as they talked intimately. Maybe the six-gun could kill one more. Pushing such a notion from her mind, she went to stow the mementos in the back of the wagon next to their former owner's body.

"Need help, ma'am?"

"No, Billy, I can do this." Amy worked for a few minutes, then swung around and sat on the back of the wagon. "Billy, who used to own this farm?"

"Don't rightly know. An old couple, if memory serves. Reckon they got tired and moved on."

"Or maybe Jeter killed them and just moved in," she said. "I'd heard a rumor to that effect."

"He was a killer, that one," Billy agreed. "But you think his wife'd stay on land stole from a dead couple? She didn't seem like that would set well with her."

"You don't take her for a squatter?"

"Not on dead folks' property. She's got some sensibilities 'bout her."

Amy snorted in disgust. What was it about Ruth Jeter that made men go crazy? Couldn't they see the woman was the perfect wife for a bloody-handed butcher and the most vicious road agent West Texas had seen in years? No self-respecting man would ever share *her* bed.

She looked up to see Ambrose emerging from the cabin, Ruth Jeter right behind.

"I appreciate all you've told me, Mrs. Jeter," Ambrose said. "You can come with us, if you like. We're headed for San Esteban."

"Thank you, but I'd better wait for Mr. Slocum. We might miss each other, and I wouldn't want to worry him none."

"You could always follow," Ambrose said.

"There're no horses or mules here. Les didn't let me keep any," she said.

"Afraid they'd be stolen while he was away?" Ambrose looked as if he intended to snap his fingers and have Amy take down every precious word.

"Didn't want me gettin' away," Ruth said simply.

"Billy there said Mr. Slocum was riding your husband's horse. Is that so?"

"The stallion was Les's favorite of all the ones he had ridden in the last few years. I'm glad Mr. Slocum got it. He deserves something after Les shot his horse out from under him."

"With the six-shooter Miss Gerardo took?"

"I suppose."

"We need to get going," Amy called. "Time is working against us, Mr. Killian."

Ruth laughed at this and said, "That sounds so much like Mr. Slocum. He looked at the watch and said the same thing."

"What watch is that?" asked Ambrose. Amy heard his "collector" tone once more.

"I think it was Les's watch. The marshal gave that to Mr. Slocum too, along with the horse. For his trouble."

"That's so," Billy piped up. "Marshal Eaton gave Mr. Slocum the watch. I seen him do it, but I thought the watch was Mr. Slocum's."

"Then why did Jeter have it?" Ambrose sounded like a prosecutor interrogating a lying witness on the stand.

"He lost it maybe. I don't know if Mr. Slocum said, leastwise not to me."

"So," Ambrose muttered, more to himself than the others. "Slocum has both Jeter's horse and his watch." Louder, he called to Amy, "Make a note to speak to Mr. Slocum about those items, will you, Miss Gerardo?"

"Yes, sir," Amy said. She started to jump down, but Billy was too attentive for her. His strong hands went around her waist and lifted, and then set her down as gentle as the caress of a butterfly wing across her cheek.

"I'll want to speak further once you get to San Esteban, Mrs. Jeter," Ambrose said. Amy didn't hear what Ruth Jeter said, but Ambrose laughed.

Amy wasted no time climbing into the driver's box. She waited impatiently for Ambrose to join her.

"What a treasure trove," Ambrose gloated. "Jeter's hat and pistol."

"Did you tell her you had her husband's body in the wagon?" Amy asked pointedly.

"Of course not. What would have been the purpose? It would have upset her unduly, and she might have forgotten all those delicious details that flowed so easily otherwise."

"Like John Slocum having both the horse and watch?"

"Yes, yes, that. I must see to buying them off Slocum before he disappears. I'm surprised he has stayed in the area this long. Drifters tend to . . . drift."

Amy rode in silence, her thoughts boiling like a stew. She wished she had never come—and that Ambrose had never met Ruth Jeter.

25

Slocum cursed his bad luck as he got behind the buckboard and pushed while the team pulled. He thought he had found a shortcut back to Ruth's cabin, but had only gotten himself mired down in loose sand. With a lurch, the wagon pulled free and began rolling along sweet as you please. Scrambling to get into the wagon proved a chore since the frustrated horses he had rented from the livery were determined to move as fast as possible. They had struggled in the soft arroyo bottom, and now wanted to stretch their logs.

Two quick steps and a jump got him back into the driver's box. He grabbed the reins and steered the horses up and out of the offending dry river bottom. The stallion trotted along behind, its long tether keeping it close, but not so near that it got tangled up.

"You should have stopped me," Slocum said to the stallion. "You know this country better than me." He found his way back into the broad, green valley where the cabin sat, and wished he hadn't been so much in a hurry that he'd risked the rockier shortcut back from San Esteban. As it was, he had wasted a full day. He hoped Ruth hadn't written him off as forgetting about her.

As he rode, he thought about the woman and the times he had been with her. There was an unmistakable attraction between them, but Slocum wondered if it existed only because of the woman's circumstances. Being married to a man like Les Jeter would make any woman lonely and desperate. For his part, he was drawn to her, but couldn't put a finger on exactly what it was that drew him back like a moth to a flame. He was horny from being on the trail so long, but the times he had been with Ruth went beyond mere physical need. That bothered him a mite, but not too much. He doubted she felt any attraction for him other than as her rescuer.

Being stranded in the middle of the Davis Mountains had to wear on her until even a drifter would appear exciting.

"Finally," Slocum muttered as he swung around a bend in the canyon, found the road up the middle of the valley, and drove to the cabin. It was a mere spot on the landscape when he sighted it, and it grew too slowly, taking most of the rest of the day to get close enough to make out details. Slocum felt a pang taking Ruth away from such a place. The farm would be perfect for raising horses. The pastures were too small for more than a hundred head of cattle, but horses were more valuable and had to be in demand up at Fort Davis and Fort Quitman up north. The Army alone would keep a man rolling in money.

Or a woman.

Slocum couldn't forget this was Ruth's only legacy from her thief of a husband. Since women couldn't own real property, she had to sell and move on, or find someone to buy the place and keep it in his name just so she could stay. He knew Ruth had no real connection to the place and its memories.

As he slowed and pulled the buckboard around, it came to him that Jeter might not have even owned this place. The stories he had heard in San Esteban hinted at the outlaw murdering the actual owners and simply becoming a squatter—but a squatter enforcing his claim with a quick pistol and a vicious liking for murder.

He had barely halted the team when Ruth came running out. The smile she gave him was genuine, sincere, and not a little disturbing.

"John!" She hurried down to the wagon and grabbed his hand. "You're back. I was beginning to think you weren't coming."

"I took longer than I should have," Slocum said. He didn't bother her with stories of how he had chosen a shortcut that turned out to take longer than if he had simply retraced his path. "You ready to go?"

"Of course I am," she said. The brunette smiled almost shyly, then got a devilish look in her eyes. "If you hadn't come soon, I'd have thought I'd made a mistake not going with that nice gentleman who showed up right after you left."

"Who'd that be?" Slocum asked, but thought he knew.

"He said his name was Killian. Ambrose Killian."

"Doesn't surprise me."

"Would it surprise you to know he paid me fifty dollars for Les's hat and gun? Fifty dollars! Imagine that!"

"Nope," Slocum said. "The man's got something loose in his head." He wondered if he should tell Ruth about the collector's single-minded need to gather about him anything Jeter had touched or owned. It wouldn't serve any purpose, he decided, so he pushed it aside. "You have what you're taking?"

"It's only a few bags," Ruth said. "I never owned much, and what I have is mostly clothing and a few other items."

"And fifty dollars Killian paid you," Slocum said. "That's good. You'll need some money."

"I've almost forgotten what it's like to need money," Ruth said. "Les brought me everything. It's been years since I actually held a greenback or even a coin."

"That'll change," Slocum said.

"Why do you say that?" Ruth looked at him sharply.

"No matter where you go, if there are two people together, money's what they want. They'll talk about money they had, money they have, or money they'll get somehow."

"How sad," Ruth said. "There are more important things in life."

"Might be," Slocum allowed. "Money was never enough for a man to buy his life if your husband pointed a six-gun in his direction." Slocum wasn't sure why he said that, but it caused Ruth to turn pale.

"I'll get my things."

"Let me help," he said, climbing down. He had to take a few seconds to stretch. He hadn't realized he had been driving for so long. His shoulders ached from using the reins on the balky team even more than his back hurt from pushing the wagon out of the sandy river bottom. By the time he had climbed the steps to the porch, Ruth had already picked up everything.

"This is all," she said. "This one's got my clothes and the other's packed with . . . odds and ends."

"I can get them," he said. Slocum took both bags. The one with the clothing was light. The other made him sag a little under its unexpected weight. He threw both into the rear of the wagon and looked around. "What else?"

"I wish I could take the goats and maybe some of the tools in the barn. But that's all."

"You can sell the tools in San Esteban," Slocum said. He walked downhill to the barn, Ruth following. He hesitated just inside the door, staring at the pile of hay where he and Ruth had made love the first time. Glancing back, he saw her staring at the same place. He doubted the same thoughts were going through her mind as raced across his.

He dropped ropes around the necks of the goats and led them out, tying the ends to the rear of the wagon. Carrying the carpentry tools and steel farming implements took the better part of the afternoon, and they eventually filled the wagon. He reflected on how much easier it would have been to bring back a couple of pack mules, but then Ruth would have had to ride out. As it was, she already sat patiently, hands folded in her lap, in the wagon.

A smile came to his lips. Riding all the way back to town with her leg pressed up alongside his wasn't such a bad way to travel.

But all the way to San Esteban she hardly said a dozen words.

"Here," Slocum said, handing Ruth a sheaf of greenbacks. "The smithy bought all the tools."

"There must be a hundred dollars." She looked up at Slocum, her brown eyes soft and moist. "You keep it. You did all the work."

"I don't want it. You'll need it. Don't let anyone rook you out of it," Slocum said, pressing the wad of greenbacks into her hand. "I've got you booked into the hotel for the night. You can decide what you want to do tomorrow."

"The stage," she said distantly, her eyes drifting to the depot.

"I'll talk to the old geezer who's the agent. His name's Sanford. He'll see that you get on the right stagecoach. Which way are you going?"

"Where are you heading, John?"

"North. To El Paso."

"That's as good a direction as any for me to go then. I don't have any family left in San Antonio." She started to say something more, but Slocum couldn't tell what it might be. "You've been so good to me. I don't know how to thank you."

"No need to thank me. I've got pretty much what I came into San Esteban with. That's as much as I can expect."

"There ought to be a reward. You said that Mr. Killian had offered one for . . . for Les."

"If there's a reward, you claim it. I don't want it."

There was an awkward silence between them. Then Ruth started to speak, but was stopped when Killian's voice boomed out.

"Mrs. Jeter! There you are. You promised me all the details of your husband's life." Killian edged between them, then turned slightly to half-face Slocum. "And Mr. Slocum, I presume? Also a happy coincidence. I understand you are riding Jeter's horse."

"That's right."

"It *was* his horse," Ruth cut in. "He was given to Mr. Slocum to replace the one Les killed. And I don't want it.

I don't want to ever see that horse again. I dreaded watching Les ride up on it and—"

"Ruth," Slocum said, quieting her.

"I'm sorry," Ruth said, tears running down her cheeks. "It's all so confused. I don't know what to do."

"Don't bother with her, Slocum," Killian said, pushing between them. "I'll pay fair price for the horse. Fifty dollars."

"That's what you gave her for Jeter's hat and gun," Slocum said.

"One hundred."

"Why do you want the stallion? Don't you know that it's a hanging horse? Jeter flopped off its back. That's the horse the marshal used to hang Jeter." Slocum took a step back when he saw the expression on Killian's face. The man combined utter evil with total avarice in a way Slocum had never before seen.

"Two hundred dollars. That's enough for you to buy a team of horses. And I'll give you another fifty for the watch."

Slocum might have taken Killian's money for the horse. He appreciated the stallion's heart and endurance. Without those traits Jeter would have been caught long since. With two hundred dollars Slocum could live well for the next year, but when Killian added that he wanted the watch too, Slocum dug in his heels.

"What do you want with my watch?"

"It was Jeter's. I want to collect the items that were most precious to him."

"He stole the watch from me. It was never his," Slocum said. "And it's not for sale. At any price."

"A thousand dollars."

Slocum stared at the man as if he were insane. There was a crazy light in Killian's eyes, but it wasn't the kind of kill-crazy that made Slocum reach for his six-shooter. It was something else, something more, something worse.

"It's not for sale at any price."

"You can't pass up that much money. It's only a watch!"

"Yeah, only a watch," Slocum said. He remembered his brother's delight when he had received the watch for his sixteenth birthday. He remembered how Robert had gone around letting everyone see what time it was, then making a big show of closing the gold case and thrusting it back into his watch pocket. That watch had been with him when he had ridden behind a foolish general, George Edward Pickett. Too many good men, Robert included, had died in Pickett's Charge. Slocum wished it had been Pickett and not his brother who had been hit by a Yankee minié ball.

Sell the watch? Slocum would show it to the devil himself when he finally was called from this life, just to let him know what time it was.

"You can't—" Killian bit off the rest of his protest when he saw that Slocum damned well *would*. He turned and spoke quietly to Ruth, who was still sniffling. She nodded and turned away. Killian followed her closely, his arm around her quaking shoulders.

Slocum started to call after Ruth, then decided not to. She had been distant since they left the farm. He couldn't blame her. For a woman who had been hidden away as she had, coming to even a town as small as San Esteban was a shock. Having her husband hanged and colliding with a man like Killian added to her disorientation. From the way Ruth had acted, she wanted nothing more to do with Slocum, and that sat well with him.

Or at least he could lie to himself and make believe that it didn't matter.

He headed for the hotel, intent on getting his gear and clearing out of San Esteban. There wasn't anything to hold him here, and he wouldn't have even stopped if the stage hadn't been robbed.

Just inside the doors Killian's assistant stood, eyes wide. She looked as if she wanted to speak to him, but didn't know what to say. From the way she had interrogated him before about Jeter and what he knew of the outlaw, this came as a surprise to Slocum.

"Miss Gerardo," he said, touching the brim of his hat. She seemed to melt with relief that he had spoken to her. Two quick, small steps brought the petite blonde to his side. She reached out and laid her hand on his arm. For all her hesitation, the way she gripped him was firm and bold.

"I need to speak to you, Mr. Slocum." She glanced over at the clerk. The man sat on a stool, artfully carving away at a small piece of wood. From what Slocum could tell, the man was whittling a dog out of the pine.

"Don't see why not," Slocum answered.

"May I call you John? This so . . . so private. Can we talk in your room, John?"

"I was about to leave town," he said.

"Then my room."

This took him aback. Such an invitation was far bolder than he expected. He dismissed the notion that it was anything more than business. He remembered how Amy had interviewed him before. It had been all business with no hint of personal involvement.

"What do you want?"

"Always straight to the point. That's what I like about you, John. One of the things." Amy batted her eyelashes a little and looked away. He swore he saw color rising in her cheeks. From his foot difference in height he was also able to look down on the creamy, sloping upper skin on her breasts. The way her flesh appeared from this angle, she must have compressed a powerful lot of titflesh into that dress.

Slocum paid his bill, turned, and couldn't find Amy. Then he looked up the stairs—and up her skirt. She was on the top step, bending over to pick up something she had dropped. He got a clear view of her bare legs, her curvy behind, and . . . more. She wasn't wearing any underwear.

She straightened and her skirt dropped to a more chaste level. Amy smiled at him and beckoned, then put her finger to her lips cautioning him to be quiet. Slocum was intrigued, and took the steps to the second floor quickly. Amy was already standing in the open doorway of a room toward the rear of the hotel. As he approached, she ducked into the room.

Slocum went to the door with no intention of entering. He found himself frozen in place and staring hard. Amy had already kicked free of her skirt and was naked from the waist down.

"Do come in and close the door. I need help getting out of this corset."

"You surely didn't need help getting out of the rest of your clothes," Slocum said. He couldn't take his eyes off the furry golden nest between her thighs. She was short, compact, and looked more muscular than he expected. There was certainly nothing to hide any of her leg muscles or those in her thighs and belly. As he stared, she turned and presented her bare rump toward him.

"You don't have to take off my corset if you don't want to, John."

"Why are you doing this?" Slocum knew he ought to light out and run. Any time a woman came on this strong with no reason, it was a harbinger of bad things to come.

He still felt himself responding powerfully, his manhood pressing painfully against his buttoned fly. Prudence said he ought to leave. Lust told him to stay.

Slocum reached out and put his hands on the woman's hips. Her skin was hot and yielding, and suddenly his flesh became even less yielding. She backed up and began rubbing her naked ass against his crotch. Slocum reached around her and stroked over smooth skin. Her corseted torso intrigued him. His hands drifted upward to cup her hidden breasts. He felt the way her heart hammered with desire, even through the layers of cloth. Squeezing down on those tempting mounds of flesh brought a tiny sob of joy to Amy's lips.

"Go on, John, please. I'm ready for you. I was ready the first time I laid eyes on you."

"Not what *I* want to lay," Slocum muttered. He reluctantly moved his hands off those quivering mounds to drop his gun belt and unfasten his fly. He found it was harder to do than he expected because of the way Amy kept backing into him, the sleek curves of her butt pressing into the circle of his groin. When he finally popped out, long and hot and hard, she reached between her legs and grabbed his balls.

He almost lost control then and there.

Her fingers stroked and dandled and then moved to the

thickness jutting outward. She tugged and pulled and then took a half step back toward him.

"In," she said urgently. "I want you inside me where I can feel you moving. I want your heat to burn me up!"

Slocum bent slightly at the waist and wiggled until he felt the tip of his meaty stalk nudge between her nether lips. Then he straightened, hips moving forward in a smooth motion that caused him to sink balls-deep into her seething interior. He gasped at the tightness. She was a small girl in many ways. The moistness all around him turned liquid as her passions grew.

He began stroking in and out, finding a rhythm that suited them both. Slocum quickly discovered that he couldn't move fast enough or drive forward hard enough to suit Amy. Clinging to her waist, he lifted her up on her toes. She let out a yelp of surprise and twisted about. Her hands left the dresser she had been braced against. With another powerful movement, he turned her half around, all the while remaining deeply hidden within her clutching interior.

Amy found she'd lost her support, and bent all the way over to put her hands on the floor. This bent her double and tightened her sex even more around Slocum. This time when he began to stroke, the friction burned all around him and then began working its way down his length. His balls churned and came to a boil. Then lightning blasted into his loins.

Hands on her hips, he pulled her back into his groin with powerful movements. Doubled over as she was, Amy got more than she had bargained for. She tried to tell him to stop. He heard the words beginning. They were smothered by her gasp and then her loud cry of total release.

He kept thrusting even after the convulsive pressure all around him slackened. It took a few minutes, but the tightness returned and Amy was once more gasping and crying out. When Slocum could no longer restrain himself, he jammed himself forward and was taken fully. He felt as if he were trapped in a collapsing mine shaft. He was crushed and heated and then he exploded.

Only when he began to turn limp did he move away from her. Amy remained bent over for a moment, as if expecting more. Then she sank down to her knees, her perky rear end still up in the air.

She turned and looked up at him.

"I never felt that way before. With any man, John."

"Not even Killian?"

Her expression changed instantly. He had touched on a sore spot.

"We are business associates, nothing more."

The way she said it told him that Amy wished it were more.

"Why?"

"Why are we only associates? That's the way we want it."

"Why did you come on to me like this?" Slocum buttoned up his fly and grabbed his gun belt. He sat on the bed. She made no move to cover up her nakedness as she swung around to sit crossed-legged on the floor. In this position she was even more lewdly splayed than before. And she obviously knew the effect she had on him sitting this way.

"I'm not saying it wasn't nice, just that it was unexpected," Slocum said, watching her more closely now for any hint about her behavior. He had an idea why she had given herself to him so readily, but hoped he was wrong.

"He . . . he wants me to get the watch from you."

Slocum stood and was at the door when she called out, "Wait, John. I couldn't do it. I could have stolen it. I could have, but I won't. I wouldn't do that to you!"

"Because I'm such a good screw?"

"Yes, no, oh, I can't get it all straight. It's not right. If you don't want to sell the watch to Ambrose, there's no reason for me to steal it for him. There. I've said it."

"Would you have tried to steal the horse too?"

"I'm sure Ambrose has some plan to get the horse. He is so completely wrapped up in getting every artifact Jeter ever owned or touched that he'll do anything."

"Artifact?"

"Jeter's possessions. His gear. His gun. His hat. The watch. And the horse. Ambrose really wants the horse since it was the one Jeter was astride when he was hanged."

Slocum felt nothing but contempt for Ambrose Killian. He wasn't sure what he felt for Amy.

"You better come up with a good story to explain why you didn't get the watch. I don't think Killian will be all that pleased with you."

"Oh, he won't do anything to me." There was a bitterness that Slocum guessed had to do with the woman's frustrated need to please her employer with word and deed—especially in bed.

"Thanks," Slocum said. "This was a nice going-away present." He hesitated, then said, "I'm on my way to Fort Griffin. Don't reckon I'll be seeing you again."

"John, don't go. Let me—"

Slocum closed the door behind him and hurried down the back stairs. The sooner he left Amy and Killian and the memory of Jeter—and Ruth Jeter—behind him, the happier he would be.

26

Ambrose Killian felt completely alive seated across from Ruth Jeter in the restaurant. Feeding her was only part of his scheme to learn more about her. While the woman lacked classical beauty, there was something more about her that fascinated him. She had belonged to Lester Jeter.

"I would like to talk at length about your former husband," Killian said. "I have a large home some distance from here. There are guest rooms. Any number of those would be more than satisfactory for you, after living in a one-room hovel for so long."

"I don't think so, Mr. Killian. I just want to get on with my life and forget about Les. As much as I can."

"Forget? Never! You must remember! I must know every detail. You can fill in gaps in my understanding of him. Your unlamented late husband was a veritable fount of contradictions. I want to examine them and eventually reveal them to the world. Everyone will want to know what turned him into the foremost road agent in West Texas. Perhaps nowhere else in Texas has ever seen his like."

"No, thank you," Ruth said more firmly.

"Oh, come now," he wheedled. "Fine food. I have the best-stocked wine cellar this side of the Mississippi. I can assign you a personal servant. You'll live like royalty, and all in exchange for a few hours a day reminiscing. If anything, talking about your husband will help drive away the bad and leave only the good."

"The offer is very kind, but I don't want to even think about Les right now. He was hung by the law, Mr. Killian. That's nothing I can brag about."

"I don't want bragging, I want truth. I want to know the warts along with the finer points. There must have been something that drew you to him, for you to marry him!"

"I was very young," Ruth said, turning more distant. "My family was gone—cholera—and there was nowhere else to turn."

"See? I didn't know that. How did he woo you? What other blandishments did he use?"

Ruth folded her arms across her chest and leaned away. Killian rattled on, oblivious to her lack of interest in his offer.

Killian turned when he heard the door of the restaurant creaking open to admit a gust of hot desert air. He held back an exclamation of disgust. His assistant should know better than to intrude in the middle of what was turning into an exceptionally fruitful interview.

"Ambrose, Ambrose," Amy Gerardo blurted out when she saw him. She made no effort to even acknowledge Ruth Jeter's presence. "I couldn't get the watch, but I found out something that will—"

"Miss Gerardo, please. Can't you see I am otherwise

engaged? We can talk later." Killian wished she had not mentioned the watch. The horse could be had by subterfuge, but if Slocum left with the watch, getting it would be difficult.

"He's leaving, Ambrose. He's leaving *now*."

"Mr. Slocum?" Ruth perked up.

"He's going to Fort Griffin."

"Not any time soon," Killian said. "He will discover that his horse—the one Jeter was hanged astride—will throw a shoe very soon. The stableman was most cooperative loosening the shoe and pulling out a nail."

"You can't do that," protested Ruth. "The horse could come up lame, stranding John in the middle of—"

"Where did you say he was headed?" Killian demanded of Amy. He eyed her closely.

"Fort Griffin. He said he—"

"Mrs. Jeter already told me he intended to ride north to El Paso."

"He told me El Paso," Ruth said, confused. "I might have misheard him. There's been so much going on."

"He lied to you," Killian said to his assistant.

"But I let him—" Amy clapped a hand over her mouth. Ruth's eyes went wide with shock and understanding. "I had to get the watch for you, Ambrose. There wasn't any other way."

"You failed. And you failed a second time allowing him to lie to you. You are fired, Miss Gerardo. Your services are no longer required."

"Ambrose! What're you saying? You can't do this. I love you! You love me!"

"Miss Gerardo, this is unseemly! Please leave. Immediately."

Killian pushed his chair away from the table.

"You don't have to throw me out," Amy said, backing away. "But you would, wouldn't you? You'd throw me out in the street, discard me like a piece of used notepaper. That's all I am to you. Something to be gotten rid of at your whim."

"You were my employee, Miss Gerardo, nothing more."

Killian hated the sight of the tears flowing unabashedly down the woman's cheeks. However had she come to the faulty conclusion that he loved her? He had never given her an instant's thought, much less thought of her in that way.

Without another word, Amy turned and left.

"I should go too," Ruth said, pushing away from the table. "Thank you for the fine meal."

"Don't go, Mrs. Jeter. Please, Ruth, there is so much I need to know."

"Perhaps later, when I am better able to talk of some things, I'll contact you."

"No," Killian said, laying the small derringer on the table. "There won't be any need for you to find me later. You're going with me now." Killian felt a small surge of desire for the woman when she sat down, frightened and looking smaller than before. This was the woman Jeter had taken as a wife. Killian would find out why, and what qualities Jeter had valued in her company as his wife.

"You're going to kill me," Ruth said in a flat voice. "All the years I was married to a cold-blooded killer, I never felt in danger. Not for my life."

"He held you captive. He was away, robbing stagecoaches and banks most of the time. How could you fear him while he was gone?"

"You'll never know," Ruth said, defiance coming into

her voice. She glared at him. "You can keep me prisoner for a million years and you won't learn one more thing."

"A million years is a long time," Killian agreed, beginning to enjoy their byplay again. "I think you will tell me all I want to know in a much shorter time. And I assure you, your prison this time will be gilded. Only the finest food, decent surroundings—"

"It'll still be a prison."

Killian looked out the window of the restaurant and saw Slocum riding slowly down the street, heading east out of town. His chance to get the watch would disappear with the drifter unless he acted quickly.

"Come along. I have no way to keep you from running off other than to threaten you. Believe me, Mrs. Jeter, I have no desire to hurt you. Quite the contrary. I find you an interesting, exciting woman."

"Exciting? Because I was married to a man you are totally obsessed with?"

"The matter is too complex to explain in a few short minutes. We will have all the time in the world to explore this," Killian said. He gestured with the small pistol.

"You won't kill me. You want what I can tell you."

Ruth gasped when he grabbed her arm and swung her about as she got out of the chair. He rammed the derringer hard into her ribs.

"I can seriously injure you. Bullets to your legs so you can't walk. A blow to your throat so you can't talk until it heals. I have time. You don't."

He steered her out the door into the hot, dusty street. Slocum had disappeared, taking the road leading to the northeast. Killian wondered whether the drifter had lied to Ruth or to Amy. From what he had seen, Slocum had lied to Amy, and she had been too foolish to know.

"Get into the buckboard," he said, clinging to Ruth's arm. She struggled a little, but not so much that he couldn't control her. "We've got to follow Mr. Slocum and relieve him of both the horse and your husband's watch."

"I might have been wrong. It must have been John's watch that Les stole."

"It was something Jeter held and carried and possessed. I must possess it too."

"Everything Les had you want?" Ruth swallowed hard. He enjoyed the look of desolation on her plain face.

"Everything," he told her. "Absolutely everything. I'm willing to wait. I am a patient man."

"A million years won't be enough."

He shoved her forward, then herded her up into the driver's box. Killian quickly followed, making sure she sat on his left side so he could put the derringer into his right coat pocket where it was readily accessible but far from her grasping hands. He was sure she would attempt to escape somehow. The gun would provide the speediest way of getting away, and he intended to deny her that route because it was more interesting to see where her ingenuity took her.

If it took her anywhere at all. Had the years with Jeter numbed her will? Killian intended to find out.

"You've got a coffin in the rear," Ruth said. "I-is it Les?"

"Of course it is. I had planned a spectacular trial and even more eventful burial ceremony. Pictures would have been taken. I was robbed of the trial, and somehow the town isn't too inclined to turn out to bury a man left dangling from an oak tree by a lynch mob. No matter that Jeter was the premier outlaw of this decade."

"You're crazy as a hoot owl," Ruth said.

Killian laughed as he snapped the reins and got the team pulling. He had paid the stableman more than enough to loosen the shoe on Jeter's stallion. How long it took before Slocum discovered that his horse was unable to continue on his futile flight away from his destiny remained to be seen, but Killian had supplies for a week or longer tucked alongside the coffin.

They rattled over the desert and took the road that led out of town past the cemetery. Killian commented on it.

"Bury Les," said Ruth. "He was no good, but he deserves to be buried. Bury him and leave John alone."

"Leave your paramour alone? The two of you were quite the item, weren't you? Behind your husband's back? Or did he care? I must find out all these little tidbits." Killian laughed and urged the team to greater speed because he had seen not only the signpost pointing to the small San Esteban cemetery, but also a man examining the right front hoof of his horse.

"John!" Ruth stood and yelled. "John!"

Killian grabbed her and savagely pulled her back down beside him.

"Warn him and I'll kill him. You wouldn't want that, would you?"

"You don't have the balls to kill a man."

Killian chuckled. The sound quieted Ruth. But Killian started thinking about what she had said. He wasn't a murderer. That would make him no better than Lester Jeter. He was a collector, a connoisseur, a man devoted to completions and discoveries.

"Having trouble, Mr. Slocum?" he called. Killian saw how Slocum's hand went for the six-shooter holstered at his left hip. Only men used to drawing and firing while on horseback slung their pistols in this fashion. The cavalry officers carried theirs awkwardly, with butts forward on their right hips. The cross-draw holster was a superior solution. He had to ask Ruth why her husband had not also worn a cross-draw holster.

"Got a loose shoe," Slocum said.

"You should have checked before you set out on the trail for El Paso," Killian said. He halted his wagon beside Slocum and reached into the bed.

Slocum looked at him sharply.

"How'd you know I was heading to El Paso?"

"Mrs. Jeter told me."

"John, I—"

Slocum turned toward her and gave Killian the chance he needed. He gripped the work-slickened handle of the shovel he had bought in town from the undertaker and swung it around and down as hard as he could. The flat metal blade struck Slocum squarely on the top of the head. He collapsed without uttering a sound.

"John!" Ruth jumped to the ground and knelt beside him. "I didn't know. I had no idea what he intended to do."

"Hush, my dear," Killian said jovially. "If you don't want your Mr. Slocum roughed up, you can drag him to the rear of the wagon for me."

Killian went around and began prying open the coffin. The lid popped up to let him stare at the decaying body of the outlaw. He smiled. He knew exactly what to do. Grunting, Killian twisted the coffin and got it onto its side so that Jeter's body tumbled out into the back of the wagon. Then he turned the coffin back upright.

"Get him sitting up," Killian said. She struggled with Slocum and did as ordered. Together the two of them got the limp Slocum up and into the coffin.

"Wh-what are you going to do?" Ruth stared at her husband's body. "Les was already in his coffin."

"My coffin," Killian corrected. "I bought it for him. I've decided it would make a better prison for Slocum, so he won't try to stop me. Get into the wagon."

"Where are you going?"

"A ways," Killian said. "A very short distance and then you won't have to worry about Mr. Slocum anymore."

Ruth reluctantly obeyed. Killian got the wagon moving down the road to the cemetery. A grin split his face when he saw the fresh grave site that O'Dell had opened for Jeter. A different occupant would be spending eternity under a few feet of dirt.

"Help me get the coffin down," he told Ruth. She looked at the grave and then at Killian. She shook her head.

"You're a monster. I won't do it!"

He took one step forward and swung from the shoulder. The impact of his fist with her chin jarred all the way along his arm, but the punch had the desired effect. Ruth caught the blow on the tip of her chin and went down in a heap, knocked out. Killian strained as he slid the heavily laden coffin to the edge of the wagon bed, then let it fall. The lid popped open again, showing Slocum inside.

"I'll wager you never thought you'd be buried in such style," Killian said, fishing around in Slocum's pockets until he found the watch. Killian pulled it away and slipped it into his own pocket. He slammed the coffin lid, wishing he had nails to secure it. Dragging the coffin to the edge of the grave proved easier than he had thought due to the dry ground. He pushed the coffin in, righted it, and then made certain the lid was closed before beginning his shoveling. Shovelful after shovelful of dirt descended to the top of the coffin until it disappeared. Working in the hot sun caused Killian to expend more effort than he wanted, but he still hummed an off-key tune to himself.

Eventually he had mostly filled the grave. Killian peeled his sweat-soaked clothes away from his body and wiped his forehead.

"That's good enough," Killian said, tossing the shovel into the grave. "I hope you appreciate all I've done for you, Slocum. I'll be certain you are given your due in my book."

Killian wiped off his hands and went to the rear of the wagon, where Jeter's body was exposed to the burning sun.

"Should I mummify you or just find a decent taxidermist? You'd be the premier item in my display either way. Who cares about guns and hats when I have the original?" Killian laughed as he wrapped a canvas cover around the outlaw's corpse. A pedestal holding the stuffed and mounted outlaw would be perfect! He knew the precise manner of presentation for it too, with Jeter's hat on his head and a hand resting on his six-shooter. It would be a museum piece that would draw scholars from around the world!

He finished wrapping the corpse, then checked to be certain Ruth was still breathing. She would make the ideal tour guide. Killian would turn his entire house into a museum, and she would be another beguiling attraction to amaze and amuse the scholars studying Jeter's criminal career.

Killian snapped the reins and got his team pulling. He could hardly wait to return home, find out all the details of Jeter's life from Ruth for his biography, and then begin to work on the display. There would be nothing to rival Ambrose Killian's Museum of the Life and Times of Lester Evan Jeter, Texas Outlaw!

27

"San Esteban," Slocum whispered. "I was on the stagecoach from San Antonio and . . ." The top of his head sent knives of pain into him every time he moved, but he kept moving, even banging the sides of the coffin. The pain helped him focus until a name formed on his lips and tasted like acid.

"Killian! You son of a bitch. You put me in a coffin."

Slocum went crazy again thrashing around, banging hard, and then settled down when the air began to turn stuffy. He was killing himself inch by inch. Slocum settled down, aware that the pain in his head refused to die down.

He listened hard and heard nothing. Rolling onto his belly, he arched up and tried to force the coffin lid away. He couldn't budge it at all. He flopped facedown, gasping with effort. Sweat stung his eyes, and he felt more than a little rising panic again.

"You will get out of this," Slocum said so loudly that it echoed inside the coffin. "You will." But he had the sinking feeling that he was lying to himself. So much dirt had been piled on top of the coffin lid that he couldn't budge it the smallest fraction.

He lay still, mind racing. The only improvement came in the way his head didn't hurt quite as much. Slocum felt his lungs beginning to burn, but he could ignore that. For a while. The darkness wore on him, but he never stopped trying to come up with a way to escape. Some cemeteries ran a pull cord down into the coffin, so if the interred was actually alive he could ring a bell aboveground. But Slocum knew nothing of the sort had been done for him—for Jeter. That thought began gnawing away at him. He wasn't even in a properly marked grave. Everyone would think Les Jeter had been laid to rest here, not John Slocum. He wasn't sure why that bothered him, but it did.

He had lived through the war and more gunfights and scrapes than he could remember, and he was going to die in another man's coffin.

Despair washed over him, making him consider wrestling his six-shooter from its holster and using it on himself. He worked to get his hand up to the six-gun and curled his fingers around the butt, then stopped.

Something was different. It took him a few seconds to realize what it was. The same sound of dirt falling was being repeated above him—but he could never hear a spadeful of dirt falling atop six feet of dirt. Someone was digging him out!

"Here! I'm still alive. Down here!" He shouted until he was hoarse, and the air turned so foul he could only choke and cough.

Then he was choking and coughing for a different reason. The coffin lid was yanked open and sand cascaded down over him.

"John! Are you dead?"

He pushed up like a stretching cat, the dirt cascading off his back in a small dust storm. Slocum shook himself off and then cocked his six-shooter as he turned.

"Amy?" Of all the people he had expected to dig him out of his grave, Amy Gerardo was about the most unlikely.

"John, I'm so glad you're not dead. I saw Ambrose burying you, but I couldn't do anything about that. He took my pistol. I don't know when, but he did and I couldn't stop him and—"

"Hush up," Slocum said. He slid his six-gun back into his holster and stood, shook again, and got more dirt off him, but what thrilled him was the harsh, dry, heated desert air. It filled his lungs and sent life roaring through his arteries again.

"I'm sorry, John. I'm just so glad I got to you in time." She looked at her blistered, bleeding hands. "I never knew it was such hard work digging up a grave."

"Get used to it," Slocum said harshly, climbing out of the hole. "You're going to need to dig one for Killian."

"Please, John, he didn't mean anything by this. It's just that he's so wrapped up in getting everything Jeter ever owned that he's lost all his common sense."

Slocum pressed his hand against his vest pocket. He was right. Killian had taken the watch.

"Where'd he go with her?"

"Her? He's got Ruth Jeter with him?"

Slocum saw the shock on the small woman's face.

"When they rode up in his wagon, she rode beside him. She wasn't with him willingly. Where are they headed?"

"His house. Where else?" Amy turned in a full circle as if she might see Killian with her own eyes. "He still has the body with him."

"Jeter's?"

"Who else? This is Jeter's coffin. He was in it coming out from town, but I saw him burying you and—"

"You didn't see Ruth Jeter?"

"No. Maybe she's not with him," Amy said hopefully.

Slocum knew better. Ruth had probably tried to stop Killian from burying him, and had been tied up and put into the back of the wagon—alongside her dead husband.

"Will your horse get me to wherever Killian went?" Slocum saw that the mare pulling Amy's carriage was already lathered.

"You're not going to leave me behind, John," Amy said hotly. "I saved you. You owe me this. And I know where the house is."

"I can find it."

"Together," she insisted. "We can get there faster, even with a tired horse, than you can get there hunting for it."

"You drive," Slocum said, climbing into the carriage. He wanted to sit and feel the sun against his face and stretch his muscles after his ordeal.

And he wanted to think about how he would dispatch Ambrose Killian.

"Stay here," Slocum said when they drove within view of the sprawling Spanish-style hacienda.

"No, John, you know I'm the only one who can talk to him. I can make him see how wrong he's been."

Slocum had spent the last few days chaffing at the delay, but Amy's horse worked as hard as it could. If they had pushed any harder they would have killed the mare. But those extra days had given Slocum the time to think of all the myriad ways to make Killian suffer. Added to this was what the man must be doing to Ruth Jeter.

"Stay here," Slocum said. "He's dangerous, and you said you two didn't part on good terms."

"He wanted her," Amy said, her face suddenly hard and her words cold. "After all I've done for him, he wanted her only because Jeter had possessed her."

Slocum jumped down from the carriage and drew his six-shooter. The exterior of the house was high-walled adobe brick enclosing an inner courtyard. The rooms were sandwiched in a square between the courtyard and the outer wall. The main entry was closed by a heavy wood door that might withstand a battering ram, but he knew there had to be other ways in. If he had to, he could drive the carriage up and scale the wall.

"The back way," Amy said, sagging under the necessity of telling Slocum everything. "There's a door leading to the kitchen that's not as heavily barred."

"Thanks," he said, reaching out and putting his hand over hers. She didn't react. All she did was stare at the hacienda as if she could see inside.

Slocum had to admit Amy most likely could penetrate the adobe with her gaze. Killian had become far too predictable in his madness, allowing Amy to know his every movement.

Slocum ran around to the rear of the house. The door was exactly where she had said. He approached cautiously, pressed his ear against the wood panel, and heard nothing. Slocum tried the latch, but it was secured. He doubted he could kick in the door, but a little finesse might work better. Taking a splinter from the door, he poked it through the latch hole and began fiddling. It seemed to take forever, but Slocum finally lifted the locking bar and opened the door. It swung inward on silent hinges.

A quick look around the kitchen showed that no one had prepared any food in the past few days. He began exploring, and found the museum with all the trinkets of Jeter's life carefully displayed. Standing on a pedestal in the middle of the room was a mummified corpse. Slocum held down his gorge.

"Jeter," he muttered. "Whatever you deserved, I don't think this was it."

He spun, Peacemaker leveled and ready. Slocum's finger relaxed on the trigger.

"You could have gotten yourself killed," he said to Amy. "I told you to wait outside."

"He's made Jeter into a statue, an object. He can't do this—"

Slocum swung away from Amy and faced the other door leading into this grisly museum in time to see Killian. The man ducked back as Slocum fired.

"Stay here," Slocum barked to Amy as he lit out after Killian, but the man had disappeared. He might have gone into the courtyard or the adjoining room. If Killian got a gun, Slocum knew he would be in for a shoot-out that might end badly for him. Killian knew every nook and cranny and could turn that knowledge to his advantage unless Slocum got to him before he could make a decent plan.

Slocum had started into the courtyard when he heard a muffled cry from the next room. Slocum hesitated, then went to the door leading into the room.

"Help!" More muffled noises put Slocum on guard. He peeked fast into the room and ducked back. Then he went into the room and hurried to Ruth Jeter. She was bound and tied to a bed. The woman had worked the gag partially from her mouth, but still couldn't speak clearly. Slocum swept it away.

"Oh, John, he's a monster!"

"Where is he?" Slocum worked furiously on the woman's rope and got her free.

"He has an arsenal on the other side of the house. He'll go for it."

Slocum jumped when a single shot echoed through the house.

"Stay here," he said, but this wasn't his day for getting women to obey him. Ruth pressed close. He didn't have time to do anything about it, and rushed into the courtyard and followed the smell of gun smoke to a room where the door stood open.

"Amy?" he called. "Are you all right?"

Slocum moved closer and saw Killian's body sprawled on the floor. Amy Gerardo stood over him, smoke still curling from the barrel of Les Jeter's six-shooter taken from the museum room.

"I'll take care of you now, Ambrose. Like I always have, like I've always wanted to," she said in a soft voice.

Slocum backed away and wrapped Ruth in his arms to keep her from going into the room. He whispered urgently in the woman's ear, "We've got to get the hell out of here now. There's nothing we can do for any of them."

"My bags," Ruth said. "I need my bags. Killian left them in the wagon."

"Come on." Slocum threaded his way back through the house, making sure he avoided the museum with Jeter's body on display. They stepped out into the hot Texas sun behind the house.

"That way," she said. "There's a stable around to the far side of the house."

Slocum let Ruth lead the way, preferring to hang back and guard their retreat. When lead began to fly, anyone might catch some of it. Ruth worked to harness the team, doing a fair job. Slocum helped and finished in a few minutes.

"Where are we going?" Ruth asked as Slocum drove the team away from the hacienda. "Far away, I hope."

"I was going to El Paso. You ever been there?"

Ruth shook her head, then said, "But it must be a good place."

"Only because it's not here," Slocum said.

"Because you'll be there too," Ruth said, smiling wanly. "Careful, don't drive so fast. My bags'll fall out."

"You can get new things," Slocum said. "I've got a few dollars, and you must still have the money Killian gave you."

"No, that's back at his house. I don't know where."

"Doesn't matter. We got away."

"Money always matters," Ruth said. "That's what Les said. Wait a minute." She flopped around and grabbed the larger of the bags in the rear and dragged it forward to hold in her lap. She opened it wide enough for Slocum to get a look inside.

He whistled long and low.

"Is that what I think it is?" Slocum asked.

"All the money Les stole. I found where he hid it."

"You're a rich woman," Slocum said.

"Help me spend it, John."

That didn't sound like a bad idea at all to Slocum.